All That Glitters

By Danielle Steel

ALL THAT GLITTERS · ROYAL · DADDY'S GIRLS · THE WEDDING DRESS
THE NUMBERS GAME · MORAL COMPASS · SPY · CHILD'S PLAY
THE DARK SIDE · LOST AND FOUND · BLESSING IN DISGUISE
SILENT NIGHT · TURNING POINT · BEAUCHAMP HALL
IN HIS FATHER'S FOOTSTEPS · THE GOOD FIGHT · THE CAST
ACCIDENTAL HEROES · FALL FROM GRACE · PAST PERFECT
FAIRYTALE · THE RIGHT TIME · THE DUCHESS
AGAINST ALL ODDS · DANGEROUS GAMES · THE MISTRESS · THE AWARD
RUSHING WATERS · MAGIC · THE APARTMENT
PROPERTY OF A NOBLEWOMAN · BLUE · PRECIOUS GIFTS
UNDERCOVER · COUNTRY · PRODIGAL SON · PEGASUS
A PERFECT LIFE · POWER PLAY · WINNERS · FIRST SIGHT
UNTIL THE END OF TIME · THE SINS OF THE MOTHER
FRIENDS FOREVER · BETRAYAL · HOTEL VENDÔME · HAPPY BIRTHDAY
44 CHARLES STREET · LEGACY · FAMILY TIES · BIG GIRL
SOUTHERN LIGHTS · MATTERS OF THE HEART · ONE DAY AT A TIME
A GOOD WOMAN · ROGUE · HONOR THYSELF · AMAZING GRACE
BUNGALOW 2 · SISTERS · H.R.H. · COMING OUT · THE HOUSE
TOXIC BACHELORS · MIRACLE · IMPOSSIBLE · ECHOES · SECOND CHANCE
RANSOM · SAFE HARBOUR · JOHNNY ANGEL · DATING GAME
ANSWERED PRAYERS · SUNSET IN ST. TROPEZ · THE COTTAGE · THE KISS
LEAP OF FAITH · LONE EAGLE · JOURNEY · THE HOUSE ON HOPE STREET
THE WEDDING · IRRESISTIBLE FORCES · GRANNY DAN · BITTERSWEET
MIRROR IMAGE · THE KLONE AND I · THE LONG ROAD HOME · THE GHOST
SPECIAL DELIVERY · THE RANCH · SILENT HONOR · MALICE
FIVE DAYS IN PARIS · LIGHTNING · WINGS · THE GIFT · ACCIDENT
VANISHED · MIXED BLESSINGS · JEWELS · NO GREATER LOVE
HEARTBEAT · MESSAGE FROM NAM · DADDY · STAR · ZOYA
KALEIDOSCOPE · FINE THINGS · WANDERLUST · SECRETS
FAMILY ALBUM · FULL CIRCLE · CHANGES · THURSTON HOUSE
CROSSINGS · ONCE IN A LIFETIME · A PERFECT STRANGER
REMEMBRANCE · PALOMINO · LOVE: *POEMS* · THE RING · LOVING
TO LOVE AGAIN · SUMMER'S END · SEASON OF PASSION · THE PROMISE
NOW AND FOREVER · PASSION'S PROMISE · GOING HOME

Nonfiction

EXPECT A MIRACLE: *Quotations to Live and Love By*
PURE JOY: *The Dogs We Love*
A GIFT OF HOPE: *Helping the Homeless*
HIS BRIGHT LIGHT: *The Story of Nick Traina*

For Children

PRETTY MINNIE IN PARIS
PRETTY MINNIE IN HOLLYWOOD

DANIELLE STEEL

All That Glitters

A Novel

Delacorte Press | New York

Published in the United States by Delacorte Press, an imprint of Random House, a division of Penguin Random House LLC, New York.

DELACORTE PRESS and the HOUSE colophon are registered trademarks of Penguin Random House LLC.

Hardback ISBN 978-0-399-17968-6
Ebook ISBN 978-0-399-17969-3

Printed in the United States of America on acid-free paper

randomhousebooks.com

2 4 6 8 9 7 5 3 1

First Edition

Book design by Virginia Norey

To my very special, most beloved children,
Beatie, Trevor, Todd, Nick,
Samantha, Victoria, Vanessa,
Maxx, and Zara,

The Flash is fun,
but don't let it dazzle you or blind you,
Always seek and be real, as I know you are,
and may the lessons you learn be gentle ones.
I love you with all my heart and being,

                    Mom/d.s.

All That Glitters

Chapter 1

Coco Martin, officially Nicole, was a striking young woman with dark hair and green eyes. She had a stunning figure, and the poise of someone older than her years. What made her remarkable and even more appealing was that she was totally unaware of her great beauty. She was modest as well as spectacularly beautiful. Men had stared at her for years and she was oblivious to them. Women would have been jealous of her, but she was so kind to everyone that they forgot what she looked like, and genuinely liked her. She had turned twenty-one at the end of last year, and had just finished her junior year as a journalism major at Columbia University. It had been a major coup when she landed a summer internship at *Time* magazine. She'd found the notice on the bulletin board in the school of journalism. The position was intended for graduate students, but after her interview, they had been so impressed that they had hired her. She was thrilled. She had started two weeks before and she was excited to have the opportunity to work at such a prestigious magazine.

It was a hot Friday in July when she boarded the jitney in New York for the three-hour trip to Southampton to spend the weekend with her parents. She was an only child, and had always enjoyed an unusually close relationship with them, even when she was very young. They treated her more as an adult than a child, and took her everywhere with them. They had had some wonderful trips together, and welcomed her among their friends when they entertained. The three of them enjoyed one another's company. Tom and Bethanie were proud of their only daughter.

Their marriage had gotten off to an unusual start when they were young themselves. They had met when they were both in college and fell madly in love, although they came from vastly different backgrounds. Tom Martin had grown up dirt poor, as he readily admitted, in the Midwest. He had gotten a full scholarship to Princeton, and it changed his life. His parents would have been more than satisfied if he had wanted to be a plumber or electrician, or at the most maybe an accountant. But Tom had never accepted his parents' limited vision for him. His friends in college convinced him that it was more profitable to manage other people's fortunes than try to make his own from scratch. After Princeton, he got an entry-level job at a New York bank and eventually, after working diligently, with Bethanie's help, he attended business school at Wharton, and in time became one of the most respected investment advisors in New York. He was a quiet, discreet man, not given to showing off, although he had a business partner, Edward Easton, who was far more visible and one of the well-known stars in the business.

Like Coco, Bethanie had been dazzling when Tom met her, a stunning beauty and a lively, creative young woman. She was studying photography in the department of visual arts at Brown University, and had genuine talent.

Bethanie was from a venerable old New York family. Both she and Tom were only children and she had made her debut the year before she met Tom. They had fallen in love when they were both nineteen, had met at a party in New York and had been together ever since. When Bethanie told her parents they wanted to get married after they graduated from college, they'd objected strenuously, and thought that Tom would never amount to anything. They wanted her to marry someone from their own social circle, not a poor boy from a simple background with ambitious dreams. They didn't see how he could go very far. Bethanie saw all his strengths and merits, and had total faith in him. Even if he would never become a material success, and remained poor forever, she loved him. When her parents flatly refused to agree to the marriage, two weeks after they graduated, Bethanie and Tom pooled what they had in their checking accounts, went to Las Vegas for the weekend, and got married in the Elvis Chapel. The Monday after, she faced her parents with the news, and they were outraged.

Tom took the bank job he'd been offered, and found work waiting on tables at night to save for business school. Bethanie refused to accept her usual allowance from her parents and took freelance photography jobs, and worked as a waitress with him at night. They lived on what they made and saved all they could. And eventually Tom went to Wharton and got his MBA. Coco had come along by then. And in the end, they proved Bethanie's parents wrong, and won their respect and admiration. When Tom became successful, he bought his own parents a house.

The two things Bethanie lived by, and had said to her daughter frequently, were "Don't play by other people's rules" and "Think outside the box." She said that one of the worst things in life was to have no dreams. Coco's parents had convinced her that she could do anything she wanted to, if she was willing to work hard and face whatever challenges came up.

Coco's parents were shining examples of perseverance, courage, and hard work to achieve their goals. Her father had certainly done that. They had never given up their dreams, or lost faith in each other. Twenty-four years after they married, they were still in love, and Tom was still in awe of his beautiful wife. She had been staunchly at his side for richer or poorer, just as she had promised in the Elvis Chapel. Their wedding pictures still made them smile.

Their parents had been older, which was something they had in common too. All of them had died when Coco was very young, and she had grown up without the advantages or complications of grandparents. Her parents had been her whole world, and she was the focus of all their love and attention. As he made his fortune, Tom had acquired a patina of sophistication, with Bethanie at his side, showing him the way.

They had a beautiful apartment in Manhattan, on Fifth Avenue, with a Central Park view, and a sprawling, comfortable, luxurious house in Southampton, right on the beach. Coco loved spending time with them. She was going out for the weekend to tell them all about her internship at *Time* and what she'd done that week. Bethanie and Tom had sent Coco to one of the best private coed schools in New York, which she had attended through high school. It was where she met her best friend, Samuel Stein. She had girlfriends too. She was

an independent thinker, but never hung out in cliques, and her closest friend since she was in fourth grade had been Sam. They had
hung out in school together and went everywhere together, even
though he was a year older and a grade above her. And despite differences of gender, background, and religion, they were kindred
spirits and soul mates from the moment they met. She told him
everything, as he did with her. He satisfied her need for male com-
panionship and was like a brother, and loyal friend, who gave her
excellent advice once she started dating.

Sam's religious Orthodox Jewish parents were uncomfortable about
their friendship from the beginning, and found it strange that a boy
and girl would be best friends. Their greatest concern was that eventually, when they got older, their closeness would turn into romantic
feelings, and they would fall in love and want to marry. Sam's mother,
Zippora, particularly didn't want that to happen, although his father
didn't want it either. When the time came, they wanted Sam to marry
within their faith. Zippora kept a kosher home. They celebrated Shabbat every Friday night, and obliged Sam to go to synagogue with
them on Saturdays. He was the oldest of four children, and had two
sisters and a brother. The others had gone to a religious school in
Brooklyn, but they sent Sam to a more liberal, nonsectarian school
in the city, and were never sure it had been the right decision. But he
had flourished there and was an excellent student, which was their
main goal for him.

Eventually his next youngest sister, Sabra, gave them real cause
for concern. She fell in love with Liam, an Irish Catholic boy she'd
met at an interschool high-school conference on diversity, and she
was determined to marry him after they graduated from college. She

was even willing to convert for him. That took the heat off Sam and his friendship with Coco, and caused the Steins even more anxiety than Coco did.

Sam was a year older than Coco, and had just graduated as an econ major from NYU. Coco had gone to his graduation and his parents had been polite to her, as they always were, but having known him for twelve years, she knew how they felt about their being best friends. They made no secret of it, and lectured Sam constantly about the danger of their being friends.

Sam had insisted that she be invited to his bar mitzvah when he was thirteen. She had sat through all four hours of the religious ceremony at the temple, and had then gone to the lavish party his parents had thrown for him at the Plaza hotel that night. Her parents had dropped her off. There had been two hundred guests and Coco had enjoyed it. It was the first bar mitzvah she'd ever been to, and she felt very grown up being there alone. She told her parents afterward that she wished she could have a bat mitzvah herself. She loved the celebration, and especially when they carried Sam's mother around the room aloft in a chair to riotous applause and lively music.

Coco's family was Catholic and had never been overly religious. Neither were Coco and Sam. Sam said he didn't think he would hold Shabbat when he grew up, and he hated living in a kosher home. He ate bacon every chance he got when he went out, but of course never told his parents. He felt that his mother's religious passion was stifling. Both his sisters had rebelled against it, but his brother, Jacob, always desperate to please them, said he wanted to be a rabbi when he grew up. He was a studious boy and Sam thought he'd do it.

Sam was expected to go to work at his father's successful accounting firm after college, and they encouraged him to become a CPA now that he had graduated. He wanted to go to business school in a few years, but the ink was barely dry on his bachelor's degree. Sam and Coco loved the fact that they had both gone to college in New York City, she at Columbia and he at NYU, and could continue to spend time together, when they weren't studying or with friends at their respective schools. Sometimes they managed to study together. Sam always helped her with her math, economics, and statistics, and she had written more than one paper for him in psychology and literature. They pooled their strengths and had both gotten good grades and maintained a strong GPA all through college. Their parents could never complain that their friendship distracted them from their schoolwork, since their grades had never suffered from the time they spent together. And it was a mystery to Sam's parents how they were so often with each other, remained friends, and didn't fall in love.

One of the big differences between them was that Sam's parents expected him to conform to their rules, their expectations for him, and their way of life, and hers didn't. There was no room in his parents' thinking for Sam to make his own choices, and they made it clear what their plans were for him, both for marriage and career.

Coco's parents wanted her to find a career that was fulfilling, be creative about it, and march to her own tune, as they had done, Bethanie by marrying someone who came from a different world and Tom by achieving so much more than his parents had ever envisioned for him. They urged Coco not to accept other people's limited views, and to fly with her own wings. It left a broad range of options and choices for her future, and her friendship with Sam had never worried them, neither due to his sex nor to his religion. They respected her ability to make good decisions and choose her own friends. Sam always said he envied her because her parents were so open-minded. He dreaded confrontation with his parents, and couldn't imagine himself marrying the kind of girl they would eventually want to choose for him, a girl from an Orthodox Jewish home. Any other possibility was out of the question. His mother always urged him to marry early and have many children, as they had done. Both his parents came from big families.

Sam had no intention of doing any of that when he eventually left home. He had only graduated a month before, and in two more weeks they expected him to start work at his father's accounting firm. He dreaded it, and for that Coco felt sorry for him. But he knew it was expected of him and he didn't want to let them down.

Coco was excited about her summer internship, and her senior year at Columbia before she graduated. She knew her parents were disappointed that, because of her job at *Time,* she wouldn't be able to join them for their annual summer trip to Europe. She went with them every year. This would be the first time she couldn't. They were leaving on Sunday, so she had agreed to spend the weekend with them before they left.

Sam's parents lived in an apartment on upper Central Park West, not in one of the fancier buildings further south, like the Dakota or the San Remo, where famous actors, producers, and writers lived, but in a very respectable building nonetheless. His sisters shared a room, as did he with his younger brother. He didn't have enough money saved yet to move into his own apartment after graduation, and he suspected he would have to live at home for the next few years. The starting salary his father was giving him would be enough for spending money, and some dinners out with friends and occasional dates, but not enough to live on yet, not by any means. He'd have to work hard for that, and he intended to. He longed for his own apartment, which still seemed like a distant dream.

Coco was planning to move out when she graduated, once she got a job, and assumed she would have roommates, which she did in the dorm at Columbia too. She didn't mind. Her parents had promised to help her get an apartment after graduation. Sam always envied how generous her parents were, but he didn't hold it against her. He just thought Coco was a very lucky girl, and most of the time, she agreed. At other times she found her parents' single-minded focus on her too possessive and intense. She hoped they would relax their vigilance in the next year or two, but there was no sign of it yet. She was sorry she couldn't go to Europe with them this year, but it felt grown up and exciting to have a summer job and stay home. She was enjoying it, and it was already clear to her that she wanted to work at a magazine when she finished school. She was even considering graduate classes in journalism.

Her father was waiting for her when she stepped off the jitney. He was a tall, youthful looking man with gray hair at his temples, and his face lit up as soon as he saw Coco. She was happy to see him, gave him a big hug, and they chatted in the car all the way back to the house, where her mother was waiting with a light dinner at a beautifully set table on the patio next to the pool. Like everything else Bethanie did so perfectly, she was a creative cook, kept an elegant home, and the house was tastefully decorated. Tom was always very generous with her. She had dabbled in decorating when she was younger, and enjoyed it. But once Tom started making big money, she had never worked again, and was available at all times to her husband and daughter. She had amazing flair with everything she did, an easy style and eye for beauty. Coco had inherited some of that from her. Her mother's grace and open-mindedness hadn't gone unobserved by her daughter. The freedom she had to be herself and choose her own path was the exact opposite of how Sam had been brought up, with his parents constantly dictating to him and attempting to restrict him.

Sam and Coco complemented each other as best friends. In some ways, he grounded her, and in others Coco encouraged him to spread his wings, in spite of what his parents said, and the limits they put on him. She tried to give him the courage to fly free of them, but he always felt earthbound compared to her. He wanted to soar as she did, but he didn't know how to do that yet. It was one of his many goals. To be free and try new things. He admired how fearless Coco was and how brave.

Bethanie and Tom enjoyed dinner with their daughter. They walked on the beach after dinner, and went to bed early. On Saturday they swam in the ocean, lay by the pool, and went out to dinner that night at a restaurant Tom and Bethanie wanted to try, and hadn't yet. During dinner, Coco told them more about her work at *Time*. Her parents were always proud of her. She had always had all the emotional support she needed from them. It was freely given, and they had always encouraged her to have confidence in herself. Her mother reminded her that there was nothing she couldn't achieve if she tried. It had been an atmosphere in which Coco had thrived.

When they were out to dinner on Saturday night, Coco's parents were excited about their trip to France the next day. Hearing them and talking about it made her miss it more than she had thought she would. But she didn't want to make a bad impression at work by asking for a vacation right after she started the job, so she had decided to pass on it this year. She had wonderful memories of their many trips together during school vacations and in the summers.

"Are you all packed, Mom?" she asked her mother when they got home from dinner. Bethanie laughed guiltily with a glance at her husband.

"More or less," she said and Tom laughed.

"You know your mom. She'll be slipping more things into her suitcase and another one will suddenly appear as we walk out the door." He always pretended to grouse about how much luggage she took, but in truth, he didn't care. She liked to wear pretty clothes, and he enjoyed indulging her. Once in Paris and the South of France, she'd buy more, he knew. It was a trait Coco had inherited from her. Tom traveled light, but all he needed for the trip were white jeans, some linen jackets, a blazer, and a suit or two. It was so much easier for a man to pack less, as his wife always pointed out to him. She often had a whole suitcase of purses and shoes, to match every outfit. But at the hotel where they stayed in Cap d'Antibes, people dressed well. It was an older crowd, an expensive hotel, and they went there every summer for a week or two. Coco loved it there too.

It was a relaxing weekend, and Bethanie made them a big brunch on Sunday. After that, Tom drove Coco back to the jitney to return to the city. They had to finish packing, and were leaving on a nine P.M. flight to Paris, where they would spend several days seeing friends, going to art exhibits, and visiting their favorite museums and restaurants. And then they would head to the South of France, followed by a few days in Venice, and ending the trip in London, as they always did. They were planning to be away for just under three weeks, a luxury of time Coco couldn't afford this summer, for a worthy cause. It was her first serious summer job.

She was in a good mood all the way back to the city after seeing them. She'd had a nice time with her parents, and she went to a movie with two of her girlfriends from Columbia that night. She knew that Sam had a date with the daughter of friends of his parents and he wasn't looking forward to it.

"How was it?" she asked when he called her after the movie.

"Painful. She was nice looking, but a huge bore. My parents' only criterion is that the girls are Jewish. I don't think she said ten words all evening. I was home by ten o'clock." He made a date with Coco for later that week, to go to dinner and a movie they were both dying to see. They never ran out of things to talk about. When they hung up, she knew her parents' flight to Paris was already in the air. They had called from the airport to say goodbye again. After talking to Sam, Coco turned on the TV in their den for a while, and then went to bed early so she'd be fresh for work the next day.

The next week at *Time* flew by and kept her busy, so she didn't have a chance to miss them. Her parents called her from Paris, and told her what they were doing, what restaurants and galleries they'd been to, since they were major collectors and passionate about art. By the end of the week, they were in the South of France, happily at their favorite hotel.

That weekend she and Sam went out to Southampton, and spent the whole time relaxing and swimming, and sleeping by the pool. They slept chastely in separate rooms, as they always had, since there had never been even a hint of romance between them. He had met a new girl that week, at the deli near his office where he'd had lunch. She was Irish Catholic, but he said he didn't care, as long as his mother didn't find out. Coco told him about several guys she'd spotted at work, whom she hadn't met yet but looked promising. Sam always said that he was closer to Coco than to his own sisters, and he could tell her anything, as she could with him. There were no secrets between them.

They had lain in the sun all weekend and relaxed. Sam had borrowed his father's car for the weekend, since his father didn't drive on Friday night or Saturdays anyway. He turned the radio on, on the drive home. The news was on, and Coco was about to hunt for a music station they both liked, when a bulletin came on, announcing a major terrorist attack in France, on the Promenade de la Croisette in Cannes. She looked at Sam with fear in her eyes.

"Don't be crazy, Coco. Don't jump to conclusions," he told her calmly. He knew how her mind worked, and that she would panic at what they'd just heard, thinking of her parents. "They were probably at their hotel." It was late evening in France, and Coco knew they were most likely at dinner somewhere, at one of their favorite restaurants, but she worried anyway. She took out her cellphone and called both of them. Each call went directly to voicemail. She was silent for most of the ride home after that, flipping through the stations for further news. What they'd heard so far was that several bombs had been detonated. The terrorists had been shot and killed. Several hundred people had been injured and well over a hundred were dead, after an initial count. It was one of the worst attacks so far. When they got to her building on Fifth Avenue, Sam parked on the street and went upstairs with her to watch the news on TV. It was heartbreaking to see; people carrying dead children, and other children screaming in fear and running after the blast, looking for their parents, husbands kneeling over their wives, parents over children, lovers dying in each other's arms, riot police everywhere.

She watched the scene intently in terrified silence, holding Sam's hand, but there was no sign of her parents in the carnage they saw on TV. Her face was tense and Sam didn't speak as Coco continued to call their cellphones, with no answer. When she called the hotel, they said that the Martins were out and not in their rooms. When she checked with the hotel restaurant, they had not dined at the hotel that night.

"Shit, Sam, where are they?" she said nervously.

"They're probably walking around somewhere," he said, but he could see the terror in her eyes, and didn't know how to reassure her.

Sam and Coco spent the night on the couch in front of the TV, watching the same footage again and again. He called his parents and said he was staying at a friend's.

The call finally came at six A.M., which was noon in France. She hesitated for a fraction of a second before she answered, praying it was them. But an unfamiliar male voice with a French accent asked for her by name. He pronounced it like a French name. "Nicole Martin." Her name was on her parents' documents and travel papers as next of kin, so if something happened to them, she would be called.

"Yes, this is she," she said, holding her breath as Sam stared at her, willing it to be good news. It had to be. They couldn't have been victims of a terrorist attack in France. It just wasn't possible and didn't make sense.

The man identified himself as a captain of the gendarmerie in Cannes. He explained that there had been a terrorist attack.

"Yes, I know," she said, wanting to scream. "Are my parents all right?" It suddenly occurred to her that they could be injured and in a hospital there. All night she had been terrified that they were dead. There was a brief pause before he responded, sounding grave.

"I regret very much to inform you, madame, they were among the victims of last night's attack. They were on the Croisette when the first bomb detonated."

"Are they injured? How bad is it?" she asked in a whisper, as Sam squeezed her hand and she closed her eyes while everything swirled around her and she waited to hear what the captain would say.

"They did not survive," he said somberly. Her eyes flew open and she looked at Sam in disbelief.

"Both of them?"

"Yes, madame. Both Monsieur and Madame Martin were killed. There will be formalities. If you will contact the American embassy in Paris, they will assist you. We are very, very sorry for this terrible act. It is a great tragedy. So many victims. Our sincere sympathy," he said. "The people of France cry with you." She nodded and couldn't speak for a moment, as he gave her a number to call, to make arrangements for the victims. The captain sounded choked himself. He had been working all through the night, and now had the grim task of notifying relatives and loved ones. Many of the victims couldn't be identified. There were human fragments all over the Croisette.

She ended the call and stared at Sam, unable to believe what the captain had told her. From the look on her face, Sam didn't dare ask her what had happened. He could see it. He put his arms around her, and she shuddered against his chest, with deep wracking sobs. This couldn't have happened, but it had. She tried to catch her breath to tell him.

"Both of them," she said with gulping sobs. He had already guessed that when she asked the captain, and then had no further questions.

"What do I do now? How do I live without them?" Sam didn't know what to do for her, other than hold her.

"Do you have to go and get them?" he asked gently, and she looked totally lost. Her green eyes were emerald pools of pain.

"I don't know. He said the embassy would help me." Sam wondered if his father would lend him the money to go with her if she had to go to France. He couldn't let her face it alone. They walked into the kitchen, and he handed her a glass of water, which seemed like such a useless gesture, but he didn't know what else to do. He felt helpless and heartbroken for her. Her parents were such great people. She took a sip and set it down. She couldn't focus on anything except what she had just heard. Both her parents had been killed. It was what she had been so desperately afraid of all night.

She sent an email to her boss at *Time,* explaining what had happened and that she could not come in and would contact them when she knew more.

She and Sam spent the next two hours sitting at the kitchen table, talking, and then Sam called the embassy in Paris for her, and they gave him a number to call in Cannes. It was an emergency number that had been set up for the families of the victims, for information, and directions about where the bodies were being taken. Not all of them had been removed yet. He handed Coco the phone when he got through. The woman who answered consulted a list and told Coco that her parents were at a military base, and the American embassy in Paris would be able to give her the correct forms for their release, in order to transport them to the United States. It sounded like there was going to be considerable red tape, but they were well organized. They had had too much practice with events like this in recent years.

Coco called the American embassy in Paris again after that. They extended their condolences immediately, and said they would email the forms she would have to fill out and have notarized to give her clearance to transport her parents back to the States. They warned her that it could take several days or even a week. They said they would call the victims' survivor number and see if they could expedite it. She felt lost again as she listened. It was a maze of words and formalities that meant nothing now without her parents. She couldn't imagine anything that would matter to her again, or her life without them.

Sam called the hotel for her, and spoke to the manager to explain what had happened, and asked them to safeguard the Martins' belongings until someone could claim them.

"Of course. Please extend our deepest sympathy to Miss Martin and the family," the manager said. But there was no family now. Only Coco.

Sam then called his father from the den, and explained the situation in hushed tones. He said he might want to borrow the money for a ticket to France. They had never fully approved of their friendship, although they'd gotten used to it in twelve years, but this was a special case that transcended all else and his father said he'd give him whatever he needed to help Coco. He felt terrible for her when Sam told him the news. Sam thanked him and hung up, and went back to Coco in the kitchen. They sat quietly together then, as though waiting for something to happen, but it already had. The rest was all irrelevant details. She would have to arrange a funeral for her parents, but she didn't want to do that until they sent their bodies back from France, and she didn't know what would happen, or even how to bring them back.

At ten o'clock, her father's somewhat flamboyant, very social partner, Edward Easton, called her. She knew from her father that Ed was her trustee in the event of his death, which always seemed unlikely. Ed explained in a serious voice that he was also the executor of her father's estate. She wasn't sure what that would be like, but it didn't matter. Ed told her how desperately shocked and sorry he was, and what a loss it was for him as well.

As quiet and discreet as her father was, Ed was the exact opposite, always center stage and very much in evidence. He was handsome, successful, social, one of the stars of Wall Street, as her father was, but the two men were completely different, and were business partners and friends. Ed was married to an important heiress, who was a billionaire in her own right, and together they made a big splash wherever they went. He was constantly on Page Six, the gossip column of the *New York Post,* and sometimes spotted with other women. Tom hadn't liked the flashy way Ed lived, but he had great respect for him in business, and always said he was an honest man. He trusted him implicitly. They had made a fortune together and Tom had wanted him to handle his estate for Coco and Bethanie. He knew Ed would be responsible doing so. It had never occurred to him that his wife would die with him, at the same time. He'd always assumed she would outlive him.

"I can't tell you how devastated I am," Ed said to Coco on the phone, and he sounded it. It was a shock for everyone who knew them. Tom and Bethanie were forty-six years old, much too young to die. "I'll do whatever needs to be done to get them home," he reassured her. "I have a call in to the American ambassador. We both belong to the Racquet Club and I've met him a few times. I'm sure he'll do everything he can to help us." Tom Martin had been a very important man in the world of high finance and was greatly respected by all.

Eleven Americans had been killed in the attack, and several others injured. It was high season, July, when the South of France was full of tourists from every country. The victims had mostly been French, but many weren't. According to CNN, the casualties included a Saudi prince and both his wives, twenty members of the Qatari royal family, several Scandinavians, the Spanish Minister of the Interior, numerous Germans and British subjects, and a tour group of Japanese schoolchildren. Dozens of French citizens were dead and hundreds injured. The death toll had risen to a hundred and sixty-four, and two hundred and eighty-seven people injured.

There had been bulletins on the news all morning, and a mournful speech by the French president. An extremist group had taken credit for the attack. None of the terrorists had survived, as they'd intended. Those who had survived uninjured among people on the Croisette at the time had been sequestered for psychiatric attention for several hours, and had just been released to go home. It was too late for any of it to help Tom and Bethanie. Reporters had said that there were body fragments scattered everywhere, which special teams were removing.

"I'll go over if I need to," Ed volunteered to Coco, "but we probably won't have to. The embassy will expedite it, I'm sure. Can I do anything for you right now?" he asked Coco, and she shook her head, barely able to speak, as Sam sat beside her. They both kept crying, and so did Ed.

"I'm okay. I have a friend here." She squeezed Sam's hand.

"I'll let you know what I hear. I'll come up to see you later," he promised. She didn't want him to, but she didn't want to be rude, and he was a link to her father. She'd be seeing a lot of him if he was the executor and trustee of her father's estate. She knew him well, but he was always a little overwhelming. She still looked dazed when she hung up. Sam took her to her bedroom and got her to lie down, and she asked him to lie next to her. He got onto her bed in her pink silk bedroom and held her. She lay with her eyes closed, but he knew she wasn't sleeping. She just lay there, in his arms, breathing and trying not to think of what had happened. She wondered if they had had time to be scared, or suffer, or if it was all over in an instant. The bombs had been powerful, and those closest to the explosions had literally vanished.

Ed Easton called back two hours later. He had spoken to the ambassador, and they were going to take care of everything. He and Coco didn't have to go over, although normally the French formalities were complicated, with considerable red tape to negotiate. Ed said the hotel was going to send her parents' belongings, including the contents of the room safe, all of which would arrive by courier. They would have everything by the next morning. The ambassador was hoping they could have the Martins' bodies in New York by the end of the week. The French government was in a state of chaos over the attack, but the emergency services were well organized in the midst of it. They had promised to send the other Americans' remains home quickly too. France was in deep mourning, and American networks had named all the American victims once the families had been notified, including her parents.

Sam tried to get Coco to eat something but she wouldn't.

At four o'clock the doorman buzzed, and said that a Mr. Easton wished to come up, and she let him. Their housekeeper, Theresa, had come to work to help her, looking devastated. Flowers had begun to arrive that afternoon. Coco hadn't called the funeral home yet. She just couldn't, and they didn't know when her parents' bodies would be arriving. The first flowers that came were from her boss at *Time* magazine, and she was touched.

Sam left when Ed Easton got there. He said he'd be back as soon as he showered and changed at home, and dropped off his bag from the weekend and his father's car. He left Coco sitting in the living room with Ed, looking shell-shocked. Ed was wearing a well-cut dark suit, a white shirt, and a black tie, and looked grim too. He'd had a flood of calls from people they did business with who just couldn't believe it.

"I'm so sorry, Coco," Ed said, reached for her hand, and held it. Just seeing him reminded her of her father, which brought some comfort, although seeing him was bittersweet. Why was he there and her father wasn't? She still couldn't wrap her mind around it. She had always known that Ed was her trustee, and her mother would have been co-trustee with him, but she had never thought that this moment would come so soon. Her parents were so young. Ed was around fifty, but looked older that afternoon, after the shocking news. Coco looked gray beneath her suntan from the Hamptons. She was shaking as Ed put an arm around her to comfort her. "I'll do everything I can for you. Let's get through the funeral, and then we can figure out what you want to do about some of your father's things."

"Like what?" She looked startled and frightened. It was overwhelming.

"This apartment, the house in the Hamptons. If you want to keep them, or sell them, or live here." She was twenty-one, so at least she could make her own decisions, but he said he would guide her to make it all easier for her. "Everything goes to you of course, now that your mother . . ." He didn't finish the sentence. The estate would have been divided if Bethanie had survived. But Coco was their only heir now, to a very large fortune. It didn't even dawn on her, and she didn't care. She wanted them, not the money they had left her.

"Do you want me to call a doctor for you?" he offered. She shook her head. She didn't want anyone or anything, except Sam with her. He was the only one who understood how she felt. He always had.

"No, I'm okay. I think I'm in shock or something."

"We all are," Ed said sympathetically in a hushed tone. "Who could possibly have expected this? The embassy said they'll get the bodies home late Wednesday night or Thursday morning. When do you want to do the funeral?" He needed to ask her the questions and she tried to focus.

"I don't know. When should we do it?" It was helpful having his advice for the practical issues. She had no idea what to do about any of it.

"Maybe Monday, in case there are any delays," Ed suggested gently. "There could be a rosary over the weekend, if you'd like that. They could have visitation set up on Friday. Were they religious?" He didn't think so. He was fairly certain Tom wasn't, but he didn't know about Bethanie, or if Coco was.

"Not really. But they're both Catholic." She couldn't bring herself to speak of them in the past tense. It hurt too much. He nodded. "We only go to church on Christmas."

"You can decide what church you want. I've already written the obituary," he said, sounding efficient. She didn't know how he'd been notified, but someone had called him. His name must have appeared on her father's papers too.

"Thank you," she said softly, and he patted her hand and stood, as the doorman rang again, to tell her Sam was on his way up. He had come back quickly.

"I'll call or text you with anything I know," Ed said and hugged her again, and then she went to let Sam in. Ed smiled at him briefly and then left. Sam watched him go, and turned to her after Ed left.

"Just out of curiosity. Did he hit on you?" he said, and she looked shocked.

"Sam! Of course not. That's disgusting. He's older than my father. Why would you say something like that?"

"I don't know. He just looks the type. He's so smooth and so slick, and he's very good-looking." She had never noticed. He just seemed old to her. And she knew his children were older than she was. They were all married and had children.

"His kids are older than I am."

"I bet his girlfriends aren't. I've read about him on Page Six."

"That's just gossip. He's married. And his wife is very good-looking."

"I don't know. I just get a funny feeling about him."

"Jealous?" she teased him.

"Hardly. Just protective. I don't want anyone to take advantage of you." She was alone in the world now, and young and vulnerable, but he didn't say it to her.

"He won't do that. My father trusted him completely." And she knew her father had been a great judge of character.

"He trusted him with money. With women I wouldn't be so sure."

"You're a freak," she said, and smiled for the first time since six o'clock that morning when the gendarmerie called from France.

Sam had brought some soup his mother had made for her. He was wearing jeans and a sweatshirt, so he could sleep in his clothes if he needed to. He was not going to leave her alone. He told his parents, and for once, they understood and were sympathetic, and offered to help however they could. But there was nothing they could do either.

She got a flood of emails and texts from friends that night and didn't answer them, although she read most of them. Sam made her eat some of his mother's soup, and Coco finally fell asleep at nine o'clock, lying next to him on her bed. He lay next to her and held her until he fell asleep too. The whole day had been a nightmare, but from this one, no one was going to wake up. It broke Sam's heart knowing that his best friend was now alone and had no living relatives. It was what Coco had been thinking all day too. She was an orphan now.

Chapter 2

Tom's and Bethanie's bodies landed in New York at two A.M. on Thursday. The funeral home Ed had chosen picked them up at JFK airport, and had the visitation room set up by that evening. Coco didn't want them to be cremated. Their bodies had been tortured enough. Ed found out there was a family plot that Tom had bought for his parents and Bethanie's, and there was more than enough room to bury them there too.

A rosary was set for six P.M. on Friday, and there would be visitation all weekend, for people to come and pray or meditate, and sign the guestbook. The funeral was set for Monday at noon. Tom's secretaries had set up a schedule to be there to receive guests and oversee the guestbook. They were expecting a huge crowd at St. Ignatius Loyola Church on Park Avenue, and Ed had selected the ushers from among their business associates, since there was no family. Coco had found a beautiful photograph of her parents on the beach in Southampton looking happy and relaxed, the way she wanted to remember them. She had them put it on the program for the mass. There was another photograph on the back of the program. It was of their wedding day in Las Vegas, and it made her laugh. Ed had called an opera singer he knew to sing the "Ave Maria." They were having Beethoven's "Ode to Joy" for the recessional, when the caskets were carried out, to be driven to Long Island for burial. Sam had agreed to go with her, and Ed had said he would be there too. His wife was in Italy, and had sent her condolences. Coco knew that she and her parents hadn't been close.

She and Sam went to the first day of visitation on Saturday before everyone else. The caskets were closed and Sam said the prayer for the dead in Hebrew next to each of them. He signed the guestbook and then they left and went back to the apartment.

Coco sat in the front pew in church, between Sam and Ed, feeling like she was having an out of body experience. Their housekeeper, Theresa, had found a black dress of her mother's that fit her, and a black hat she'd never seen before. Coco couldn't remember anything about the ceremony and afterward she stood shaking hands with people for what felt like hours and didn't recognize half of them. Most of them were people her father had known in business. And then at last, they stood in the cemetery, while the caskets were lowered into the ground on ropes, and she sprinkled a handful of earth on each of them, and collapsed sobbing in Sam's arms. And then it was over. Ed stood very near her, and patted her shoulder repeatedly. She felt as though her body belonged to someone else, and her mind was dead. The only part of her left alive was her heart and it was broken in a million pieces. There had been no preparation for this, no warning, no sign of ill health, or of a storm coming that would claim both of her parents and destroy her life.

Sam sat with her all that night. He never left her, and she stayed in bed for several days afterward. Sam stayed at the apartment with her, and Theresa prepared meals for them that Coco didn't eat. She thought about going back to work, but knew she couldn't. She couldn't get her mind clear enough to concentrate on anything, or even think. She called her boss the week after the funeral, and said she just didn't have it in her to come back to work. He understood and told her again how sorry he was, and to call him when she felt better, whenever that was. She was a bright girl, and he would have liked to have her on the team, and to hire her when she graduated. She promised to call, but didn't know if she would. She thought it might always be a bad memory for her and a painful association that she had worked there when it happened. Sam had said in a shaking voice that if she had gone with them, she would be dead now. He couldn't bear thinking about it, and was grateful she had stayed in New York. Her summer job had saved her life.

Ed came by to see her every day, in the afternoon, and Sam came at night after work, once he'd started working for his father. He spent the nights in the guest room after the first few days. She liked knowing he was there, even if they didn't talk or she fell asleep, or they sat and stared at the TV. They tried going out to the Hamptons, but somehow it was worse there, and they came back the same day. She kept expecting to see her parents walk toward her on the beach, and felt suffocated when she realized they never would again. It was over. Life as she had known it was over, and changed forever. Trying to get used to it was agony. Trying to accept it was all she thought about now, and she couldn't.

She and Sam went for long walks on the weekends, and at night, by the river, when she couldn't sleep. The nights were hot, and she would stare into the blackness of the water sometimes, thinking about them, and wishing they were back. Every day and every hour was painful. Some days were worse than others. And the nights were endless.

Sam's mother continued to send her soup, and she ate a little of it, but nothing else, and she got thinner by the day. By the end of August, she looked worse than she had when it happened. Sam wasn't surprised but he was dismayed when Coco told him she had decided not to go back to school, and take the semester off.

"Do you think that's a good idea?" He didn't, but he didn't want to push her. "What will you do with yourself all day?"

"Same thing I do now, walk around the apartment and stare at the furniture, or out the window. I just don't think I could concentrate. I'd flunk out. It's like my mind is just a bowl of mush. If I went back, I'd fail all my classes."

"It might force you to focus. Maybe that would be a good thing," he suggested cautiously. He didn't want to upset her. She was in terrible shape.

"I'll go back next semester. What difference does it make if I graduate six months later? Who cares?" It didn't make any difference to anyone now, least of all to her.

"I care, you care. Just so you finish," he said, a little firmer with her, and she nodded. He was her only counselor now, and they had both been brought up to believe education was important. It was to their parents, but she no longer had any.

"Yeah, whatever."

"Your parents would care," he reminded her.

"I know. I'll go back, just not right now."

Sam was working at his father's accounting firm, and not enjoying it. It was boring, and he was worried about her all the time. She wasn't bouncing back, but maybe that was to be expected. It had been about six weeks since they'd died, which wasn't long. On Labor Day weekend, they went to the Hamptons again for the day, but they didn't spend the night this time either. She didn't want to, so they came home.

She smiled at him on the way back. "Are you tired of me yet? It must be a drag to play combination nursemaid/psych attendant," she said sadly.

"Stop that. I love being with you." He looked serious as he said it.

"I'm lousy company," she said mournfully.

"Not always."

"How is it working for your father?" She was turned inward, and hadn't asked about anyone else since it happened, not even Sam.

"Pretty dull. I don't know how he has made a lifetime of it." He could be honest with her. "It's actually depressing."

"What would you rather do?"

"I don't know. I always said I'd do this, but it's hard. I don't think I have much choice. It's what they expect of me, but I can't imagine doing this for the rest of my life."

"You're twenty-two. You don't have to sell your soul forever."

"They think I do. It's good enough for my father, so they think it should be enough for me too. They want me to be an accountant. And my brother isn't going into the business with him. He's serious about becoming a rabbi."

"What does he know? He's fourteen. That's like wanting to be a fireman or a baseball player. He'll probably outgrow it."

"I don't think so. He studies with the rabbis every day. He loves it. I would shoot myself. That's even more boring than what I'm doing." Both his sisters were in college now, so only the two boys were at home. "And my parents are thrilled he's so religious and scholarly. So we all have our roles to play. Mine is working with my father in his business."

"Even if you hate it?" He nodded. "Remember what my mother always said, you don't have to play by other people's rules."

"You do if they're your parents and they support you. At least that's how it works at our house."

"You could get another job, Sam," she said gently. She hated knowing that he was unhappy. He seemed so trapped by what his parents expected of him. It wasn't fair. He was such a good guy, and he didn't want to disappoint them. He was giving up all his dreams, which was another thing her mother had said not to do. But Sam didn't know what his dreams were, only what they weren't. His dream for the moment was not working at his father's accounting firm for the rest of his life.

"What about you? What are you going to do when you finish school?"

"I don't know, still journalism, I hope. I wanted to see what magazines are like at *Time*. But I just couldn't do it this summer." In a way, nothing had changed, and everything had. Maybe she wouldn't work after she graduated. Nothing interested her now, or seemed to matter. But if not, how would she fill her time?

"You'll have to graduate, Coco, or the only job you'll ever be able to get is flipping burgers at McDonald's."

She smiled. "You sound like my father. Actually, that might be fun. I'm going to graduate," she said to placate him. Sam thought graduating was everything.

"You have to go back to school to do that." He was worried about her taking a semester off. It didn't seem like a good decision to him.

But he couldn't force her. No one could now. She could do whatever she wanted. Ed questioned her about it too when she told him she had taken the semester off.

"You might feel better if you were busy," he said carefully.

"I'm afraid I'll flunk all my classes if I go back now. I can't concentrate on anything." She had never had bad grades, and didn't want to now.

"That'll get better with time," Ed said on one of his daily visits to her. "Would you like to go out to dinner one of these nights?" he asked her. She hadn't been out since July, and it was mid-September. She didn't want to see people. The only friend she'd seen so far was Sam. She hadn't called any of her girlfriends or returned their calls, so they had stopped calling. She was worried about being a burden to Sam, but he insisted she wasn't. He had dinner with her at the apartment every night.

"I'm not very good company," she said to Ed, who nodded. He was always patient with her, and very kind. He was the only father figure she had now, to advise her and watch over her.

"I think you need a change of scene. Doctor's orders." He smiled at her. "I'll take you to dinner tomorrow night." She didn't want to go, but he insisted, and the next day he had his secretary call to say he'd pick her up at seven. She told Sam he had the night off, because she was having dinner with Ed Easton. Sam was surprised, but he thought maybe they had to talk finances, so he didn't question it or argue with her.

Ed picked her up right on time. She was wearing a plain black dress, another one of her mother's, and it hung on her. She was startled when he took her to La Grenouille. She used to go there with her parents for special occasions. It looked so beautiful and so festive that she felt guilty being there, but the meal was delicious. And he was right. It cheered her up being out. They went early, and he had asked for a quiet back table, so everyone didn't stop and say hello to her on their way into the restaurant. Her parents had loved La Grenouille too. And many of their friends were regulars.

They talked about lots of different things, and not about her parents or their estate for once. She was smiling when they left the restaurant, and looked more relaxed and young again, despite the dreary dress. The evening had done her good. She had noticed that all the headwaiters knew Ed. He obviously went there a lot. He had a very active social life, which was what landed him on Page Six frequently. He took her home in a cab.

She was smiling on the way home. "Thank you, that was lovely," she said, and meant it. He noticed that she looked more like herself again. Her youth and extreme beauty shone through her grief.

"We'll do it again," he promised. He hadn't wanted to push her before this, but now he could see that she needed to be prodded, to get her out of the house. "I think we should do this a couple of times a week," he suggested. It sounded like hard work to her, babysitting her the way Sam had been, to get her through her sorrow. "How about Friday? Marielle is going to the house in Connecticut for the weekend, and I have to stay in town." She and her parents had visited them there. It was an enormous estate.

"You don't have to do that, Ed," she said gently. "I'm okay. I've just been very sad."

"That's understandable. But now we need to get you un-sad, or at least feeling better. Do you like the ballet?" he asked, and she nodded. "I have season tickets and no one ever wants to go with me. Marielle hates it. I waste the tickets most of the time. We'll do that one night. And maybe a play." It sounded above and beyond the call of duty to her, and she felt guilty taking up his time. It was already nice enough that he stopped in to see her every day on his way home from the office. She was familiar with her father's will now. He had left everything in such good order that there were very few decisions to make, except about where she wanted to live. She was still living at home, and had never had her own apartment, and didn't want to, especially now. She wanted to live in theirs forever. But she felt lost and alone in the big apartment. She was grateful that Sam still stayed there with her most nights, but eventually he would get tired of that too, or his parents would complain. They had been sympathetic so far, and hadn't objected. But Sam hadn't had a date or a night off in two months, except when she'd had dinner with Ed at La Grenouille. He asked her about it the next day.

"Did it go okay with Ed last night?"

"It was very nice. We had a good dinner and came home early. It was kind of nice to be out."

"We could do that too, you know, start eating at restaurants." They'd been eating the meals Theresa left for them for two months, and sometimes Sam brought in burgers or pizza. Coco didn't care what she ate. She nodded at his suggestion, but he could see that she didn't really want to go out for dinner. She watched movies with him at night now, which was a good distraction.

On Friday, Ed's secretary called her again, and said he would come by for her at seven-thirty. She said they were going somewhere informal this time, and Coco felt awkward refusing, so she didn't.

She sent Sam a text that she was seeing Ed again. She wore black jeans and a sweater, and Ed took her to a small cozy Italian restaurant. She had a nice time with him, and he called her on the weekend afterward to see how she was. She was sounding better, and more like herself. She went for a long walk in the park with Sam both days. The weather was still warm and it felt good to be out in the air. She felt like an invalid who was slowly recovering from a terrible accident.

Sam had to have dinner with his family on Sunday night, and he'd been home for Shabbat when she had dinner with Ed on Friday. She was surprised when shortly after Sam left on Sunday, the doorman rang and said that Mr. Easton was on his way up.

"Is everything okay?" She looked surprised when she let him in.

"Fine. I was just thinking about you, so I thought I'd drop by. Is Sam here?"

She shook her head and smiled. "I gave him a night off."

"He's certainly a faithful friend," Ed commented. He was wearing a black turtleneck sweater and jeans, and looked years younger than he did in a suit. He had a good haircut, and smelled faintly of cologne. She was wearing jeans and a sweater too, with her long dark hair down her back. She looked startlingly pretty, and as usual was unaware of it.

"We've been friends since I was nine and he was ten," she said about Sam. "He's like my brother."

"You're not in love with him?" he asked and she smiled.

"No, we're just friends."

"I shouldn't be," he said as they sat down in the small den her parents had loved to use, lined with books, with a fireplace. "But I have to admit, I'm relieved to hear it. I thought maybe he was your boyfriend."

"Not at all. Why are you relieved?" she asked innocently, and he moved slightly closer to her on the couch, and put an arm around her casually. She didn't feel threatened by it. He was a familiar figure to her now, more than ever, like Sam, except there was something subtly different about the way Ed looked at her, and she wasn't sure what it meant. He had been very attentive to her ever since her parents' death, and taken his role as trustee and advisor very seriously. He looked into her eyes then before answering.

"You haven't noticed anything, Coco?" he asked gently, speaking softly. "I didn't want to crowd you while you were getting over what happened. I'm falling in love with you, more every day. I have a hard time staying away from you, and not showing up here every night." She looked stunned, and before she could react, he kissed her, and felt her body with his strong sensual hands. No man had ever touched her quite that way, or made her body come so alive at his touch. She was breathless when he stopped kissing her, with his hand still on her breast.

"I didn't . . . I didn't realize . . ." She didn't know what to say. She had never thought of him that way, and suddenly she didn't want him to stop. She felt both safe and aroused at the same time. He kissed her again, and then they were lying on the couch together. She'd had sex before, but not often, and it had never felt like this. She felt drunk from his touch. "What are we doing, Ed?" she asked in a small voice. "Marielle?" He was a married man.

"We've been over for years. We stayed together for the children, and now we have an arrangement. We have an understanding. For all intents and purposes, I'm a free man." She felt better when he said that, and only mildly guilty when she abandoned herself to him. He smelled wonderful, he was so handsome, and he knew exactly how and where to touch her. She had never thought of him this way before. Even before he took her clothes off, she could sense that he was an expert lover. And then suddenly, they were making love, and she felt as though she were flying through space with him. He drove her to the edge of ecstasy and then pulled her back, then led her to the edge again, he played her body like a finely tuned instrument. When it was over finally, she knew that something extraordinary had happened between them. She lay in his arms smiling at him, and he kissed her again, more peacefully that time.

"I've never felt for any woman the way I feel about you," he said with raw emotion in his voice, ran a finger down her belly again, and touched her irresistibly. And then it all started again.

They made love until midnight, and then wandered into the kitchen naked, and ate ice cream. It was odd being with him that way, but he made it seem normal and natural. And then he led her to her bedroom, and made love to her one more time.

"I've wanted you for so long, Coco," he said, admiring her afterward. "Sometimes I think your father wanted us to be together, which is why he made me your trustee. It's almost like being married to you," he said. "Maybe one day that could happen too. I may be old enough to be your father, but I don't have fatherly feelings for you, most of the time." She wondered what her father would have thought, if he would have been pleased, or shocked. He wouldn't have made Ed her trustee if he hadn't trusted him completely, which gave some sort of benediction to their union, and made it almost sacred, with her father's blessing.

"I don't care how old you are," she said in a soft, sensual voice. She was dazzled by him, and totally at ease with him. He had introduced her to things she had never done or felt before.

"When can I see you again? I'll come by for lunch tomorrow." She nodded, and he finally tore himself away from her at two in the morning, and kissed her longingly again before he left. There were stars in his eyes too.

He came back the next day at lunchtime, and they locked themselves in her father's office so Theresa wouldn't walk in on them, and made love on the couch for two hours before he had to go back to the office. It felt crazy and fun and wonderful and exciting. His passion for her was almost frightening at times, and overwhelmed her like a tidal wave, and then gently left her on a beach of softest sand afterward. He was masterful with his tongue and hands.

"I'm so glad you're not in school," he whispered to her.

"So am I." She giggled like the young innocent she was. She wondered about his wife at times, but he said it was over between them, and she believed him. He was an honorable man and she knew he wouldn't be doing this with her if he had a viable marriage.

He lived up to his plan of taking her out to dinner twice a week, and showed up every day at lunchtime. He arrived one night at midnight, after Sam had left, and spent the night with her, which proved to her that he really did have an understanding with his wife, or he couldn't have spent the night. She never doubted it for a minute. And it was convenient that Sam had recently stopped staying with her at night.

She told no one about what they were doing, although Sam questioned her a few times. But she was careful not to let anything show to him. She didn't want Sam to know. He had been odd about Ed since her parents died and suspicious of him, almost as if he was jealous.

"Are you okay? You seem so distracted sometimes," Sam commented. He assumed it was part of the grief process but it worried him.

"I'm fine, I'm feeling better," she said matter-of-factly, and she looked it. She wasn't happy again but she seemed healthier and more alive, but she didn't dare tell Sam what she was doing. He was always uneasy about Ed, and she knew he wouldn't approve. Either jealous or possessive, or overprotective, like a big brother. And he was young, he wouldn't understand.

She and Ed had been lovers for two and a half months by Thanksgiving, and she felt as though her whole life had changed. He was the most exciting man she had ever known. He still showed up on Page Six occasionally, which he said was to keep people off the scent. He thought they should remain discreet for as long as possible. He said people would be envious of them, and their thirty-year age difference would cause comment and criticism, which he didn't want to expose her to.

"It doesn't matter to me at all," she reassured him. He was so much more exciting than any boy her age.

"One day, I hope we'll be married, and we won't have to explain it to anyone," he said with a hopeful expression.

"Are you really going to get divorced?" She looked impressed. He had mentioned it several times. She didn't feel guilty because he was so clear that their marriage had been over for years. And the idea of being married to him was exciting and made her feel safe.

"I was going to get divorced anyway. Tell me when you're ready, and I'll file." She felt too young to be married, and she didn't think it would be proper to marry less than a year after her parents' deaths, and he agreed when she said it to him. "We'll talk about it next summer then. I can hardly wait," he said, pulled her close to him, and kissed her to seal the deal.

She spent Thanksgiving with Sam and his family, while Ed was at his Connecticut home with his. In the December issue of *Vogue,* there was a handsome photograph of him with Marielle at their country estate, which he said had been taken in the summer before he got involved with Coco. He said they had agreed to the interview to keep up appearances for their children's sake. The photograph meant nothing, he said, and Coco believed him. She had no reason not to. He had never lied to her. He and her father were both honest men.

Their dinners at La Grenouille became more and more regular. They went to the Italian restaurant often too. He came by frequently at midnight, when he said he couldn't bear the night without her, and Sam always left around eleven. Sam still came by every evening after work, but didn't always stay for dinner now. When he did, he left before Ed showed up, but he had no idea she was seeing Ed. She kept it a secret. Ed went to the country on weekends and said he did work there, and could get more done than in the city. For Christmas he gave her a Cartier love bracelet set with diamonds, and a matching ring that looked like a wedding band. When Sam questioned her about it, she said it was her mother's. Ed had put the bracelet on with a little golden screwdriver that came with it, so she couldn't take it off. And he said the ring was her promise ring, with better things to come in future, once people knew about them. They had no set plan about when to tell them.

He went skiing in Switzerland with his children over Christmas. It was a hard time for Coco without her parents, but since Sam's family didn't celebrate it, he spent the time with her, so she wasn't alone. Ed came by to say goodbye to her before he left for Europe, and Sam was there and after he left, Sam looked at her strangely.

"Is something going on with you and Ed?" It had hit him like a bolt of lightning when he saw them together. The look in Ed's eyes gave him away.

"Of course not. Why would you say that?" Coco said, looking uncomfortable. They had kissed stealthily when he got on the elevator. He was on his way to the airport. A car was waiting for him downstairs with his bags.

"He looks at you like he owns you," Sam said, suspicious.

"Don't be silly. He's my trustee."

Sam looked at her intensely. "Be careful, Coco. He scares me. I think he's a player. I smell it from a mile away." But since Sam was as innocent as she was, she paid no attention to him. And she was determined not to tell him the truth. It was her secret with Ed. It was the first time she had ever lied to Sam, and she felt guilty about it. Her birthday was a few days before Christmas, and she spent it quietly with Sam. She didn't want to celebrate it, so they had dinner at home.

Ed called her on her birthday, on Christmas Day and New Year's Eve, and texted her in between. He had business in London for a week after the holidays, and by the time he returned, she hadn't seen him for almost three weeks. He barely got through the door the first time he saw her, before they were making love all over the apartment and finally made it to her bed.

"Oh my God, I missed you so much. It was unbearable without you. I can't go away without you again." But he did, to Saint Bart's in February, on a yacht with friends, for Easter in Rome, with his children again, and in June, he mentioned in passing that he had rented a house in Tuscany for two months, so his children and their spouses and his grandchildren could come and go. For the first time, she looked at him questioningly.

"Will Marielle be there too?"

"Who knows with her? She does what she wants and makes her own plans. Although she'll want to see the children too. I think she'll be on a boat in Greece in July. Maybe you and I can go somewhere then."

"Are you still planning to divorce her?" Coco said quietly. She had decided not to go back to school for spring semester either, and she had done nothing in the past nine months except make love with Ed and watch TV with Sam.

"I'm not sure this is the right time. She's had some health issues. But it's certainly a possibility. Maybe in the fall," he said, reaching for her, and she pulled away.

"I don't want to be rude, Ed, but I don't want to be your piece on the side. I still see you on Page Six a lot, and you were in *W* with Marielle last month when you went to Spain to see friends. You didn't tell me she was going to be with you. I think you're more married than you've told me." She had thought it for a while, and wondered if Sam was right. Ed had the perfect arrangement in hiding with her. No one had any idea that they were involved, and he could have her whenever he wanted. She had been his willing plaything for nine months. The anniversary of her parents' death was in a month, by which time, he had said, he wanted to marry her. She was beginning to think he was playing her for a fool, with Marielle's "health issues," which made it a bad time to file for divorce, and a house in Tuscany for two months, where his wife would be too. Coco stared at him and he didn't flinch or falter.

"The only one I love is you. How can you doubt that?"

"I don't. But I think you are still very married, and possibly intend to stay that way. You've had plenty of time to do something about it since September, and you haven't."

"I'll do it in the fall," he promised.

"I don't believe you," she said bravely. Everything about him was exciting. He lived a jet-set life, but he shared that life with Marielle, not with her. Maybe Sam was right and he was a player. If so, the joke was on her, and he had taken advantage of the fact that he was her trustee, and she was a naïve twenty-two-year-old girl. She was not in his league. But she was not a fool.

"I'm not so sure my father would have liked this," she said quietly and firmly. "Or that you'd have done this if he were alive. You were his partner. He trusted you."

"I think you're being unfair," he said, looking sullen, as he got out of bed, walked across the room, and reached for his clothes.

"I don't think I'm the one being unfair here, or dishonest. I'm not married and staying that way. You are. If you loved me and were honest, you'd have seen a lawyer by now." She was very clear about it. It had been troubling her for a while, and she had finally said it.

"I have seen a lawyer," he insisted, but he looked like he was lying now, even to her. "He advised me to wait." When he said that, she could see what he was, and what he was doing. It was all a game to him, and who knew how many others there were, the women he was in the papers with, whom he claimed were only decoys. She suddenly felt like an idiot and realized that he had treated her like one. He dressed and she didn't stop him. Then he came toward her, and tried to caress her and she moved away.

"I think we need to stop until you get your life in order. I love you.

But I'm not stupid, Ed. This has been easy for you." She had been constantly available to him for almost a year.

"And you had something better to do?" he said sarcastically, and it hit her like a slap. "Like movie nights with your little friend Sam? I've wined and dined and entertained you for the last year, with the best sex you'll ever have." There was a mean look in his eyes she hadn't seen before, and what he said was rude and disrespectful.

"Is that all it is? You abused my father's trust and mine, and took advantage of the fact that I have no family and no father to defend me now. I trusted you, but maybe I was wrong." She seemed suddenly very grown up and felt it as she faced him. She was shaking, but he didn't know. It took courage to challenge him, and she loved him now.

"You're not a child, Coco. You're a woman. We're both adults. You knew I was married, you always did. You decided to break the rules with me. You can't blame me for that now."

"You said you wanted to get divorced and marry me, right from the beginning."

"Maybe I will someday, when I want to, not when you tell me to. That's up to me. For now, this suits me the way it is." He was suddenly cold and arrogant, and almost cruel.

"It doesn't suit me," she said in a trembling voice, realizing now who he was. Sam was right. He had played her like a harp. She had been the fool here, imagining that he loved her, and believing everything he said.

He turned in the bedroom doorway then and looked at her with contempt. "You need to grow up, Coco. Your innocence is charming, for a while. But if you want to play in the big leagues, this is how it is. It's been fun. Goodbye." He walked to the front door and out of the apartment, as Coco felt like someone had squeezed all the air out of her. He was a bad guy, and always had been, just great in bed. She lay there for a long time thinking about it, realizing what a fool she had been. She wanted to hate him, but she didn't. She hated herself.

She got up and took a shower and dressed. She was quiet when Sam came to see her that night. By the time he came, she had taken off the Cartier bracelet with the little gold screwdriver, and the ring Ed had given her, and put them away. She wanted no reminders of him anywhere. It had gone on for almost a year and suddenly it was over.

"What's up? Are you upset about something?" He always knew. She started to tell him, stopped herself, and then decided to tell him the truth. She told him a modified, slightly tamer, less X-rated version of the last nine months, and admitted to the affair with Ed, that he had played her and lied to her, and she had just been a diversion for a married man. Sam looked furious, not at her, but at Ed.

"I told you the guy's a player. What a son of a bitch. He took total advantage of you and the state you were in, and the role your father entrusted him with. What a pig."

She smiled at the intense look on his face. "I was the idiot," she said, feeling ashamed. She'd had an affair with a married man for nine months, thinking he had an "arrangement" with his wife and he was going to marry her. He had won in the end, and she felt like a fool.

"You're just young, Coco. The guy is thirty years older. He knows how to play the game."

"I fell for it because he was exciting," she said, remorseful.

"You need to play it safe next time. The exciting ones are usually dangerous, and he is. But at least you figured it out in the end. I still love you," he said, and put an arm around her.

"You're not mad at me for lying to you about him?"

"You had to experience it for yourself. You'll know better next time." She nodded, and they grabbed popcorn in the kitchen, and sat down to watch movies together. She was grateful he was her friend. Ed was everything Sam had said. He lived in the fast lane, and had run over her like a bus. She was surprised to find that her heart wasn't broken but her pride was badly bruised.

Chapter 3

The anniversary of her parents' death was a hard day for Coco. She and Sam drove out to the Hamptons, where she felt especially close to them. They had shared such happy times there. She remembered every moment of the year before vividly, and the last time she saw them. She and Sam walked on the beach together and she cried. She still missed them acutely and she knew that her experience with Ed would never have happened if her father were alive. He would have protected her. Sam tried to, but she wouldn't listen. She hadn't heard from Ed in a month, and it was awkward having him as her trustee, but she didn't need any advice from him about the estate for now. She was thinking of trying to get a change of trustee, but she wasn't sure how to do it. She doubted that he would fight it, for fear she would expose him and how he had taken advantage of her, which wouldn't have sat well with a judge.

She had learned a lesson from it, and made a vow to herself. No married men no matter what they said about "an arrangement" with their wife. And no more exciting guys. She was going to keep her eyes open for a "normal" one if she fell in love again. Sam was right.

As they walked down the beach on the anniversary of her parents' death, Coco said sadly, "Who will walk me down the aisle, if I ever get married?" Tears were rolling down her cheeks, and Sam smiled.

"I will. That's an easy one. Just make sure you marry the right guy. We're both too young to get married anyway. That's a big responsibility. I'm not ready for it, and you're a year younger than I am. We're still babies." He had recently met a girl he liked. His parents knew hers. He mentioned her to Coco a few times. Her name was Tamar Weiss, and miraculously, she was Jewish. He was usually attracted to girls who weren't. He hadn't told his mother about going out with her or she'd have been all over him, wanting him to get married. She wanted all her children to marry early, and have lots of babies. Sam's sister Sabra was still insisting that she wanted to get engaged to her Catholic boyfriend, and convert for him. Sam's mother was going crazy over it, which kept the heat off Sam for now, and he could date Tamar in peace, while no one paid attention. He told Coco that Tamar was a nice girl. She worked in a bank, came from an Orthodox family, and had a lot of siblings. She wasn't exciting, but she seemed like a solid, reasonable, intelligent person. He enjoyed her company, and when Coco asked him if he was in love with her, he said he wasn't.

"Your choice of words, 'solid and reasonable,' scares me. Can't you notch that up a little? You don't need to fall in love with a stripper, but how about someone a little jazzier than 'reasonable and solid.' She sounds like a Seeing Eye dog."

"Jazzy is dangerous, Coco. You just learned that with Ed."

"Yeah, but 'solid' is going to bore the shit out of you after a few years, if it takes that long."

"Maybe not. My parents aren't exciting and they've been together for twenty-five years. That's solid."

"Your mother is a little bit exciting," Coco said, thinking about it. She had lots of personality and opinions.

"No, she's not. She just screams a lot. My father ignores it. I hope my sister has the guts to defy them. I really like Liam. My mother will have a coronary if she marries him, but Sabra's pretty stubborn. She might just do it. You need to go back to school in the fall, by the way. Your father would want you to. He'd be upset that you've been out of school for a year now." She nodded. She'd been considering it too, but she wasn't sure she wanted to go back, or needed to, although she knew her father would have wanted her to graduate. But school seemed boring to her now.

Instead, she called her boss at *Time* from the summer before, and asked if he had any internships available. She could at least do that for the rest of the summer. She was tired of sitting around the apartment, especially now that Ed was out of the picture. He had eaten up a lot of her time, which had kept her from doing anything else, including seeing her friends, except for Sam, who showed up faithfully almost every night, and had for a year.

"Funny you should ask," John Campbell, her old boss, said when she called him at *Time*. "We do have an opening. I don't know if it would appeal to you. It's in the London office. We can take care of the visa from here. We don't pay living expenses for interns, so no one from here has wanted it. I don't know if that works for you or not." He knew enough about her and her late father to suspect that money wouldn't be a problem. "They want an American, and we haven't been able to find one. Would that screw up your plans for school?"

"I don't have plans for school right now. I've been debating it. This internship might be just what I need." Her life in New York seemed flat at the moment. She had been mourning her parents for the last year, and hiding with Ed. She hadn't seen anyone, and she didn't want to go back to school yet. "How long is it for?"

"As long as you want. It's open-ended."

"When does it start?"

"As soon as you can get there."

"What would I do?"

"More or less the same as you were going to do here. It's kind of a jack-of-all-trades/girl Friday position, pitching in where needed."

"It sounds perfect," she said, excited about it.

"The salary is ridiculous, which, as I said, is why we haven't found anyone." But she could afford it. She didn't need the money. She needed to get busy and do something useful with her time. "Give it some thought and call me."

"I'll call you tomorrow," she promised. She wanted to sleep on it, but it sounded like exactly what she needed. And London would be a nice change from living with the ghosts in her apartment.

She talked to Sam about it that night, and he reluctantly agreed with her. His preference was that she go back to school, but if she wasn't going to, then getting out of town might be good for her, in case Ed showed up again. A year after her parents' death, she was in better shape now and could take a job for a while until she went back to school.

"Just promise me one thing, that you'll go back to college at some point. You've only got two semesters left to do. You should finish and get your diploma," Sam said, in his older brother role.

"I will, at some point," was all she would commit to.

She called John Campbell the next day, and told him she wanted the internship in London. He was delighted.

"Give us a few weeks to get your visa in order. Why don't you plan on starting mid-August." That gave her a month to get organized and pack. She'd have to find a place to live when she got to London. It sounded exciting, and she called Sam at work and told him she had accepted, and would be leaving in a month.

Much to her surprise, a week later, she got a call from Ed. She didn't dare not take it, since he was still her trustee, and the call might be about the estate. She took the call cautiously, and sounded cool when she answered. It had been five weeks since their unpleasant scene when they ended their affair. He sounded surprisingly friendly in the circumstances, and as though nothing had happened.

"How are you, Coco?"

"Fine, thank you. What's up?" She cut to the chase and didn't want to chat with him or play games.

"Nothing, I just wanted to check in and see how you're feeling. Things got a little out of hand the last time we saw each other. I'm sorry about that." He made it sound like she'd been drunk or in a bad mood.

"It's fine. We needed to clear things up." She didn't tell him that she still felt like an idiot and thought he was a bastard. She was just grateful that no one knew about them, except Sam.

"I hope you're feeling better. I was wondering if we could get together. Marielle is in Greece, and I'm leaving for Italy in two weeks.

I'd love to see you." He was incredible. He wanted to start where they'd left off, with nothing different in his situation, except that his wife was on vacation so he was free.

"I'm sorry, I can't. I'm leaving too. I'm going to London."

"How about dinner tonight?" He sounded faintly desperate. He didn't like rejection. And she didn't like liars and cheaters. She remembered everything Sam had said while she hadn't listened to him.

"Sorry, Ed. I can't make it." Then she couldn't help adding, "You're still married." Even if he weren't now, she wouldn't have gone to dinner with him. He had used her to add spice to his life. He was a bad guy. Sam was right.

"Well, maybe when you get back," he said hopefully.

"I don't think so. And when I get back, let's talk about a successor trustee. I think that would be a good idea."

"If you think so," he said, sounding vaguely annoyed. He wasn't going to argue the point with her. He knew she was right to ask for a new trustee, given what had happened between them. She hung up after that, and didn't hear from him again.

She spent the rest of her time in New York packing. She closed the house in Southampton, and left the apartment in the city as it was. She didn't know when she'd be back, a few months, longer, maybe even a year. It all depended on what would happen in London. John Campbell was giving her a new lease on life. After a year of deep mourning, she needed it, and couldn't wait to start the job. Sam needed to pursue his own life too, and not just babysit for her, although he never complained, and loved seeing her almost every night.

He drove her to the airport when she left. They clung to each other for a long time before she had to go through security.

"Take care of yourself," he admonished her. "Don't do anything crazy, and watch out for the exciting ones!" he teased her.

"You too. Watch out for the boring ones." They smiled at each other with all the love they'd shared since they were children, and then she went through security, and waved at him. After she disappeared into the crowd, he felt sad to see her go. She was so much a part of his daily life. He walked to the garage to get his car, and drove back to the city. He hoped everything would go well for her in London, and that she would remember the lesson she had learned with Ed. He hoped she'd meet a good man now, and he was going to see where things went with Tamar. He was convinced she wasn't as boring as Coco said.

Chapter 4

C oco had given herself a few days' leeway to find a place to live
before she started work. She was lucky because with the money
she had inherited from her parents, she could afford to live in a good
neighborhood, rent a cheerful, safe apartment, and have a place she
truly liked. For others, it wasn't as easy, which was one reason why
no one had leapt at the internship in London. It was an expensive
city. With the help of a realtor, she rented an adorable mews house
that was nicely furnished and would be a lovely home for her in London. It wasn't showy, but had everything she wanted. And it was
available immediately.

She left the hotel, unpacked her bags, and was settled in when she
started work at *Time*. Her boss was a woman in her late thirties, Leslie Thomas. She gave Coco a stack of filing to do, and a long list of
calls to make on her first day of work. Coco was off and running and
had a good first day. Everyone was pleasant and polite to her. They
introduced themselves as soon as they saw her, and by the end of the
week, she knew who they were and what they did. She was, as John

Campbell had described the job to her, the office jack-of-all-trades. She did everything from changing the occasional light bulb to making dinner reservations for her superiors. Leslie gave her some small captions to edit on her second day there, to gauge her creativity and writing skills. Coco was above all willing, grateful for the job, and thrilled to be there. She was honest about the fact that the internship was her first real job, at twenty-two. She didn't pretend to know things she didn't, which Leslie liked about her. She was hardworking and sincere, and eager to learn.

"Where are you staying?" Leslie asked her. Coco had already figured out that her boss's accent was upper class. There was a definite distinction between social levels in England, and someone had whispered to her that Leslie's father was in the House of Lords, which meant that she came from a distinguished family, but not necessarily that she had money, and she had said that she lived in East London, which was comfortable and respectable, but not fancy.

Leslie was attractive, single, and had no children, and had mentioned to Coco that she was divorced. She was thirty-eight and had no boyfriend at the moment.

"I found something in Chelsea," Coco answered, referring to where she lived, without saying it was a house, even though very small. It was more like a dollhouse, but had everything she needed, and was perfect for her. But the neighborhood made it clear that Coco wasn't poor or struggling.

"I'm giving a party on Saturday night, if you'd like to come. Most people leave town on the weekend, if they can, but the weather has been so beastly, I'm hoping enough people will be here."

It had been raining nonstop since Coco arrived. She didn't care. She had so much to discover about her job and the people she worked with that the weather hadn't bothered her so far, although it might after a while. It had been blazing hot and sunny in New York, and was perfect August weather the last time she went to the Hamptons with Sam. It felt more like winter in London. She'd worn a light wool coat to work every day. She thanked Leslie for the invitation and jotted down the address. "Nothing fancy," Leslie added, "jeans and a nice top are fine," which was more or less the same dress code as with her friends in New York, although not at the restaurants where she'd gone with Ed, where she had to wear a nice dress and high heels. But he was older, and moved in a different crowd. His wife was known to be one of the best dressed women in New York, which set a standard Coco couldn't match. But she had youth and her natural beauty on her side, which Ed preferred.

By the end of her first week at *Time,* Coco was starting to feel comfortable and confident in her job. She and Sam had FaceTimed several times, she showed him around her tiny house. He was impressed. The rooms were small, but it had a cozy atmosphere with a sense of history to it, and there was a fireplace in every room. Central heating had been added a century after it was built, and it had been modernized since. She told Sam she was going to a party on Saturday night. It sounded like fun to him, and he was happy for her. He had a date with Tamar Weiss that night himself. He'd been out with her a couple of times since Coco left.

When the day came for the party, it was still pouring. Coco wore a black sweater and jeans, and high heels. She had her long dark hair loose down her back, and she wore a heavy raincoat. She ran to find a cab on the street nearest her house.

By the time she got to Leslie's apartment in East London, about forty people were already there. They were a good-looking group of young people, mostly in their thirties, and Coco guessed that she might be the youngest person there. Everyone greeted her warmly when Leslie introduced her and Coco said she was freshly arrived from New York. They asked where she had been working before, and she explained that she was officially still a student at Columbia, but had gotten the job through the *Time* bureau in New York.

"They must have been desperate to get rid of you, or thought you were fantastic to send you to us," a handsome blond man in his early thirties teased her. His name was Nigel Halsey-Smythe. He was very handsome and seemed intrigued by Coco. He was obviously taken by how beautiful she was. "I'm a younger son," he rapidly explained with a grin, as he handed her a glass of wine after introducing himself. "In our system here that means a fancy name and no money. My older brother got it all, so he's got the family seat in Sussex, the estate, and the title, and I'm left to eke out a living. I sell advertising upstairs at *Time*. We're paid mostly on commission, which means that if we go to dinner, you'll have to pay. Although you probably make less than I do, so we'll have to go to parties at art galleries with champagne and free hors d'oeuvres." He was funny and she was touched by his honesty about his situation. In the British system, younger sons often had no money. The eldest brother got everything, while everyone else had to struggle and got nothing. As they talked, she learned that he had gone to Eton, the best boys' boarding school in England, and Cambridge, one of the finest universities. He also mentioned that he was thirty-three years old. He said he'd never been married, although his older brother had been married twice. "Younger sons are not in high demand," he said, pretending to be mournful, and they both laughed. He introduced her to a dozen other people. There was a plentiful buffet with Indian food, and she noticed that the caterer was pouring good French champagne. The assembled group, which grew in size rapidly, was an interesting mix of aristocrats, working-class people, mostly from the magazine, and a number of foreigners, including a group of Italians and two very pretty French girls who worked for British *Vogue* and looked like models themselves. They had a cluster of men around them at all times. Coco felt like a bumpkin compared to them. Nigel saw to it that she met nearly everyone, and they settled in a corner on a couch with some others to talk.

"So how long are you here for?" he asked her. He had made her the focus of his attention for the evening so far, and went through the buffet line with her. He seemed mesmerized. They were balancing their plates on their knees, as Leslie continued to greet new arrivals. A waiter from the caterer relieved guests of their dripping raincoats and umbrellas in the front hall. It all felt very British to Coco, and she wished that she could FaceTime Sam so he could see the scene. It was a whole different atmosphere from their student milieu in New York. This was much more sophisticated and international than what she was used to in her college life, and she was grateful to have Nigel at her side. He gave her the lowdown on everyone, and he seemed to know them all. Whose father was a lord, who had a title, who was a nobody, who had a fantastic job, or a fabulous country house and gave house parties where people killed to be invited. How aristocratic their families were was very important to him, but he didn't act like a snob. He just liked knowing about everyone and was curious about Coco.

"Great manor house, terrific food, no central heating, and no money, like most of us," he described one couple. "The roof is going to cave in on them one of these days. The place leaks like a sieve," he

said of one of the houses where the owners gave the best parties, according to him. "Do you ride?" Coco nodded, slightly in awe of all of
them, but surprisingly comfortable with him. She liked his openness
and lack of pretension, and his good looks had caught her attention
when she walked in. She'd noticed him staring at her until he walked
over to meet her. She was flattered by his attention, and his description of people's circumstances made her laugh. "So, what does your
father do? Banker, lawyer, head of some vast American corporation,
Wall Street genius, famous artist, or a mere mortal?" He was constantly playful, but interested in all the details to place where she fit
into his world. Leslie seemed to have a very eclectic group of friends.
Coco could tell that one was just as likely to meet someone with a
title as a photographer with a heavy Cockney accent in her living
room. It was fascinating. Nigel seemed to fit into the upper echelon
of the scale, despite being a younger son, as he so easily confessed.
He didn't have the title or the money, but he clearly had the blue
blood and noble heritage.

"My parents died last July, a year ago," Coco said quietly in answer to what her father did. Nigel sobered for a minute, and gazed
sympathetically at her.

"Oh, I'm sorry. How awful for you. Both at once?" She nodded. "It
must have been an accident. Terrible bad luck. Do you have siblings?"

"No, I don't," she said softly, trying not to sound tragic about it,
although it was. "Cannes, last July." He knew instantly what that
meant, and touched her hand gently, although he barely knew her.
The kind gesture brought tears to her eyes. "We used to go to the
South of France every year. I wasn't with them last year. I had a summer job at *Time*. I didn't go back to school last year because of it.

I was thinking of starting again this September, but I'll wait till January now. This is a wonderful change of scene after all that. It was a hard year."

He nodded and then smiled at her. "Thank you for warning me. We'll have to do our best to convince you to stay here. University is so boring, and we have much more fun here. Do you hunt?"

"I never have."

"We can arrange that when the season starts. I have lots of friends who hunt. My brother is the master of the hunt in our region. But we don't speak so we can't go there. It's great fun, if you like to ride. I usually avoid my brother at all cost. We hated each other growing up. I almost got over it, but then he inherited everything, and I can't stand his greedy little pig-eyed wife," Nigel said somewhat bitterly. Leslie pulled her away from him then, before Coco could comment, as they set their empty plates down and a waiter whisked them away. Nigel conceded with regret as Leslie removed her. "We can talk about my family some other time," he said, as Coco followed Leslie.

"Don't let Nigel monopolize you. He'll talk your head off. He knows everyone in London. He has a complex about being a younger son, but he's very sweet," she said, smiling. Coco had enjoyed him, and she liked hearing all the pertinent insider information he had shared with her. It added local color. Leslie introduced her to the two French girls from *Vogue,* who were very stylish and avant-garde. They spoke perfect English, and greeted Coco warmly, despite the flock of handsome men around them, most of whom were dressed like Nigel, in jeans, tweed jackets, and brown suede shoes. It was a good look and Coco liked it. She thought that most of the men in the room were sexy and handsome and seemed more polished than their counterparts in New York, although most of the men she knew there were students or recent graduates like Sam. Ed, of course, was at a whole different level, and wore a suit most of the time, except on weekends. There wasn't a suit visible in Leslie's living room. They were all much more casual, and the Italians looked more stylish than anyone else. Leslie made a real effort to introduce Coco to as many people as she could, although it had gotten difficult to move around her living room, so many more people had arrived as the evening wore on.

Nigel came to say goodbye to her before he left, asked for her cellphone number and said he'd text her and take her to a party sometime soon, or maybe they could have dinner together. She gave him her number willingly, and stayed for another hour after he left. One of the Italians had been flirting with her at a distance, but never came over to talk to her. She ended up chatting with a very interesting group of women who worked for Condé Nast, and an auctioneer at Christie's who was in the art department. Coco could see that Leslie knew lots of interesting people, and Coco wasn't alone for a minute all night. She left after midnight, and the party was still going strong, but she'd had two glasses of wine and one of champagne, and she was tired. She slipped away quietly, after thanking Leslie for a fantastic time. Several people were smoking joints by then, and the whole group seemed slightly drunk, some more than others. The alcohol had flowed generously all evening, and people had settled into smaller groups, some sitting on the floor.

Politics was a popular subject, and Leslie seemed to know a number of people in fashion. Coco noticed that all of the men in the fashion business wore heavy oxfords and no socks. The rest of the guests were more traditionally dressed. Leslie herself had worn a short tight black knit Alaïa dress that showed off her figure and her hair was as dark as Coco's. She wore it in a knot, with no makeup. She was an attractive woman and didn't look her age. Coco liked her, and had had a great time at her party.

She fell asleep minutes after she got home, and tried to describe it all to Sam the next day. He was impressed, and said he'd had a nice evening with Tamar. They'd gone to a movie and had dinner at a kosher restaurant on the Lower East Side, since she was Orthodox, and would only eat kosher meals, which would delight his mother if he told her about Tamar, but he didn't intend to. He didn't want to fuel his mother's obsession about his getting married, especially to an Orthodox Jewish girl.

"No more BLT sandwiches or lobster for you, if you stay with her," she teased him and he laughed.

"My mother would have a heart attack if she knew what I eat when I'm with you. That sounds like a pretty racy crowd you fell in with last night," he said, half impressed and half worried for her. "Be careful not to get in over your head." But fortunately, no one knew her circumstances, so fortune hunters weren't likely to go after her. She just looked like an exceptionally pretty young woman, and dressed like everyone else their age. Unless they knew who her father was, which most people didn't, they wouldn't suspect that she had inherited a fortune. He was glad that she was happy and having fun, and meeting new people, which had been the whole point of going there, and staying occupied. She had spent a year of intense mourning, now she needed to get back into living. The world she was exploring sounded like fun for her. At times, Sam envied her the options she had in her life. In contrast, he felt like he had none at all.

"You have to come over and visit," she urged him. She'd only been gone for ten days, but already missed him. He was so much a part of her life, and stood in as her family now, that she felt as though she had lost a limb being away from him. She didn't miss Ed nearly as much as she did Sam, and she was still angry at Ed, and herself for falling for him. She could see now how innocent and trusting she had been, and he had taken full advantage of it, and still wanted to, if she'd let him. She was no longer as naïve, at least not about him. But Sam wasn't sure how much more alert she would be, if the bad guys were packaged differently in a new setting. She was only twenty-two, and it would be easy for her to be taken advantage of in a fast international crowd in London. It sounded to him like she had fallen in with some of them the night before.

"Just be careful," he warned her again, and promised to come over when his father would let him take time off from work and he could afford a cheap ticket, if he could find one.

Nigel made good on his promise and called her on Monday, at work. He told her how much he had enjoyed meeting her, and hoped to see her again soon. Hearing from him put a smile on her face as she started her second week of work. The next day, he came down from upstairs and showed up in her office right before lunchtime, and invited her to have lunch with him. She had no plans so they went to a pub nearby, and he had her laughing all through lunch, describing house parties he'd been to. He was the most engaging, ingenuous, funnily innocent man she had ever met. He had a boyish quality about him that was very endearing, and he was very sympathetic about her losing her parents. His own parents had died when he was young, but had been much older than hers, since he was the youngest son and his only brother was fourteen years older than he was, from his father's first marriage. They walked back to the office together, he disappeared upstairs to the advertising department, and she went back to work for Leslie, and did some filing.

On Thursday he texted her, apologized for the short notice, and invited her to a party on Friday night. "Nothing posh," he said in his text, "probably just mash and bangers or fish and chips, in the garret of an artist friend." It sounded like fun to her, and he picked her up at seven-thirty at her mews house, looked around and was impressed.

"I say, Coco, this is very nice indeed. You must be paying a fortune for it. These old mews houses are very hard to find." It was nicely decorated, which she was enjoying too, and came with everything she needed, a fully stocked kitchen, nice linens, and everything she could have wanted.

"The rent isn't too bad, and it feels like a dollhouse. I love it. The owner moved to Hong Kong for two years. I was lucky to find it."

"You certainly were." They had a drink before they left, and when they got to the party in a shabby neighborhood, they walked up four floors to the artist's studio. There must have been a hundred people squeezed into the tiny space. The smell of marijuana was heavy in the air, and the crowd was even more eclectic than it had been at Leslie's, a little more down-market, but mostly very arty. Even in clean jeans and a nice blue sweater, she felt overdressed. Nigel was in a tweed jacket and jeans again, and seemed comfortable wherever he was, in any kind of group. The artist was Indian and had a Chinese girlfriend, who had posed nude for many of his paintings. She had a spectacular body and a lovely face.

The meal was fish and chips, as Nigel had predicted, and after an hour, he suggested that they slip away and go out to dinner. They left and he took her to a good French restaurant, and contrary to his earlier warning, he ordered a very good bottle of French wine, and paid for the meal. She suspected that he had exaggerated about being dead broke. He was very aristocratic, had lovely manners, and seemed to know every titled aristocrat around the world. He had been to the Hotel du Cap in the South of France, nearly as often as she had. She was surprised she had never met him there, but they had spent their days there in their private cabana, and rarely met the other guests.

"I'm not sure I could ever go back without them," she said sadly. "That was so much a part of all my summers with my parents. It would be too weird and painful without them." He nodded and touched her hand again.

"You're a brave girl to have gone through what you did for the last year."

"There's no other choice. Things happen and you have to deal with them. But it was very hard," she said. She told him about Sam then and what good friends they were, and how he had been at her side for all of the past year. She didn't mention Ed, who seemed irrelevant now, and a bad memory. She didn't want to admit to her own stupidity, falling for the classic line of a married man, about having an understanding with his wife, planning to divorce, and never having felt for any woman what he did for her. It was all so trite and such a cliché, she realized now. At least Nigel was single, thirty-three years old, and had never been married. She wasn't sure yet if they would be friends, or something more, but she was enjoying his company immensely, and he was so charming, amusing, and boyish that he seemed more like her age than his own. He wasn't afraid to admit to his fears or feelings, which she found refreshing. There was no hidden agenda with him. He said whatever he thought.

"What do you want to be when you grow up?" she asked him over dinner, since he didn't seem as though he was fully an adult yet.

"Rich and happy," he answered very quickly. "Rich and miserable seems like such a waste," he said and she laughed. She didn't ask him how he intended to become rich, since he claimed to be poor now, although she didn't quite believe that either. He was expensively dressed, and he lived in a stylish part of town. But he obviously had less than his older brother, due to the British laws of primogeniture, which had existed for centuries.

"What do you want to do?" she asked him directly.

"Have fun. As you've seen firsthand, life can be cut short. I think it's important to live life to the fullest, and enjoy every moment. I can't bear people who whinge all the time." She had already learned that "whinge" was the British word for whine, and he didn't. He constantly seemed to be enthusiastic, look on the bright side, and make everything fun. He never complained, which was refreshing, except about his brother, whom he very obviously disliked. But he appeared to have countless friends, and he was fun to have around. He was apparently a popular houseguest, and she could see why. "What about you?" He turned the question on her.

"I don't know," she admitted. "I guess I have to finish college at some point, though I seem to have run out of steam on that. I want to work for a magazine, and I am, even though it's an entry-level internship. I don't have a burning desire for a career, but I want to work. I don't think I've found my passion yet, but I still have time, and I haven't even graduated."

"Marriage and kids?" he asked, curious about her. She seemed to have a sensible way of looking at life, which he liked.

"Not for a long time," she answered his question. "My parents married right out of college, at the Elvis Chapel in Las Vegas." She grinned and he laughed.

"I've always wanted to know someone who did that. I love it. How terrific."

"They eloped. My mother's family was fancier than my father's. She was a debutante, etcetera, etcetera, and they didn't approve of my father, who grew up poor, and they thought he would never amount to anything. So they got married anyway, and he proved them wrong. They were very happy, and getting married early suited them. I've never wanted that for myself, and I'm way too young to think about kids. They had me at twenty-five. I can't even imagine having children three years from now. It would scare me to death. I'm not ready for that kind of responsibility," she said honestly. But she did have the responsibility of a large inheritance she had to make decisions about. She had people to advise her, but never mentioned any of that to Nigel. She was extremely discreet about her circumstances.

"Some women are so desperate to get married. It's a bit unnerving. I don't care when I marry, as long as it's to the right woman," he said sensibly, "and I'd like to have children. I just haven't met the right woman yet. I don't have to worry about an heir for the title or the estate, since I don't have either one, which takes the pressure off." He was totally free and open to the possibilities of what life presented to him, and he was candid about admitting he didn't like his job. He seemed more interested in his social life and his friends.

He was a very relaxed person without an agenda, which made him easy to be with. She liked him a lot. He was half pal, half flirt, which she liked too. His flirtatious side made her feel like a girl, and his acting like a pal the rest of the time made him good to talk to, though not as good as Sam. But they had no history with each other as she and Sam had. "By the way, there's a very grand house party next weekend, if you'd like to come. Fabulous house, a castle actually, one of the finest in England. They keep it going with tours of the house and grounds, which is quite awful really, but very lucrative. They give wonderful house parties, and you'll meet some fun people. Separate bedrooms of course, if you like. I think they have forty guest rooms, so it won't be a problem. I think you'd enjoy it." He made it sound so appealing, she couldn't resist. She had heard of the castle when he told her the name. He seemed to move in only the best circles, and was accepted everywhere. She was touched by his generosity in including her. She told him she was happy to accept, and took him up on the offer of separate bedrooms, since they had just met.

She mentioned it to Leslie when she went back to work.

"You'll never be bored with Nigel. I think he goes to three parties a night. He knows everyone in London. He's a good guy, very good family, though his older brother got everything of course when their father died. That's how it works here. But Nigel will always land on his feet. He's always such a positive presence. I adore him. I'm glad you two hit it off. He'll introduce you to everyone, and you won't have a free night for a year." It was the busiest Coco had ever been, but it was a great start to her time in London, and Leslie's endorsement put her at ease about him. Leslie and Nigel had been childhood friends, like she and Sam, though not quite as close in age, since they were five years apart. She said she'd gone to school with a cousin of his. People from good families all seemed to know one another or be connected somehow.

He texted her what she needed to bring for the weekend, so she'd be properly dressed and wouldn't feel awkward, which seemed thoughtful to her, so she didn't have to guess. She packed everything he suggested and a few extras, for formal dinners, casual lunches, hiking, hunting if she chose to tag along. She had it all in two suitcases when he picked her up on Friday afternoon in a magnificent racing green vintage Jaguar. She felt incredibly chic as they drove the three hours to the castle he had told her about. She'd read up on it the night before. It sounded fabulous, and the family that owned it was interesting as well. The castle had been built by the family in the fifteenth century, and enlarged two hundred years later. All of the contents and structure were original. She couldn't wait to see it in real life and not just photographs.

"I love your car!" she said, as they drove along. He had the top down, and she was wearing a scarf and felt like Grace Kelly in *To Catch a Thief*. With his blue-eyed, blond good looks, and easy aristocratic style, there was something naturally glamorous about him. He was effortlessly sophisticated and elegant without ever showing off.

"I'm so glad," he said about the car. "Her name is Josephine, and she's the love of my life. I give you fair warning, if we ever fall in love, she will always come first. I hope you can live with that," he said, grinning at her, and leaned over to kiss her cheek to soften the blow, as she smiled at him.

"It sounds like I'll have to."

"I'll let you drive her if you like," he said generously and Coco shook her head.

"I wouldn't dare. I'd be afraid to hurt her, or do something wrong."

"She's rather temperamental, I'll admit. It's part of her charm."

"Do you like temperamental women?" she teased him.

"Only Josephine," he answered.

"Good, because I'm not."

"I can tell." He smiled at her. "That's why you're here." It was an honest statement and she laughed.

They arrived just in time to change for dinner. There were about thirty people milling around the enormous drawing room, and their hosts were warmly welcoming, and delighted to meet Coco. They were a marquess and marchioness, and Nigel had briefed her beforehand on how to address them. They were in their early forties, and made everyone feel very much at home. Nigel said they had a genius for getting the right people together. Liveried servants showed them to their rooms, and Coco noticed that they were in separate hallways, which was apparently standard for couples who were not sharing a room. They would need a compass, a map, and roller skates to find each other, she whispered to him on the way to their rooms, and he laughed.

"No worries. I know the house very well. It's full of shortcuts and secret passages, if I need to get to you quickly."

"I'd probably end up in the dungeon and no one would ever find me if I tried to find you."

"I promise to get up a search party if that happens," he said, as they stopped at her room, which was a large, very English-looking room filled with handsome antiques, beautiful dark red damask fabrics, and a canopied bed. He hurried off with the footman to get to his own room and change for dinner. He disappeared down another hallway with a wave, as she closed her door. It was all a new experience for her, and she felt a little bit like Alice in Wonderland as she opened one of her suitcases and a maid in a black uniform and white cap appeared. It was very *Downton Abbey,* and a throwback to another era, like the house itself, which was enormous, and very much a castle. The photographs she'd seen online hadn't done it justice.

"Would you like me to unpack for you, miss?" she asked Coco, who was embarrassed to have someone else unpack her bags.

"No, thank you very much." She smiled at her. "I'm fine." The maid was about the same age as Coco and the two young women smiled at each other like two guests at a costume party. She disappeared and Coco rushed around to have a quick bath, unpack her dress, put on makeup, brush her hair, and dress for dinner. She wore a green silk dress the color of her eyes, with a string of her mother's pearls, her own diamond earrings, and high heels. She wore just a little mascara, red lipstick, and brushed her hair until it shone. She looked very elegant and quietly sexy as she made her way along the hall, and down the grand staircase, where she saw Nigel looking up at her and smiling. He'd been waiting for her in a perfectly cut dark blue suit. He was very handsome, and they were a striking couple as they walked into the drawing room together, and their hosts greeted them again.

They made the rounds to meet the other guests. Nigel knew everyone with one or two exceptions, and everyone was happy to see him. He and Coco were the only single people there. The others were all in couples, his age or the age of their hosts. Coco was by far the youngest guest, but as soon as they spoke to her, they were impressed by her. Their hosts were particularly happy to see Nigel with such a charming girl. The hostess whispered to her that he had a penchant for either young actresses who acted like spoiled brats with no manners, or heiresses who were even more spoiled. They all thought Coco, with her easy, polite ways and obvious good breeding, was a breath of fresh air. "Lovely girl . . ." were the whispers among the other women, and they made note to invite her to their own homes, with or without Nigel, since they weren't an item, according to their hostess. Two of the guests said they wanted to introduce her to their sons.

After dinner the ladies withdrew to the drawing room, according to tradition, and the men joined them half an hour later, after port or brandy and cigars. Late into the evening, card tables and parlor games were introduced. There was a great sound system, and some of the guests who were so inclined danced. No one went to bed before three A.M., and it was nearly four when Nigel walked Coco up the stairs and down the hallway to her room. He paused at the door with a smile and raised an eyebrow, asking a silent question.

"If you invite me in now, it will spare you the embarrassment of getting lost and winding up in the dungeon," he whispered, as he kissed her cheek in a slow and sensual way.

"I think I'll stay here tonight," she whispered back.

"And I should go back to my room?" he asked, and she nodded. "Oh, cruel woman . . . What if I have a nightmare, there won't be anyone to comfort me."

"There's a whiskey bottle in my room, and a bottle of brandy, in a small bar. There's probably one in your room too. You could try that," she said demurely and he laughed.

"Ah, Coco, you have no heart." But he was only teasing her and she knew it. It was much too soon to fall into bed with him, and she had no intention of doing that, especially since she was sure that many women already had. He was very charming and famously handsome, and she suspected that few women resisted him, and most fell prey to his charms. She didn't want to be one of them. Not too quickly anyway. "See you at breakfast, after a long, lonely night." He kissed her cheek again, and headed down the hall to his room, as she gently closed the door to hers.

Chapter 5

The rest of the house party at the castle was magical. They had a small, very good live band to dance to on Saturday night. Nigel warned her that most of the weekend parties he went to were not as well done as this one. They had started at the top. Their hosts had a lot of style, and made the weekend fun for everyone.

The men went hunting on Saturday morning, and a few of the women joined them. Coco chose to be one of them, and stood discreetly behind Nigel. She chatted with their hostess, who was a very interesting woman. She was involved in a number of social causes and had a master's in psychology.

They explored the nearby village that afternoon, danced away the night after dinner, and this time at Coco's door, Nigel kissed her properly, not just on the cheek, and she enjoyed it thoroughly. She still didn't let him spend the night with her, much to his dismay. It tantalized him and just made him want her more. By the second day of the weekend, he knew that she was the woman he had been waiting for all his life. He was incredibly nice to her, and they had a wonderful time together.

On Sunday all the guests were present for a big breakfast. Some stayed for lunch, and afterward, Nigel and Coco left after thanking their hosts profusely. The marquess and marchioness said pointedly to Coco that they looked forward to seeing her again, and hoped she would visit them soon. She had left an envelope in her room with a tip for the maid, as her mother had taught her to do. She intended to send flowers to their hosts on Monday.

On the way back, Nigel couldn't stop talking about how much he had enjoyed the weekend with her. "Their weekends can be quite boring sometimes, even if lavish and well run, because their guests are almost always married and a little older. They were a good group this time, although we were the youngest people there. But you were fantastic. Everyone fell in love with you," he smiled at her, "and so did I."

"I had a wonderful time too. I really loved our hosts. They're such nice people. I liked all the guests." It had been a memorable weekend, one she knew she would never forget, no matter what happened with him. She had heard what he had said about falling in love with her, but she didn't want to address it yet. She knew he wasn't serious after knowing her for two weeks. But he brought it up again himself when he dropped her off at her house.

"I meant what I said," he said gently. "Coco, I'm falling in love with you."

"Let's take it slow for a while," she said, smiling. He didn't know about the affair with Ed, but it had only ended three months before, and she didn't want to rush into anything. She wanted time to get to know Nigel, not just at parties, but with time alone. If it was real, it would unfold. And if it wasn't, she didn't want to get hurt again, or to hurt him. There was a vulnerable side to him too, beyond the good manners, good looks, and good breeding. She knew by then that he'd had a lonely upbringing, at boarding school since he was seven, with cold parents who had died when he was young, and the older brother who treated him like a nonentity as soon as he'd inherited the title and what was left of the family fortune. Nigel had had almost no love in his life and she didn't want to tell him she loved him until she was sure she did, or to mislead him, or rush into it before she was sure of how she felt herself.

"Please don't be so sensible," he said longingly, as he kissed her outside her front door. "I'm in love with you. Let's seize the moment." He was almost begging her, and it touched her profoundly.

"I don't want to rush into anything until we're sure."

"You're too young to be that reasonable," he complained. "What happened to the impetuousness of youth? You must be lying about your age." She laughed. It was hard to resist him, but she forced herself to. He carried her bags inside for her, and took them upstairs. They sat on the couch in the small library, and had a glass of wine, and kissed in front of the fire he had made, and then reluctantly he left her, and texted her right away. "Call me at any hour, if you need anything. I do house calls, especially at night." She laughed and answered him, thanking him again for the best weekend imaginable.

"How was it?" Leslie asked her the next day at work.

"Absolutely fabulous. Magical. I had the best weekend of my life."

"Nigel is good at that. And the castle is incredible, isn't it?"

"Everything was perfect." Coco glowed.

"Nigel must be head over heels in love with you by now." She smiled knowingly at Coco.

"So he says."

"He probably means it. He's always very upbeat, but I think underneath that, he's a very lonely guy. He says he wants to get married and have babies. I think he probably does."

"I'm too young for that," Coco said, "and he wants to move too fast."

"If you make him wait, he'll love you forever. That always works with men," Leslie said wisely and went back to her office. But Coco wasn't trying to play him or inflame him. It really was too soon for her.

Two dozen red roses in a vase from a fashionable florist were waiting for her on her doorstep that night when she got home. She knew he was in late meetings, but he called her at ten o'clock when he got out, and wanted to drop by.

"Can I trust you?" she asked, and he laughed.

"No, but I'll try to behave. I've had fifteen years of slutty women I never cared about. Now I'm in love, and I actually found one with decent morals. What miserable luck." But it was also why he was falling in love with her, because he couldn't have her easily, and she was falling in love with him too. She wanted to savor it. No one had ever been as loving in his attentions to her. She wanted to know his flaws as well as his virtues, and give it a little time.

He was there half an hour later and they chatted about their respective days at work. His roses were almost bigger than her dining table, and looked beautiful. She thanked him. She had sent flowers to their hosts for the weekend.

They kissed and cuddled and he left at midnight. They had dinner several times that week. When she told Sam about the weekend, he sounded suspicious. "Why is he rushing you? Is there something behind it?"

"Don't be so paranoid. My boss went to school with his cousin and has known him for years. She says he's a lonely guy. His parents sent him to boarding school when he was seven, which people do here. I think he's starving for love. In any case, I'm being sensible."

"Good. Get to know him. Wait," he said in his big brother voice.

"I am."

They stayed in town the following weekend, and did several of the things she had wanted to do since she arrived. They went to the Victoria and Albert Museum, saw the queen's jewels at the Tower of London, which was touristy but fun, and they wandered in Hyde Park. On Sunday, they had tea at Claridge's.

Afterward, he took her to his apartment, so she could see it. She was somewhat shocked when she did. It was in a good location, in a fashionable neighborhood, but the apartment itself was small and dark, with paint peeling off the walls. There was nothing personal about it. It looked more like a hotel room than a home, and she was sad for him when she saw it. It showed her how empty his life was. He had an active social life and many friends, but there were no photographs of his family, mementos, or family heirlooms. It supported Leslie's theory that he was a lonely man. Then they went back to her cozy little house that looked more lived in after a few weeks than his did after five years. It struck Coco too that there was nothing on the walls at his place. There was no décor, and he had bought everything at Ikea. It looked more like a student apartment than the home of a thirty-three-year-old man. He said he never entertained there, only at his club, and she could see why.

Once back at her house, he built a fire, and they sat peacefully together, kissing and talking. He said they had been invited to another house party the following weekend, by guests who had been at the castle with them. This one would be more human scale and less grand, but sounded like fun too. It would be more of a mixed crowd with some younger single people there, closer to his age. It sounded like fun to her and she agreed. She was thoroughly enjoying her budding relationship with him, and her introduction into his world.

The second house party was different, but just as much fun. There was a prosperous-looking older man there in his sixties, who had a girlfriend Coco's age. He was British and she was Russian and was an interesting girl. She had been the mistress of a well-known Russian businessman, and had a four-year-old daughter by him. The rest of the guests were a good mix of people. Coco loved the life she was sharing with Nigel, and the people he was exposing her to. She was enjoying her job, and liked working for Leslie. She was getting an inside look at the magazine business, although she wasn't doing anything important herself, but she liked the atmosphere and the people. Most of all, she was enjoying Nigel. When they came home from the second weekend, they sat kissing for a long time, and it was harder and harder to remain sensible. He looked at her seriously for a minute.

"Would you go away with me next weekend, Coco?"

"I think we just did." She smiled at him.

"Not to a house party. Just with me, the two of us. I'd love to take you to Paris. It's my favorite city in the world."

"That sounds like a plot to seduce me," she said, laughing.

"It is," he admitted freely. "I don't want to just fall into bed with you some night, although I would be thrilled if you did. Or get lucky at a house party, because we'd had too much to drink. I want to take you away and make love to you, to get us off on the right foot. Would you do that?" he asked, his eyes pleading with her.

She kissed him and nodded and then whispered, "Yes, I would." There was something so touching about his request, this time she couldn't resist him. And they'd known each other for a month and spent a lot of time together.

He was so excited, he looked like he was going to explode. He planned it all meticulously. They left early Friday evening on the Eurostar and arrived in Paris in glorious, warm, end-of-September weather, and took a cab to a small romantic hotel he knew on the Left Bank. They had dinner at Le Voltaire on the quai of the Seine that night, and walked along the river afterward, as the Bateaux Mouches glided by all lit up, full of tourists.

Then they went back to their room at the hotel, with a romantic four-poster bed covered in toile de Jouy fabric. He carefully un-dressed her like a work of art he had longed to possess since he first saw her. He made love to her tenderly, and they were both engulfed by the passion that had been growing for the last month, like a hurricane waiting to happen. The romantic little room was perfect for their first night of love. He looked at her in the moonlight and had tears in his eyes when he told her he loved her, and as she held him in her arms, she told him she loved him too, and meant it. They both had so much to give to each other. They made love again until the sun came up, and then they slept at last, in each other's arms. They both felt as though they had come home at last.

When she woke up in the morning, Nigel was sitting on the bed, admiring her. He had brought her café au lait and croissants from downstairs and she smiled as she woke up.

"I must be dreaming," she said happily.

"No, this is my dream, Coco. I've dreamt it all my life, and now you're real." It was like a fairy tale, for both of them. It was exactly what they wanted, and the place and time were perfect.

They walked past the Invalides that morning, and went to the Jeu de Paume, and then walked to the Petit Palais to see a visiting Renoir exhibit. Then they stood outside Notre Dame, looking at it with awe. It wasn't repaired yet after the fire, and he spoke to her solemnly.

"Coco Martin, on this day I vow to love you forever."

"I love you, Nigel," she said softly in response. She was speaking of that moment, and made no promises for the future, because she no longer trusted the future, ever since her parents' deaths. There was no forever. But she knew she loved him, and he believed her.

They did a little shopping after that, and went back to the hotel. He had bought a small sketch of Paris for her at one of the book stalls along the Seine as a souvenir of the time in Paris they would never forget. It was a perfect beginning for their relationship. They made love again before dinner, and ate at a small romantic restaurant, and then went back to their hotel room and made love again. He was an expert lover, but didn't make it seem that way. His love for her was genuine, and so was their lovemaking.

They got up early the next day, and walked around the Left Bank, and at noon, with great regret, they took a cab to the train station, and took the train back to London, their hearts full of memories of the trip to Paris where their life together began.

Coco didn't keep her relationship with Nigel a secret from Sam this time. She told him the day after they came back from Paris, and he was panicked. She sounded madly in love with him, and it was easy to see why. Nigel was doing everything right. It sounded like a movie or a fairy tale, but not like reality to Sam.

"Coco, wait! Slow down! Take it easy here. You've known the guy for a month. He takes you to parties at castles, introduces you to half of London, the fancy aristocratic half. It sounds like everyone he knows has a title, and now he takes you to Paris for a weekend, and sweeps you off your feet. Dracula would seem like Prince Charming in that scenario. He may be a wonderful guy, but let's see a little real life here first. The 'normal' stuff, remember? You've got another exciting guy on your hands here. How does he act when he has a cold, or when you're in a shit mood and pick a fight with him? I know you feel like a fairy princess right now. Who wouldn't with a guy swearing to love you forever in front of Notre Dame? Shit, I would fall for him if he said that to me. I just don't want you to make another mistake like Ed and get hurt. Slow down, and give it time."

"I am. I'm not going anywhere." It bothered her that Sam was so distrustful of him. She was certain that Nigel was real.

"You need to be sure there's no ulterior motive behind this. Ed wanted to have a twenty-one-year-old sex toy. What is this guy after, if anything? You can't forget that your father left you a hell of a lot of money. You need to be sure that's not the draw here." She was disappointed by Sam's reaction. She was sure that there was no ulterior motive with Nigel. He just loved her.

"My boss has known him since they were kids, she went to school with his cousin. She says he's a great guy. He doesn't know I have money. He just thinks I'm a young girl working in London."

"Don't be so sure. You don't look like a pauper. I'm sure the place you're renting is more than a girl in your job could afford. And you've been places and done things that poor girls can't. Trust me, he *knows*.

He may not know how much you've inherited, but he's figured out some of it. And it sounds like he loves the good life and admits he has no money. If he's for real and not after anything, I will run you down the aisle, not walk you. Just give it time, and see what he does. You've got another highflyer here. Normal guys don't take you to Paris to make love for the first time, or take you to castles for the weekend."

"No, they lure you into the back of their car, and you get knocked up at sixteen," she said, and he laughed.

"Well, not quite." Despite her strong religious convictions, he had finally managed to have sex with Tamar on a night that her parents were in New Jersey with relatives, sitting shiva for a great-aunt who had died. She lived at home too, which gave them few opportunities, so they took what they could. He said he loved her, but was in no rush to do anything about it. Unlike Coco, whom he didn't trust not to do something extreme now that her parents were gone and not there to reason with her and hold her back. Her father would have kept a close eye on her. And without them, she was desperate for stability in her life. Sam wasn't convinced she was looking for it in the right places. Certainly not Ed, a married man in his fifties, cheating on his wife. And Nigel was a dark horse in the race. She didn't know him well enough to judge him objectively after a month. Sam was sure her parents would have agreed, even though they had married young, but they had known each other for several years before they eloped. "I just want you to take it slow and be sure."

"I am taking it slow. At least be happy for me that I've met a nice guy."

"I am happy for you, if he turns out to be everything he appears to be. Right now, he's a dazzler. That can be blinding. Like Ed."

"This is nothing like Ed. He's not married, and he's not a liar."

"That's a good place to start," he said, but Sam wasn't convinced.

"How's Tamar?" she asked to get the spotlight off her for a minute.

"Great. She got a promotion at the bank. She wants six kids, and a kosher home. I introduced her to my mother, now my mother thinks I should marry her immediately." It sounded like a death sentence to Coco, and an end to his freedom. She was just as worried about him as he was about her. "I think I need to come over and meet this guy. I want to see him for myself," Sam said seriously.

"Any excuse is good. I would love you to come over. Do you think your father will let you?"

"I'll tell him I have to." As her self-appointed guardian and big brother, he wanted to meet this guy and make his own decision about him. He could tell that Coco had stars in her eyes, and he didn't blame her. "I'll let you know if I can do it."

True to his word, a week later Sam texted her that he'd be there in a week, for a four-day weekend. They would be closed for a holiday in New York, and he was stealing an extra day, and had gotten a cheap ticket. She couldn't wait to see him, and told Nigel how much Sam meant to her. Nigel was spending every night at her house now, since Paris, and they were both loving it. They made love as soon as they got home from work. She made breakfast for him in the morn-ing, and they cooked dinner together, or went out. As people met Coco, invitations for both of them began flooding in. He introduced her to so many people that she was suddenly sharing in his booming social life. She had to convince him to pick and choose. They couldn't go to everything, although he would have liked to. She realized that he liked going out more than she did, but she never had a bad time when she was with him. He was easygoing and kind, and the people he knew were wonderful to her, and thrilled for him. They all told him how lucky he was to have found her. They made a perfect couple and he agreed. He was in heaven, and so was she.

When Sam came, Coco picked him up at the airport. She was taking two days off from work. She wanted to spend as much time with him as she could. Whatever the excuse, even his suspicions about Nigel, she was thrilled to see him. He had taken a late flight on Wednesday and arrived on Thursday morning. He had slept on the plane, so he wasn't tired. After she picked him up at Heathrow, they went out, had lunch at a small Indian restaurant, and walked around the neighborhood. When Nigel came home from work, Sam was eager to meet him. Nigel had brought home a bottle of good malt whiskey, and a bottle of French wine. They were going to cook dinner at the house.

Coco could see that the two men were taking each other's measure, and she left them alone to figure each other out. She loved both of them, and she knew Nigel could hold his own. She wasn't worried, as she busied herself in the kitchen. They had opened the bottle of whiskey by the time she served dinner, and both men looked pleased and relaxed.

She had bought steaks, which she knew they would like. They were both hearty eaters. She had made string beans and mashed potatoes, and miraculously, it had all come out just right. With the French wine at dinner, it was the perfect meal.

Nigel talked about his job in answer to Sam's questions, and Sam admitted that it was challenging working for his father and doing everything his way. He wasn't enjoying it, but felt it was his duty to work in the family business with him, and his father's distrust of any kind of technology made everything more complicated. Sam was trying to modernize the business, with tremendous resistance from his father. He said they argued about it every day. Looking at him, Coco realized that he looked stressed and not very happy. And his sister had finally just gotten engaged to her Irish Catholic boyfriend, and his mother was irate, so things were tense for him on the home front. He said his parents were pushing him about Tamar.

"You're ten years younger than I am," Nigel commented, as they ate Coco's delicious dinner that she had prepared with the utmost care to get it right for the two men she loved. "Why are they pushing you to get married? At twenty-three, I was still raising hell, chasing barmaids and cocktail waitresses," he said, and Sam laughed.

"It's Orthodox tradition to get married young and have a lot of children, like Catholics. My father is more relaxed about it, but my mother is very religious, and definite about her point of view. My sister marrying a Catholic isn't helping, and my other sister says she won't get married until she's thirty, if then. Knowing her, maybe never. My brother is the family scholar, so they think he's a saint. Which leaves me, as the standard-bearer of all their hopes. I believe in doing things slowly, so I'm in no rush to get married." He looked pointedly at Nigel, to get his message across, even if subliminally.

"At your age, I wasn't either. At mine, you start to think about it, if you want kids."

"Coco is younger than I am," Sam said directly, and she looked mildly embarrassed. Sam was definitely acting like her big brother, even though he was only a year older. But she had no one else to look out for her interests, and she knew he meant well. "At twenty-two, she's too young to have children."

"I think when you meet the right person, it's the right time," Nigel said quietly. "The right one doesn't come along ten times in a lifetime. It never has for me until now."

"That might be true. But good things don't happen in a hurry," Sam said firmly. Nigel nodded and didn't comment. "I think if it's right, it can wait, for a while anyway." There was a moment of silence after that, and then the conversation moved on to other things. On the whole, the two men in her life liked each other. Nigel insisted on brandy after dinner. By the time they all went to bed that night, Sam and Nigel had had a lot to drink.

Nigel had already left for work the next morning when Sam got up. Coco had taken that Friday off too, so she was waiting for him when Sam appeared in the kitchen squinting in the sunlight and she laughed.

"Oh God, I'm so hungover," he said with a pained expression. "I forgot the way the Brits can drink. There was an English kid in my econ class at NYU who could drink anyone under the table. I think Nigel must be related to him. Coffee, quick, this is an emergency." He looked better after he'd drunk it, had a piece of toast, and taken an aspirin. He still had a headache, but it was tolerable.

"So what do you think?" she asked him nervously. She wanted Sam to love Nigel too.

"I like him. He's a good guy, and he's obviously nuts about you. But you still don't know him after so little time. Don't go off half-cocked and do anything crazy."

"I'm not going to," she said firmly.

"I think he would, and he may try to talk you into it. I think you need to run a check on him. I'm worried about his finances. He talks about how poor he is. He may be exaggerating, but if he isn't, his expectations of you may be excessive or unrealistic. Your father would have worried about that too." That was always the key with her, what her father would have done, or thought, or disapproved of.

"He's not marrying me for my money, Sam. He doesn't know how much I have. And he hasn't asked me to marry him. You're jumping the gun here." But he had hinted at it, and his intentions were obvious, although they seemed honorable. He kept hinting at marriage. And he said he wanted kids. Soon. So Sam was worried.

"Don't be so innocent. People guess or talk, or know things. He may have run a check on you. People do that. And they marry people for a lot less than you have. I don't want that to happen to you. If you marry him at some point, you'll need an airtight prenup. And you should get married in the States so it's legally binding. You should do that with anyone. Don't even think about it without a solid contract." He really did sound like her father.

"He hasn't asked me to marry him, so you have nothing to worry about."

"I think he will. And so do you. The other thing that worries me is that he doesn't have a career. He has a job, and one he hates. If he decides to stop working if you marry him, there isn't a damn thing you can do about it. You need to think about this stuff, Coco, and get a sense of what his plans are, and his goals, and his values. How would he feel living off a rich wife? Would that be fine with him? You don't want a dead weight around your neck, with a guy who doesn't want to work. It happens, more often than you think. For him it may seem stupid to bother working with everything you have, once he realizes it. It sounds like he has no real interest in his career or any career. At his age, he should. You and I are just starting out. He's ten or twelve years into his work life, at what should be the high point of his career, not the low point. Instead, he's a low-level advertising guy and hates his job. That's not good news for you. And you may be very good news for him. I don't want to see that happen to you. You deserve better than that. He seems more like a play and party guy to me. He's charming as hell, and he loves you, but you should have someone who contributes more than that. He wants kids, but how is he going to support them, and you?" She knew that her mother had lived on her father's meager earnings when she'd married him, and worked herself. She wasn't sure how ambitious Nigel was. He talked about people, and their social plans, and the house parties they were going to, not about work, or building anything for the future, or saving money. Sam was giving her good advice.

"I feel rude snooping into his financial situation. He says he has no money. His brother got everything, and he got nothing when his father died. What more do I need to know? He already told me. He's not hiding anything."

"That's the British system," Sam commented, and poured himself another cup of coffee. "I don't think this is about being rude. You have to protect yourself. He leads a very high-end life with a lot of jet-set people. This is not the 'normal' guy we were talking about. He's another highflyer, a flashy guy like Ed, but maybe with no way to get the plane off the ground, unless you pay for it. Check it out. Ed could do it for you. It's not that complicated."

"This is none of Ed's business," Coco said immediately. It complicated everything that she had slept with her trustee, and shouldn't have. She regretted it now. "I'll see what I can figure out." Sam nodded. He had raised some good points.

"Have you met his brother?"

"No, they hate each other, and they don't speak, if they can avoid it. His brother got everything, and gave him nothing."

"That's not good news either. He seems like a sweet guy. I like him. His life is a little fancy for me, with dukes and duchesses, and counts and castles. That all matters a lot to him. Is that what you want, Coco?" He was surprised. It seemed so unlike her. But Nigel was very seductive and glamorous in a boyish way, and the people around him and their lifestyle were very appealing too. They seemed to play all the time. It was a throwback to another era. Nigel readily admitted that many of the aristocrats he knew had lost their money but refused to give up the lifestyle that went with it. He didn't seem to mind since they gave a lot of the parties he went to.

"It's kind of fun. A lot of it is very superficial, but I've met some interesting people with him. And I love him. He's kind of like Prince Charming. He's generous with me. He paid for everything in Paris and he always pays when we go out to dinner." But he had a miserable, seedy little apartment. She suspected that he was spending his entire salary on her. And the house parties they went to cost him nothing.

"Just make sure Prince Charming has a little something in the bank and won't be totally dependent on you. Or if that's the case, at least you'll know what to expect. It's hard to talk about money, but if you're thinking about this long-term, you should know." She nodded, and knew he was right. Maybe Nigel found it hard to talk about it too. It was embarrassing for both of them. He had said he was poor since they met, so he hadn't misled her. No matter how in love with her he was, he wasn't proposing marriage, so she didn't need to worry about it. And by no stretch of the imagination could she see herself married at twenty-two. So Sam was worried for nothing, but she was grateful for his concern.

They talked about Tamar too. Sam said he loved her, but Coco wasn't convinced. She was the kind of girl his parents wanted him to marry, but Coco thought he needed someone more interesting than a religious bank clerk who wanted six kids. It sounded like a dismal future to her, and to Sam too. She didn't want to see him give up his dreams just to please his parents, and she hoped he wouldn't.

They went out and explored London together after Sam showered. It was nice just being together, and talking, and sometimes just walking along together, lost in their own thoughts. He had given her much to think about, and he was right that Nigel just wasn't the "normal" guy she had hoped to find. But she loved the Prince Charming aspect of him, and it was hard not to be dazzled by the people he knew, the places they went together, and the friends he introduced to her. He led such a glamorous life, whether he had money or not. She wasn't sure she cared about that one way or another, although she appreciated Sam worrying about her. She and Nigel weren't getting married, and she didn't spend a lot of money to live, and even if they did get married one day, how expensive could it be? Her parents hadn't been extravagant with all they had, although they had lived well, had nice homes and bought important art, and were generous with her and each other. Nigel didn't seem to spend a lot of money. They usually went to inexpensive restaurants when they went out, and cooked at home several nights a week. Their busy social life cost them nothing, except flowers for their hosts afterward and she paid for those. She thought Sam was overly worried.

The three of them had dinner out that night at a nice Italian restaurant, and Nigel picked up the check, although Sam offered to.

They ate dinner at home again on Saturday, and on Sunday, Sam flew back to New York. She went with him to the airport and had tears in her eyes when he left.

"I wish you lived here," she said sadly.

"Come home soon then," he said with the big brother look in his eyes that always went straight to her heart. He was the only family she had now.

"I love you, Sam," she said, as the tears crept down her cheeks.

"I will always love you, Coco," he said with a lump in his throat, and she knew he meant it. She nodded, and a minute later, he walked into the security line. She watched him until she couldn't see him anymore. He waved for a last time, and, crying openly by then, she waved and touched her heart. He nodded, and then he was gone, back to his own life. She cried most of the way home in the cab.

She was glad Nigel was out when she got home. He was meeting friends to play tennis at their club. She wanted some time to think about Sam and her parents, and everything Sam had said. It all made sense. And she hoped he wouldn't marry Tamar. She sounded like such a dull girl.

On the plane already in the air, heading back to New York, Sam was hoping she wouldn't marry Nigel. Something told him she was going to get hurt. And there was nothing he could do to stop it. His heart was heavy as he left.

Chapter 6

On Coco's twenty-third birthday in December, after three months of house parties, hunting weekends, and going to nearly every fancy party in London, Nigel took her to dinner at Harry's Bar, and dancing at Annabel's afterward. He was a member of both clubs, along with several others. He had wanted to give her a party, but she said she didn't want one. Her birthdays made her too sad now, since her parents' deaths, and she preferred to spend it alone with him. They had been to a constant round of Christmas parties for the past two weeks, and had been invited to various friends' ski houses for Christmas and New Year's, and hadn't decided where to go yet. Christmas was hard for her now too. Nigel wanted to go to Gstaad or Courchevel, where his friends had houses and had invited them. Coco didn't really care where they went, and she was enjoying the quiet evening with him on her birthday. He invited her to dance at Annabel's, and startled her when he stopped dancing, and dropped to one knee on the dance floor. She realized then that they had been playing a song she liked and there was no one else around them, as the people at tables around the dance floor stared at them. Nigel had warned the manager of what he planned to do, requested the song, and they had asked the other clients to sit this one out. In the spirit of romance, they had agreed, excited to be part of the surprise.

As Nigel dropped to one knee, Coco stared at him, not sure what he was doing. He held her hand and looked at her with his big blue eyes. "Coco, my darling, will you marry me?" She was so stunned she didn't know what to say, and was speechless for a moment. "Coco?" He pressed her for an answer as tears filled her eyes. She wanted her parents to be there to share it with her, or Sam, or someone she loved and knew well. Nigel looked at her so imploringly with tears in his eyes too that she couldn't turn him down. She couldn't do that to him and break his heart. She loved him, and wanted to be his wife, just not quite so soon, but the right man had come along, and she didn't want to lose him. She nodded, as the tears spilled down her cheeks and she couldn't stop them.

"Yes . . . yes, I will," she whispered, as he got to his feet, took her in his arms and kissed her. The whole room applauded, and then he led her back to their table as everyone around them smiled and offered congratulations even though they were strangers. Another couple sent them a bottle of champagne to celebrate their engagement.

"I didn't know you were going to do that," she said, as she wiped her eyes on her napkin.

"Neither did I." He beamed at her. "I decided yesterday when I was trying to figure out what to get you for your birthday." He took a small ancient-looking navy leather box out of his pocket and set it on the table. "It's the only thing of my mother's that I have. I hope it fits." He opened the box, and took out a beautiful antique cushion-cut diamond ring of a very respectable size. "It was originally my grandmother's." He slipped it on her finger and it fit perfectly, and she stared at it and started to cry again.

"I wish my parents could see it, and meet you," she said as he held her tight, as the ring flashed on her finger. It was a beautiful stone, and bigger than any of the jewelry her mother had. Her parents preferred art to jewelry.

"I wish I had met them too," he said respectfully. "When do you want to get married? Let's do it soon. I want you to be my wife as soon as possible. We're going to have such a beautiful life."

"I don't know. Next summer? June?" She said it off the top of her head.

"Why wait that long?" He looked disappointed. "We could invite everyone we know to my club for a big reception. Do you want a church wedding?"

"I . . ." She choked on her words for a minute. "I can't have a big wedding without my parents. It would kill me. Can't we do something very small, just us and your family? We can do something later for friends, but not at the wedding."

"I doubt my brother would even come, with his dreadful wife. And I don't want them there. They would ruin it. I don't have any other family. Just friends. They're my family now." He looked a little dismayed and hurt that she didn't want a big wedding, but she had no family either. He wanted to reciprocate for all the fabulous parties they'd been to with a big event of his own, the bigger the better, but it was clear that Coco didn't want that and wouldn't agree to it. "If you don't want a big wedding, then why wait? Why not January?"

She looked shocked. "The only one I want is Sam, and maybe Leslie, my boss, since she introduced us." They had gotten close and

Coco liked her a lot. "I don't know if Sam could come over, although he promised to give me away. And I'd like it in a church." There was a small church that she had discovered and liked. What she described was not the splashy, important wedding he had envisioned, but the main thing was that they get married. They could give a huge party later, when she wouldn't feel her parents' absence quite as acutely as on the day of their wedding. They had only been gone for a year and a half. He and Coco had only known each other for three months. He said that people were probably going to comment on that, and even wonder if she was pregnant. But this felt so right to him. Despite her mixed emotions about her parents, it felt right to her too. She remembered Sam's admonition then that she get married in the States with an airtight prenuptial agreement to protect her, but there wouldn't be time now, and all of Nigel's friends were in England, for the reception. He wouldn't know a soul at their wedding if they did it in New York.

"Let's say a month from today, in January," Nigel said happily. "That gives us time to plan whatever we do. We could go skiing for our honeymoon," he said, looking excited. "I'm sure someone would lend us a chalet."

"I'd like to go to New York after that. You could see the apartment, and my parents' house in the Hamptons. It's my house now." And would be theirs, and their children's.

"I didn't realize you still had an apartment and a house of theirs," he said, looking intrigued by both. She had never mentioned them. "That should be fun," he said. He looked like a child at Christmas, as she sat next to him, with his grandmother's diamond on her hand. His mother had given it to him before she died, for his future wife. He had been saving it in case he ever had to sell it, if he needed money, but this was a much better use for it, as the symbol of his love for her, and a prelude to their marriage. Coco looked dazed when they went home to her place that night. They never used his, it was too grim, and he'd been talking about letting it go. He was with her all the time. But she didn't know how long she was staying in London, so he had kept it. But now she would be staying forever, as his wife. She hadn't even thought about that yet. New York was still her home. But Nigel expected to live in London with her. He was so profoundly British, she couldn't imagine him living anywhere else, and he wouldn't want to.

She agreed to the January wedding date, because she couldn't think of a reason not to. She had qualms about marrying so quickly, but she got swept along on the tidal wave of his excitement. There was a lot to think about and plan, even for a tiny wedding. She called Sam the next morning and told him the news. He was shocked.

"In January? You'll only have known him for four months then. Coco, that's crazy. Why the rush? Are you pregnant?"

"Of course not. Nigel doesn't want to wait," she said with a sigh. "He wants to do it then. He's like a kid when he talks about it. And why not? We're going to get married anyway. January or June? What's the difference? Can you come then?"

He sounded upset when she asked. "No, I can't. My father's having knee surgery then. It's not serious, but he's going to be immobilized for three or four months. I have to run the business, and my mother is all stressed out about him. I can't leave them. I probably couldn't come till May."

"I think Nigel will go nuts if he has to wait that long. We're not really having a wedding or a big reception. Just a small church ceremony and lunch with a few friends afterward. That's all I want since my parents won't be there. I can't do a real wedding without them, and especially if you can't come either." He felt guilty, but he just couldn't make it. "We'll give a party later when you can come."

"I'm sorry to let you down," he said apologetically.

"You're not letting me down, and this is very short notice."

"Did you look into that matter I suggested, the financial check?"

She understood immediately. "No, I didn't. We've been so busy, and I didn't think there was any rush. It doesn't really matter. He says he has nothing and I believe him. What's to find out?"

"Well, you'd better do something about a prenup in the U.S.," he said sternly.

"I will. My dad always said that too. I'll email Ed today, he can get something drafted and send it over."

"Have you told Nigel about that yet?"

"No, I haven't, but I will."

"And you should probably get married in the States to make sure U.S. laws apply."

"I don't think he'll want to."

"Talk to Ed. Or any New York lawyer. Just make sure you're covered."

She looked pensive when they hung up.

She brought the subject up that night at dinner, and Nigel didn't look bothered by it.

"Because of what my parents left me, I need a prenuptial agreement, particularly one that's valid in the U.S." She was afraid he'd be insulted by it, but he wasn't, which was a relief. It also told her that despite Sam's fears, Nigel was an honest man, and not after money, if he didn't balk at a prenup.

"Of course. I'll sign anything you want. What they left you is your money. I would never think of infringing on it." She was relieved as soon as he said it. She had sent the email to Ed after she talked to Sam, and he called her the next morning, and sounded very surprised.

"You're getting married? When did that happen?"

"I am. It happened once I got here. He's a very nice man."

"Does he have money of his own?"

"Apparently not," she answered coolly, "so you'll have to do the prenup accordingly to protect what I have."

"I'll take care of it right away." There was a moment's pause then. "And, Coco, good luck."

"Thank you." She sounded distant and cold.

"When is the wedding?"

"In January." He didn't dare ask her if she was pregnant, but he thought it.

"I'll get the contract to you right away. Thank you for letting me know. It's different here but they have contracts in Europe too, denying community property and establishing separate property in a marriage."

The agreement he had drawn up by their lawyers reached her five days later. It was a very stringent agreement that stated that all funds, investments, property of any kind and capital that was hers at the time of the marriage remained her separate property, and Nigel relinquished all claim to any of it. They both had to list all their assets as well. Ed had included the full list of hers. She wondered if Nigel would sign it. She handed it to him that night and was even more shocked when he signed all three copies of it right after he read it, and promised to add a list of his assets, which he said again amounted to nothing. He owned nothing. He just picked up a pen, signed the contracts, and handed them back to her.

"Don't you want to have it looked at by a lawyer?" she asked him, startled by his reaction.

"No. I'm not marrying you for your money. I don't even know what you have, and I don't want to know." He hadn't even bothered to read her list of assets, but he noticed that it was long. "We're going to have a beautiful life together. We love each other, that's all I need to know."

He had made everything easy for her, and the rest fell into place too. They agreed to the small church she liked in her neighborhood. She asked Leslie to be her witness since Sam couldn't come, and she was touched. Nigel remained firm about not inviting his brother, and asked two old school friends as his witnesses instead. And after the ceremony, the five of them were going to lunch at Savini at the Criterion, in legendary historical opulence, among the columns and beneath the gold ceiling. The elegance of the nineteenth-century setting suited him and he had suggested it. And Coco loved it. They were going to Courchevel to stay with friends the next day. Sometime in the spring or summer, they would plan a real honeymoon. But for now, all they wanted was the simplest and smallest of ceremonies, and after that they would be man and wife. It was as though Nigel was desperate to hang on to her and terrified to lose her now that he had found her. And although it was speedy, Coco was sure she was doing the right thing. She had no qualms at all. And he had given her a formal letter stating he had no assets, and twenty thousand pounds in the bank, which was nothing compared to her.

Coco went looking for a dress in the designer section of Harrods, and found a perfect white wool Chanel suit. She found a hairdresser

who was going to put tiny white orchids in a chignon. She bought
white satin Manolo Blahnik high-heeled pumps with rhinestone
buckles, and a small bag to match. She had everything she needed.
The florist was going to make a bouquet of the same white orchids
she would wear in her hair, and a boutonniere for Nigel. They kept
everything simple and low-key, in deference to Coco's feelings about
her parents not being there, and Nigel agreed.

Despite the careful planning, and the simple ceremony, their wedding day was hard for Coco. She cried from the moment she woke
up, thinking of her parents and how heartbroken she was that they
couldn't share the moment with her. Nigel tried to console her and
couldn't. She spoke to Sam four or five times before the ceremony at
eleven, although it was the middle of the night for him. He thought
she was moving much too quickly, and it was a mistake, but it was
too late for that now. She was doing it, so all Sam could do was support her. His father had had the surgery two days earlier and wasn't
well, and there was no way he could have come. But he felt terrible
not to be there. He kept telling her that everything was going to be
okay, but he didn't believe it himself. She was marrying a man she
barely knew, whose financial stability was nonexistent. He was a
pauper compared to her and had made no attempt to hide it, to his
credit.

The disparity between them worried Sam, and the short time she
had known him. And what would his future be? Parties forever and
an insignificant career? Or no job at all? Sam would have liked to see
her marry someone more solid. But Coco was dazzled, and felt rud-
derless without her parents. She was looking for a secure base, and

Sam couldn't see Nigel providing it. At least he felt sure she had gotten a good prenup, thanks to Ed. Sam was surprised that Nigel had signed it. So her money was protected, as was everything she owned. In a crazy moment, he wondered if the marriage might actually work. Stranger things had happened. Sometimes people jumped into marriages hastily, and they lasted forty or fifty years. He hoped it would for her. Maybe Nigel would turn out to be the right man after all, in spite of Sam's concerns. He hoped so. And Coco was sure of it.

"I'll come over when my dad gets back to work," he promised, and by the time Coco left for the church with Leslie in her car, she had run out of tears. She was quiet, thinking about her parents. She had never missed them as much as she did on that day.

"It's going to be wonderful," Leslie said confidently, as she walked her into the small church. When Coco saw Nigel standing at the altar, waiting for her, she smiled, and she slowly relaxed and believed it too. She was sure it was going to be perfect, because they loved each other. She could feel her parents watching over her and sharing the day with her.

Nigel beamed when she walked in. She had never looked more beautiful. The ceremony only took half an hour, and then they walked out of the church as man and wife, with their three witnesses. Nigel had bought a narrow gold band for her at Tiffany, and they had gotten one for him too.

Then the five of them went to lunch. Nigel ordered Cristal champagne, and they all had a superb lunch. Coco had paid for it, as the bride, since her father wasn't there to do it, and Nigel couldn't. But he had selected exquisite French wines of the finest vintages, and the menu, with caviar for the first course. When they got back to her house at five o'clock, they were both more than a little drunk. They made love and fell asleep immediately.

They were leaving for Courchevel in the morning, and she was his wife now, Coco thought as she fell asleep next to him. His wife. She loved the sound of the word. She knew that nothing could go wrong. She had a family now. She had a husband, and for the first time in eighteen months, she felt safe again. And she knew Nigel would protect her forever. He had vowed he would.

Chapter 7

Their week in Courchevel was perfect. The snow was crisp, the sun warm on their faces. The friends they stayed with, and their other guests, celebrated the newlyweds constantly. It was a fantastic vacation, and there were parties for them every night. Several of their acquaintances had houses there, and were there at the same time, so their honeymoon was a weeklong celebration with Nigel's social circle. As soon as they got back to London, Nigel surprised Coco over breakfast with a question.

"Where are we going to move to?"

"We're moving? Why?" She looked confused.

"We can't live here as a married couple. It's an adorable matchbox. We need a proper house that we can entertain in. This was suitable as a temporary place for a girl your age, here for a short time, but we need a respectable home suited to our status now." He sounded definite about it. It had never occurred to her. She had two homes in New York. But they lived in London now. And Nigel wanted them to have a proper home.

"I don't know. I never thought about it. I don't even know who to call."

"I'll start calling some estate agents, and see what's on the market." He was matter-of-fact about it, as though she had agreed to the plan, which she hadn't. She was still a little stunned when they left for work. A serious house in London was going to be a big expense and undertaking, and she assumed that he expected her to pay for it, since he had no money of his own. How did he know she could afford it? What if she couldn't?

From then on, Nigel saw two or three houses a day, sometimes as many as six, during his lunch hour and after work. He told her not to worry about it. He would vet them first, and only bother her with the good ones. She tried to pretend it wasn't happening, but Nigel was deep into it.

In March, six weeks after the search began, he said there were two houses that he wanted her to see. He set up the appointments for a Friday morning without asking her, and Coco called Leslie and said she would be coming in late. She was still working at *Time* and enjoying it, and now that she was staying in London, she saw no reason to quit. Leslie liked having her on her team.

Coco was stunned when she saw the houses. They were both large, imposing family homes, with enormous reception rooms, many bedrooms, in excellent condition, in the best neighborhoods. Both of them were worthy of a captain of industry, a financial titan, someone like her father or Ed Easton, or an aristocrat with a huge fortune. She had no idea that he'd been looking at houses that large, worth that kind of money, and she nearly gasped when the realtor told her the asking price for each of them. One of them even had a ballroom. Nigel pointed out that they could give dances. There was one she liked better than the other, the slightly smaller one. She said nothing to the realtor and she turned to Nigel when they left the last appointment, without making a commitment. At twenty-three, she couldn't imagine owning that kind of house, married or not.

"Why do we need a house that size? Shouldn't we wait till we have children? We're fine where we are for now, Nigel. Those houses are incredibly expensive, and we don't need anything that big."

"Of course we do. Do you have any idea how many dinner parties and house parties we've gone to in the last six months? If we're going to have an active social life and be part of the London scene, we have to reciprocate. We need a home we can entertain in. Dinners, dances. We can't go around like thieves, going to everyone else's parties and giving none of our own." But few of the houses they'd been to had been as lavish as these two. They would need a full staff to run them, and somewhere between four and six children to fill them, or a constant flow of houseguests. It was all way beyond the way she or her parents had lived. Nigel clearly had very grand ideas about their status on the London scene.

"I don't even know if they would be a good investment," she said in the cab to the *Time* building.

"I can assure you they are, or I wouldn't have shown them to you," he said tersely, looking insulted. "And I know you can afford them." How could he be so sure? She wasn't even certain of it, whatever she had.

"How do you know I can?"

"I read our contract and I knew anyway. You weren't here on the salary *Time* is paying you. I know who your father was. His fortune was not exactly a secret." What he said shocked her profoundly. He'd done research. She didn't say it, but she was shaken. Sam had been right.

She called Ed that afternoon, when she knew he'd be in the office, and he took her call immediately. She told him about the houses, and the asking prices, and asked him if she could afford it. He still had not replaced himself as her trustee, and she had been too busy to pursue it, and forgot about it. She had bigger things to deal with.

"Yes, you can afford it, but I'm not sure that's the point here. Do you want a house that big in London? Are you planning to stay there? Are you starting a family right away? That's a lot of house you're looking at, in both cases." She had told him the square footage and the price.

"We're not starting a family, for sure. And I don't know if we're going to stay here. My husband wants to. We haven't decided yet. He likes being prominent on the London social scene. But I want to spend time in New York too."

"Those are still two very large houses. To answer your question, yes, you can afford either one of them. But do you want to?" She didn't. But her husband did, desperately. It was their first big difference of opinion, and a very expensive one.

"Thank you," she said crisply, and pursued the conversation with Nigel that night when he got home.

"Of course we want to stay here," he said immediately. "Where else would we want to live?" He acted as though the question was ridiculous.

"I'm American. Until now I've lived in New York. I still have two homes there, my parents' apartment and a large beach house, and all I have here is a temporary job. Since you're married to me, you could get a green card, and work in New York, if you wanted to." She realized they should have discussed it before, and hadn't.

"I don't want to live in New York." He looked shocked. "Why don't you sell your parents' apartment and the beach house to defray the cost of a house here? We're never going to live there." He dismissed the possibility summarily, and she felt a sudden pang of homesickness for New York. It seemed reasonable to him to live in London, but not entirely to her. She had roots in New York, memories, and homes. But her husband was English. She realized that they should have discussed it thoroughly before they married.

"I don't want to sell my property there. I love my parents' apartment. It's been my home for my whole life. And the beach house too."

"Are you telling me you can't *afford* a house here? Or don't want to?" He looked devastated and like he didn't believe her.

"No, but I'm telling you it's a lot of money. We don't need a house that big. We could buy something smaller, and buy a bigger house when we have children. *And* I want to spend time in New York too."

"How long do you want to wait for kids?" he asked her, worried.

"Several years. I told you that before. I'm twenty-three years old. I'm not ready for babies. I haven't even finished college."

"Are you ready to be married, Coco?" he asked accusingly, as though she was letting him down. It was another conversation they should have had before, but they hadn't. "You're sounding like a child." He sounded disapproving as he accused her of it.

"I'm ready to be married because I love you, but I didn't realize you wanted to buy a house, and certainly not one that size. I need to think about it." She did not want to be pushed into it, or bullied. But she didn't want him to be unhappy either. He was her family now.

"You'd better think fast, or someone will snap those houses up.

I've been looking for two months, and they're by far the best I've seen," he said coldly, as though she was cheating him of his due. There was suddenly an atmosphere of tension around them in the tiny mews house, and it went on for days. He didn't argue with her about it. He didn't speak to her at all. They stopped making love. She had the sense that it was going to be a cold war until she gave in. The only thing that gave her some comfort was knowing that even if she bought one of them, they were both beautiful homes and probably were a good investment that they could always sell. But he was forcing her hand. And living in either of them would be a much grander lifestyle than the one she wanted, even as a married woman.

After several sleepless nights, while they barely spoke to each other, she decided to tell him to look for something smaller that would be easier to manage. She would have preferred to stay where they were for another year or two. She was waiting at the breakfast table to tell him, after another sleepless night, and he looked so miserable when he sat down that she didn't have the heart to tell him she wasn't going to buy either house. It was the first major financial decision she'd ever had to face, and didn't feel equal to it. They'd been married for less than two months, and he expected her to spend a fortune so they could show off to their friends.

"Coco," he said, looking exhausted, "I'm not asking you to throw money away, or to give it to me. Both of these houses are excellent investments, and the house will be in your name," he reminded her. She had never bought a house before and it scared her, especially with so much pressure from him.

"I don't even know how to run a house that size. Or if I want to live here. I came here for a few months," she said, feeling suffocated and panicked.

"And now you're married to an Englishman, and you do live here. I can run the house for you. If there's one thing I know, it's big houses," he said confidently. "The house in Sussex was ten times that size." And now his brother had it. Nigel was trying to re-create what he had lost. It was a fresh insight into him. And he expected her to do it for him. Coco was beginning to understand that now. It was a very tall order, and a lot for him to expect of her.

"I don't feel ready for a big house like that," she said with tears in her eyes, and he smiled at her.

"I'll do everything for it. We both want to have a beautiful life together. A house like that is part of it." She was in over her head. She suddenly knew that she had run out of the energy to do battle with him. She had the money, and he had the endurance and determination to fight her on it forever until he got what he wanted. He wanted one of those two houses, or one like them, and nothing was going to stop him. She felt her resolve melting. He couldn't force her to do it, but in a way he had. He was stronger than she was, and bigger, and older, and wanted a big house and a big life desperately. Far more than she did. It was part of his identity, the one he wanted, at her expense.

"All right," she said with a long, tired sigh. She told him which one she preferred, the one without the ballroom, and he conceded, as though making a sacrifice for her.

"I'll call the estate agent. Coco, you won't regret it. You'll thank me one day, when the house is full of our children, and we're giving the most spectacular parties in London." She didn't want parties or children at the moment, so it didn't sound like good news to her, and it was a huge amount of money, which he didn't mind at all.

They signed the papers a week later, which gave her plenty of time for buyer's remorse, but she didn't want to disappoint him. She felt pushed to the wall. They were going to take possession of the house sixty days later in May. In April, he gave her a list of all the things he wanted to do in the house, built-ins and marble fixtures, chandeliers, and changes he wanted to make. He had been interviewing contractors. She almost choked when she saw their estimates.

"Don't worry about a thing," he said, smiling at her. "I'll oversee everything. They say they can have us in by August."

"Why don't we just move straight to the poorhouse? Do we need to have all that done to it? The house looked perfect to me."

"Trust me. It will be even better when we're finished. You're going to love it." She didn't love it. She loved him. And then he hit her with another bomb. "We'll need furniture too of course." She hadn't even thought of that for a house that size. It was a daunting prospect, and would be an expensive one. They were going to be hemorrhaging money for the next five months. She remembered a remodel her mother had done of the city apartment, and her father's complaints about how expensive it was. Now she understood. She had only known Nigel for seven months, and had no idea how expensive his tastes were. He had very grandiose ideas. But as soon as she agreed to buy the house, he became warm and loving again, and wanted to make love to her all the time. The floodgates had opened and he couldn't get enough of her. The cold war was over, but it had cost her dearly. He never doubted for a moment that she could afford it. He had done his homework well.

They took possession of the house in May, and the workmen started almost immediately. It was a mess within days. The whole house was torn apart for Nigel's improvements. It looked like a bomb had hit it. The pristine quality she had liked about it had vanished.

The disruption added measurably to the tension between them. Their nights in the mews house were more stressful than pleasant as they argued about the work on the new house. The weekend parties they went to constantly, more than ever now that they were the golden couple everyone wanted to entertain, only meant that she had to put a good face on the strife between them.

They were barely speaking to each other again on the first of June, when Nigel came home from a Saturday lunch with some of his male friends looking sheepish. She had no idea why he looked that way, and didn't ask him. She was already tired of problems with the contractor and workmen at the house, doing work that hadn't needed to be done anyway. It seemed like a total waste of time and money, and a lot of both.

"Do you want to go out to dinner tonight?" he asked her, which surprised her. They hadn't gone out to dinner alone since April. They had done nothing but argue about the house, and eat at home. And most nights they didn't bother to eat dinner, after they argued about the latest estimates from the contractor. Their lovemaking fell by the wayside again. She was paying for everything and money was flowing out the door. She had read somewhere that remodeling and moving were two of the greatest life stressors other than divorce or loss of a loved one. She was tired of hearing about the house she hadn't wanted in the first place. She wasn't sure she wanted to have dinner with him, and hear more. She was sure he had come up with some new expensive plan for the remodel.

She hesitated and he looked at her, and sat down on the couch. "I have something to tell you."

"The house burned to the ground," she said in a choked voice, almost hoping it had.

"Of course not. It's going to be gorgeous and you're going to love it. No, I had an opportunity today that I couldn't pass up. I would have called you, but I didn't want to tell you on the phone. A friend of mine invited one of my old mates from Eton for lunch. A great guy. He moved to Australia after he left Oxford. His parents died recently and he was here to settle their affairs. They had an absolutely gorgeous house in Sussex. My friend needs money, and he told me to name my price. I quoted an absolutely, ridiculously low amount, and he took it on the spot. We shook hands on it, so it's a done deal. We'll need a country house anyway, Coco. I know this is a lot all at once, but trust me, it's a gorgeous place. I couldn't pass it up. It needs a little work, but not much."

"You did *what*?" She stood across the room from him and stared at him, unable to believe what he had just said. "You bought a house in Sussex over lunch? It's a done deal and you didn't even call me? And you expect me to pay for it? Are you out of your mind, Nigel?" This time she wasn't frightened or upset. She was furious. She couldn't believe he'd done something like that. Now they were about to have two houses she didn't want. He was out of control. He had signed off on their prenup as though it didn't matter to him, and had been spending millions of dollars of her money ever since. "What were you thinking?" She owned the house, but he was costing her a fortune, and not even apologetic about it. He kept telling her how lucky she was that he was improving her investment. And now he wanted to buy another one, or just had.

"Coco, we need a country house. It just turned up a little earlier than we planned."

"We never planned to have a country house. We never even talked about it. For what? Why do we *need* a country house?"

"To give house parties like the ones we go to every weekend. We can't mooch off my friends forever," he said primly, and for that exact moment she almost hated him.

"I don't mooch off anyone, Nigel. I don't even know if I can afford it."

"I think you can."

"You don't know that. I don't even know if I can. And a handshake does not constitute a 'done deal' when it requires someone else's money. This is a nightmare."

"Do you love me?" he asked, looking woebegone.

"That's beside the point. I don't love what you do, or how you spend my money, *without even consulting me*! What kind of marriage is this?" It was a very expensive one to be sure.

"I'm asking you to trust me. I know houses. You're going to end up with two of the prettiest houses in England."

"And the largest staff and the highest expenses. How big is the place in Sussex?"

"It has four good houses on it, pastureland, and beautiful stables. He even threw in the horses. There are only six there now, but there's room for a lot more. And there's a lake."

"This is insanity." He told her the price he had agreed to, and she had to admit, it sounded low to her too, but she didn't want a country house or to spend more money. She couldn't be married to a man who incurred expenses to that degree without even asking her.

She slammed out of the house and went for a long walk. He was gone when she came back. She hoped he had gone to find his friend from Australia to tell him he had to renege on the deal. He didn't come home until midnight, and he was drunk.

"Did you get out of it?"

"Out of what?" He looked confused as he got into bed.

"Out of the house in Sussex. I thought maybe that was where you went."

"Of course not. I gave him my word as a gentleman, I can't go back on that."

"What if I refuse to pay?" She felt desperate and trapped. What if he bought more houses?

"I suppose then he might sue us for breach of promise. I gave him a note on it, and signed it."

"Nigel," she said, feeling frantic, "this has to stop. You're going to ruin me."

"According to my discreet inquiries, you have a lot more than that." Her stomach turned over as he said it. And when had he re-searched that? Before or after he married her? Sam had been right from the first. Nigel was after money. A lot of it. And a lifestyle she didn't want and feared she couldn't afford long-term.

She went downstairs then and slept on the couch, and he was too drunk to get out of bed again. When he got up in the morning and came downstairs, she was gone. She had called Leslie Thomas, her boss, and went over to her house. She had no one else to talk to. She told her what had been happening, and Leslie looked dis-mayed.

"You know, these men from the old aristocratic families don't know how to live without money. They're used to their houses and their farms and their land just being there, and the lifestyle that went with it. When it's all gone, they somehow expect it to be magi-cally restored to them again. I think it crushed Nigel when his brother got everything, even though he knew he would. And I think he ex-pects you to be that magic, to re-create for him that world that he grew up with. It's not very realistic. I'm not sure that he even realizes he's taking advantage of you. What do you want to do now? Divorce him?"

Coco shook her head miserably. "I love him, but he can't keep doing this. I don't trust him now, he can't keep buying houses with my money."

"Can you explain that to him?"

"I'm not sure he'll listen. I'm trying to. He refuses to hear me." She looked depressed about it. "We shouldn't have gotten married. It was too fast. We didn't know each other well enough. It was all very romantic, and now it's anything but."

"I thought so too, that it was too fast, but I know how Nigel is when he wants something. And he wanted you. I'm sure he still does. Maybe all you can do is tell him that if he buys another house like that, you'll divorce him, and stick to it." Coco nodded. There wasn't much else she could do now except leave him. But even after the house he'd just bought in Sussex, she didn't want to leave him. She loved him. "Your calling me this morning is fortuitous," Leslie said to her. "I've been wanting to talk to you." Coco wondered if she had done something wrong or was being fired. "I'm leaving *Time*. It was a big decision, but I've wanted to start my own business for a while. I came into some money recently from an aunt, and I'm going to give it a try. I want to start a relocation business, for people moving to London who need to set up house. I'll find them a location, stage it for them, or decorate it, and get it all set up before they arrive. I have a friend who's been doing that in Paris, and making very good money. There's a real need for it. Corporations move people here all the time, and others just move here for personal reasons, as you did."

"It sounds like fun," Coco said, thinking about the plan, but disappointed that Leslie was leaving *Time*. She liked working for her, and she liked her job, although she knew her internship would end sooner or later. She had already been there for ten months.

"That's why I wanted to talk to you. I think you'd be great at it. Now that you're a permanent resident here, would you consider coming to work for me? I'd love to have you." Coco's eyes lit up. It sounded like a good idea, and she wanted a long-term job.

"I'd *love* it!" She beamed at her.

"You would? Fantastic!"

"When are you starting?"

"The end of this month. I plan to open up the business at the end of July. I'm giving them four weeks' notice tomorrow. You could give them two weeks' notice, as an intern. I'd rather they not know that I'm stealing interns from them. And I'd pay you a proper salary. You'll be legal doing that now, since you're married to Nigel."

They talked about the business for a while. It sounded exciting. Leslie was going to work out of her house at first, to keep the overhead down. She only lived ten minutes from Coco's mews house by cab, and not too far from their new one. The offer of a job was the best news she'd had in months. The four and a half months since her wedding had been rocky, and expensive.

"What are you going to do about Nigel?" Leslie asked Coco gently before she left.

"Kill him if he buys another house."

"Hopefully, he'll behave now. If not, you should get out. I never realized how irresponsible he could be."

Or how greedy, Coco thought. He wanted everything, a city house, a country estate, and God only knew what else he had in mind, and he wanted it all right now, at her expense. He knew too well that she could afford it.

Leslie hugged her before she left, Coco was excited about the job offer, and Leslie had suggested a decent wage.

Coco was in better spirits when she let herself into her house. Nigel was at the kitchen table with a ferocious hangover.

"Where were you?" he asked her.

"I went to see Leslie Thomas," she said.

"What about?" She didn't tell him about the job. It was none of his business.

"Something to do with work." He nodded, which made him wince, and she went upstairs and showered and changed. When he came upstairs and lay down on the bed, she asked him a direct question. "How were you planning to pay your friend for the house in Sussex?"

"I told him you would. We'd been drinking a lot by then. I said you would pay in three installments, by wire transfer. It was his suggestion. He needs the cash." She nodded and didn't respond. She went out after that, and spent the day walking and thinking, and didn't come back until six o'clock that evening. Nigel was out, and hadn't left a note for her. He knew that he had gone a giant step too far.

She called Ed Easton the next day on her cellphone from work, and told him about the house in Sussex. Nigel was right. He had gotten it at a very low price, but he still shouldn't have done it without consulting her.

"Your new husband is spending your money like water," Ed commented. "As your trustee, I have to warn you that's not wise."

"Am I broke yet?" she asked with a sigh.

"Far from it. But you will be one day if he keeps this up."

"I'm planning to shut him down." She asked him to transfer the price of the house to her bank account in London, and he said he'd take care of it. He couldn't resist adding a comment, maybe because she had ended it with him, or maybe because he believed it.

"I'm glad we got the prenup we did. I felt a little guilty about making it so tough on him, but now I'm glad I did."

"So am I," she said clearly. "Thanks, Ed." And then she hung up. Even if things weren't going smoothly with Nigel, she had no regrets about Ed, and knew she never would.

Chapter 8

L eslie gave the magazine notice on Monday and told them that she would be leaving at the end of June. Starting her own business had always been her dream and she wanted to pursue it. She had just turned thirty-nine, without a husband or children, and she figured it was the right time to give it a try. She had no encumbrances, and thanks to her late aunt, she had the money now to do it.

Coco told Nigel that night that she was going to pay for the house in Sussex, but if he did anything like that again, she would leave him. She wasn't going to let him ruin her financially so he could show off to his friends. He thanked her profusely, and swore he wouldn't buy any more houses or make any more financial commitments without consulting her. He acted almost like a child who had been punished, and she realized that even though he was ten years older than she was, he was immature and irresponsible. It wasn't a happy discovery, but it was what she had to deal with. Nigel was a charming child as long as he got his way, and a very nasty one when he didn't. He manipulated her by withholding love.

He was supervising the contractors at both houses, so at least Coco didn't have to worry about it. She was planning to give notice at the magazine two weeks after Leslie had, so they could leave at the same time. She hadn't told Nigel about her new job yet. Communication between them was still strained, and they hadn't made love since he bought the house in Sussex. She was too upset about it. The day before she was planning to give notice, he came home looking as though the world had come to an end. He poured himself a stiff drink, sat down on the couch, and glanced at her with a miserable look on his face.

"Is something wrong?" She wondered if he was sick.

"You could say that. They announced some departmental changes in advertising and marketing today. Cutbacks. I got fired, Coco. I'm out of a job, after five years." He was taking it hard, and she felt sorry for him. His ego had taken a big hit. He didn't earn a big salary, but it paid for all his expenses, so he didn't need to ask her for money.

"I'm sorry," she said gently. "You'll find another job." He nodded, and then halfway through his scotch, he cheered up a little.

"I guess it'll give me more time to stay on top of what the contractors are doing at both houses." The city house was supposed to be ready in August, and Sussex in September. But overseeing the renovations wasn't meant to be a full-time occupation in lieu of a real job. She didn't like the idea of his staying out of work to check on the houses. That should have been in addition to his regular employment.

"I think you ought to look for another job," she said as politely as she could. "We have a lot of expenses with the two houses. It's nice if you contribute where you can."

"Does it really make a difference? What point is there to my working, with everything you have?" She didn't like his referring to her inheritance that bluntly, or thinking of it that way. And this was what Sam had been worried about, that Nigel might decide she had so much money he didn't need to work.

"I work. I think you should too," Coco said quietly.

"Yours is just a token job," he said dismissively.

"Actually, I'm starting a new job in July," she said. He looked surprised, since she hadn't told him yet. "Leslie is starting a business, relocating people moving to London, finding them a place to live, decorating, and setting it all up so they have nothing to do when they get here. It will be both corporate and personal. She asked me to come and work for her. I'm giving notice tomorrow and I'll start with her in two weeks."

"Why didn't you tell me?" He looked hurt, and turned from attacker into victim.

"We haven't exactly been speaking to each other much. She asked me the day after you told me about Sussex."

"Well, I think I'll wait to look for a job until September. There's no point job-hunting in the summer, anyway. There's no one around," he said, as he poured himself another scotch.

"I think you should get your CV out there now," she said, wondering how long he would be out of work, with the excuse of the two houses they were remodeling, and how hard he would look for a new job. It worried her. She didn't want him viewing her as the supplier of all benefits, and to become totally dependent on her. She wanted him to work too, on principle. Their situation seemed to have degenerated rapidly since they'd gotten married five months before. He stayed downstairs drinking that night after she went to bed, and he was dead to the world when she left for work the next morning. They had let him go on the spot the day before. He had cleared his desk and been escorted out of the building. That was company policy when you got fired. She knew it must have been humiliating and felt sorry for him.

Coco gave notice herself that day, and they were very nice about it. They were grateful she had stayed that long in a minor job and had been diligent.

Sam texted her that night. As he had promised, he wanted to come over. He could take some time off in the last week of June. His father was back at work, and in good shape again. Sam wanted to see her, he hadn't been to London in nine months, which seemed like a long time to both of them.

So much had happened since then. She had married Nigel. They had bought two houses. She was changing jobs. Sam's life was moving more slowly. He had run his father's business on his own for the past six months. He said he had learned a lot from it. But now his father was back, doing things his way again. Sam sounded discouraged about it. He had been dating Tamar for just over a year now.

Coco picked him up at the airport when he arrived, as she had before. They hugged each other so hard, she was afraid they would break something. He looked thinner, tired, and pale, but he was thrilled to see her. She had had her last day at *Time* the day before, so she was free to be with him the whole time, and didn't have to go to work.

She drove him to the city house they had bought on the way to her place. The contractor and his men were working at full speed when they got there. They had a large crew working on it to meet the deadline. Sam was amazed when he saw it.

"This place is huge. Why do you need this much space? Are you having quadruplets?"

"Apparently Nigel thinks we are." She didn't look happy about it. She was still uneasy about how much they had taken on, and how many people it would take to maintain it. By her calculation, at least three, and Nigel thought one of them should be a butler, which made her even more uncomfortable.

There was no question, the house was beautiful, but they didn't need it, and it had been expensive, especially with the remodel. She hardly saw Nigel now that he wasn't working. He was going to the pub a lot at night to meet up with friends.

"I'll drive you out to see the country house in Sussex tomorrow." She'd only been to see it once herself. It was beautiful and peaceful, but she feared that Nigel's remodel to modernize it would be extensive, and provide another excuse for him not to work.

"Why all these houses?" Sam looked baffled. He knew she had inherited a large fortune from her parents, but she wasn't given to showing off like this. It was obviously all Nigel. He took their social life very seriously, although it had slowed down recently after he was fired, and she quit her job.

"I think he wants to impress his friends. He wants us to entertain, and give house parties in the country. That's a little grand for me, and a huge amount of work to entertain fifteen or twenty or thirty people for a weekend. And it costs a fortune. He just lost his job, by the way. He wants to take the summer off, and start looking in September."

"How do you feel about that?" Sam asked, concerned.

"I don't like it," she said honestly. "He pressured me into buying this house, and made a commitment to a friend to buy the place in Sussex without even telling me till after he did it. Things are a little rocky. I told him that if he makes another purchase like that without consulting me, I'd leave him. He spends a hell of a lot of money." She looked worried and Sam wasn't surprised.

"It sounds like he's gotten very grand since you two got married. He wasn't like that before, was he?"

"He likes the good life, and we certainly went to some very fancy homes on our weekends away together, but now he wants to give parties like that, not just go to them. He likes to live a glamorous life, and he has a very good idea of what I've inherited from my parents from the declaration of assets in our prenup, and he did some research before."

Sam was disturbed to hear it, but not surprised. "And you didn't," he reminded her. "He sounds very entitled. He didn't strike me that way last year." He had been respectful of Coco then, but his ideas had been somewhat grandiose even before they married.

"He promised me he wouldn't do it again. I hope he means it. I want him to get a job. It's embarrassing to have to push him about it. He said something about how pointless it is for him to work, given what I have. But I'm working. I think he should too." He had some savings, but he would be totally dependent on her when that ran out, which would be soon.

They both knew she had married him too quickly and didn't know him well enough. It had been obvious even then that Nigel liked living in the fast lane, and wanted a *Great Gatsby* kind of life, which Coco didn't. She'd let him pull her into it, but she didn't want to buy houses left and right to keep him happy. That kind of spending fright-

ened her, no matter how much money she had. With her parents'
example, she wasn't irresponsible about her money.

"Ed says I'm okay, but I won't be forever if Nigel keeps spending
this way."

Sam was worried for her as they drove back to her mews house,
which was a far cry from the mansion she had just bought.

"When are you moving in?"

"Supposedly in August. The country house will be finished in September, and I'll have to hire people to run it." It was a very luxurious
lifestyle for a twenty-three-year-old girl with a brand-new husband
without a penny to his name, or a job. But he had always told her
that he had no money. She just didn't know that he was going to
spend hers like a drunken sailor, and then get fired on top of it.

Nigel was out when they got home, which didn't surprise her. Sam
had a glass of wine, and they sat on the couch and talked with his
arm around her. They talked about his family, working with his father, and Tamar, who was devoted and loyal, and even willing to help
with his father's business on the weekends. She was helping them
with the billing. It made Sam feel even guiltier that he didn't want to
marry her.

"I'm twenty-four. I'm not ready to settle down yet. She's a year
younger than you are, and she wants to get married and have babies.
I can hear my youth flying out the window every time she says it,
along with my freedom."

"Why don't you date someone else for a while? Give yourself a
breather?" He liked the idea but felt guilty about that too.

"It would probably kill her. And my mother would kill me." He
smiled ruefully at Coco and she laughed. His mother was fierce when
she wanted to be, and she ruled her family with an iron fist. "My

mother is crazy about her. She's more like my mother than either of my sisters. Sabra is marrying Liam. Rebecca told my father she wants to convert and become a Catholic. And not even for a guy, she said it's more in keeping with her personal beliefs. Last year she was considering becoming a Buddhist. And Jacob still wants to be a rabbi. They're all driving me crazy. I miss you, Coco. It's not the same without you. I have no one sane to talk to except when I call you."

"It isn't the same for me either," she admitted, and they both knew she had made a mistake with Nigel. His lavish spending terrified her. He wanted all of London society to be impressed by them, but that was a costly venture, and Coco was footing the bill.

Nigel was different with Sam when he came home that night. He was quieter and less engaging, and seemed slightly annoyed that Sam was there, as though Sam was spying on him. It wasn't entirely inaccurate, but he was really there to see Coco and offer her whatever support she needed, and help her figure out what was going on. Things had changed since she and Nigel got married.

"That's quite a house you two are working on," Sam commented with a smile when they sat down to dinner at a pub nearby.

"Coco thinks it's too big for us," he answered glumly. "But it won't be when we start having children. And we can give some spectacular parties there. We'll be the talk of the town," he said, lighting up as he said it. It was all there in what he said and his facial expressions. He wanted to make a big splash, a *very* big splash, at her expense. It didn't embarrass him that she was paying for everything. He wanted to show off at any price. It was his way of making up for his brother inheriting everything. Now he had more.

Sam commented the next day when they drove to Sussex that he could see that Nigel was different. He blamed the magazine for firing him, and was bitter about it. But he liked not working. And he was annoyed that Coco was making a fuss about buying two houses at once, and thought he should get a job. He was well aware that she could afford what she'd spent, and had no remorse at all over pushing her to do so. He felt entitled to all of it, and was no longer funny and charming, and he was drinking way too much, with an edge to him when he did. And he made constant references to how rich Coco was, which embarrassed her and made Sam angry on her behalf.

The property in Sussex was beautiful and had a sense of history to it, but needed a lot of work due to deferred maintenance. The bones were there, though. When they got it fixed up, it would be an impressive estate, which it once had been, a long time ago.

"He got a great deal on it," Coco said, trying to make her peace with it. They owned it now, so there was no point complaining. They had to either fix it up and use it, or sell it, maybe even at a profit. Sam was impressed when he saw it. Coco had agreed to keep it and do the work, so they could give the weekend parties that Nigel was dreaming of, like those his wealthy friends gave. He had found a rich American wife to help him achieve his dreams. Sam suspected that had always been his intention, but he didn't say it to Coco. It was too late for that now, and it would only upset her. She was married to him, and said she loved him, although things had been a lot less pleasant lately.

Over dinner that night, Sam suggested that they come to New York that summer and spend some time in the Hamptons, but Nigel said he didn't want to go anywhere until the houses were finished. They would be staying in London for the summer. Coco had told Sam he could use the house in Southampton if he wanted, but he said it would feel too odd, and sad, to be there without her. She was what mattered to him, not the house.

Their four days together flew by, and she got plenty of time alone with Sam. Now that he wasn't working, Nigel disappeared a lot, and said he was working on the house. She wasn't always sure it was true, but didn't question him about it. It was easier not to. He got nasty now when she pressed him about anything, like what he spent.

When she took Sam to the airport, he looked at her with all the love he had always felt for her. "Call me if you need me, Coco." He didn't like the atmosphere between her and Nigel. It was tense most of the time now, and occasionally the looks he gave her were ugly. He was angry, not grateful for what she was doing for him. He felt entitled to it all.

"You too."

"Don't do anything stupid or buy him any more houses."

"Don't worry, I won't. And don't you do anything stupid either, or let your mother boss you around." He laughed at that.

"I'll try to come back in the fall to see how the houses look." She hugged him tight then, and they almost cried when they left each other, but didn't this time.

She was sad after Sam left, and went home thinking about him. Nigel could see it, and a few days later, he came home and said he had a surprise for her.

"We still haven't taken our honeymoon, and I thought it would be more fun with friends. We need a vacation. So I chartered a boat for us, with a fabulous owner's cabin, and five guest cabins." He looked triumphant as he said it.

"What kind of boat?" She liked boats, but this one sounded like a big deal to her. Her father had chartered one for them in the South of France once years ago, and they'd loved it. But she knew it had been incredibly expensive.

"It's a motorboat," Nigel said, smiling at her. "Two hundred and forty feet with a crew of nineteen. We can go wherever we want in the Mediterranean. Italy, France, Croatia. I think Saint Tropez would be fun. We have it for two weeks at the end of August, and when we come back, the house in town will be finished and we can move right in. We should start thinking about a housewarming party." Using various parts of the house, they could seat a hundred for dinner and dancing.

"Nigel, that's an enormous yacht. Chartering it for two weeks must have cost a fortune."

"It did, but it's our honeymoon. We deserve it, and we can take five couples with us. I've already made a list. It's mostly the people who entertained us all winter." He pulled a brochure out of a drawer and showed it to her. It was spectacular. She could imagine what it cost, and he expected her to pay for it. He had done it again, but not with a house this time. He hadn't bought it, he had only chartered it, thank God.

"Nigel, how much did the charter cost?" Her voice was low and tight.

"Do we have to talk about that now? Are you trying to spoil it? You always do these days," he said nastily, as though she'd refused him anything, which she certainly hadn't. He had pressured and intimidated her into everything she'd spent.

"I'd like to know. You're going to have to tell me eventually." He told her and she nearly fell out of her chair. "And you didn't think you needed to ask me first?"

"I thought you'd be excited." She was, about the price of the charter more than the boat. She didn't give a damn about taking five
couples with them to impress them. Saying it was for their honeymoon was a thin excuse, and she saw right through it. He wanted to
show off again. Those five couples would talk about the trip for
years, and invite them for weekends again and again.

"Nigel, the boat is gorgeous, but it's insanely expensive." It was
twice the price of the work they were doing on the house, which was
bad enough. "Are we committed to it?"

"I signed the contract this morning. I wanted to surprise you." And
since they were married, technically, she was responsible for any
debt or expense he incurred. So she was on the hook. She was no
match for him. He outsmarted her at every turn.

"I'm going upstairs to lie down," she said quietly. She didn't want
to fight with him. But he had crossed the line again, in a major way.
She wondered how many times he would do it. The boat sounded
like a fabulous idea. It even had a grand staircase, a swimming pool,
and a helicopter landing pad, but she would never have chartered a
boat that size, and certainly not for two weeks.

"Please don't be mad at me," he said softly, as she walked away to
go upstairs. She turned to look at him. It was hard to believe that he
didn't understand what he was doing, and the kind of money he was
spending. It was astronomical. "I just wanted you to be happy. You
should have some fun with your money."

"That should be up to me to decide when we're talking about
houses and amounts like this. I'm sure the boat is beautiful. I just
don't want to blow my inheritance like this. It's supposed to last for
my lifetime, and our children's lifetimes. It won't, if you keep spending it like this, and you can't do it without talking to me about it. I

don't want a honeymoon with ten of your friends along for the ride."
She was growing up fast dealing with him.

"Why not? You go to their homes. Why can't we take them with
us?"

"I'm going to have a hard time explaining this to my trustee. He
may put me on an allowance if you keep blowing money like this."
She could see Ed doing it, and she wouldn't blame him. She had
been extremely careful and reasonable before. Nigel was becoming a
major money drain, and she was scared of where it could lead.

"Just tell him it's our honeymoon. He'll understand."

"No, Nigel, he won't. And neither do I." But she was beginning to.
Nigel had had a plan when he married her, and she was it. The question was what to do about it now. She had to figure it out. He hadn't
asked her to give him the houses, he was content to spend as much
money as he could on a lavish lifestyle, which only he cared about.
Coco didn't. Nigel had seen an opportunity with her and seized it,
and now he was running with it, as fast as he could.

Chapter 9

The trip on the boat Nigel had chartered was nothing less than fabulous. He organized it perfectly, with a night for them alone before the others joined them. They picked the boat up in Monaco, where it was docked next to several even bigger yachts, which dwarfed it. All of them belonged to famous yacht owners, but the *Moonbeam* was a spectacular boat, and only a year old. It had been built by a famous shipyard, and had every comfort imaginable. Marble bathrooms, a spa, a hair salon, a movie theater, exquisite furnishings, priceless contemporary art, two Cordon Bleu chefs, and an impeccable British crew. The cabins were enormous and supremely comfortable with beautiful sheets and cashmere blankets and exquisite décor. They were waited on hand and foot. The champagne flowed from the moment they set foot on the boat, and Nigel had ordered caviar for their guests every night. There was nothing Coco could do about any of it, so once she accepted that the expense was inevitable, she tried to enjoy it as best she could. They had Jet Skis, water toys, a small sailboat and a submarine on board, and a helipad for the owner's helicopter. It had indoor and outdoor swimming pools, and a fleet of masseuses, hairdressers, and manicurists in addition to the nineteen-person crew. It was the most luxurious experience Coco had ever had.

The meals were extraordinary, like a three-star restaurant every night. They made a detour to Saint Tropez to do some shopping, and after that they headed to Italy, with a night in Portofino, Corsica after that, and then on to Sardinia, where they met up with friends on other yachts. Nigel knew people everywhere, and whenever they were in port, they gave lunch parties every day, with heavily laden buffets and the finest French wines.

All their guests talked constantly about how perfect everything was, and Nigel relaxed with Coco again. She tried to do the same. They made love for the first time in a month. And in spite of what it was costing her, Coco had a fantastic time too. It would have been impossible not to. They all felt like Cinderella after the ball when they got deposited back on the dock in Monaco, after two of the most perfect weeks most of them had ever spent.

They were driven to the airport in a van after the crew said good-bye to them. The captain had been extremely efficient and very pleasant. They had work to do when the charter guests left. The owner and his family were coming on board the following day, and sailing to Greece, to spend a month there.

The group was silent on the way to the airport, as reality hit them after two weeks of sheer heaven.

"You have to admit, it was incredible, wasn't it?" Nigel whispered to Coco in the van, looking pleased with himself. He had thoroughly enjoyed it, and told the captain they'd be back next year. Coco couldn't believe how cavalier he was about what they had spent. It didn't bother him at all. He hadn't even thanked her, and acted like their benefactor for organizing it. The guests barely thanked Coco.

The flight to London seemed like an affront after the comforts of the boat, and it was raining when they arrived. Nigel had spoken to the contractor, and he had said everything was ready for them. Even the new furniture they had ordered was in place, where the decorator had told them to put it. They went straight to their new house from the airport, and she and Nigel were both thrilled when they saw it. It was beautiful, and even the art they had purchased had been hung. Coco had spent a fortune, and it showed, which was Nigel's intention. But it was worth it. They would have the house for years, and as Nigel said, their children would grow up in it. This made a lot more sense to her than two weeks on someone else's boat with nothing to show for it except memories, and with people who weren't even her friends. They were his. Nigel was surrounding himself with people who took full advantage of the benefits he offered, at Coco's expense.

They were planning to move out of her rented mews house the next day. They spent an hour walking around the new house with the architect and contractor, inspecting things before they went home. They were both in great spirits after seeing the house, and they had congratulated the contractor on his fine work, and for completing the job on time.

Their daily cleaning lady had left them some cheese and salad and a roast chicken in the fridge at Coco's house. It was depressing serving themselves the haphazard meal after the opulence of the yacht. Everything was packed in cartons.

"I can't wait to move in tomorrow." Nigel looked at her lovingly and she smiled. She was admittedly more relaxed after the boat trip, they were on better terms, and excited to be moving into their new home, whatever the cost. The money was spent now and the house was exquisite.

She spent the next morning finishing packing a few last things and by noon they were moved in. Nigel had packed his clothes and nothing else. He had no other possessions. He had given up his apartment and thrown everything away. He had no family souvenirs and nothing of value.

They had a sandwich in their new kitchen, and then she drove over to Leslie's house. They were meeting a new client at three o'clock. They had gotten several clients from a corporation where Leslie had connections, and two Americans who had heard about them from a friend. Their relocation business was taking off.

Leslie smiled when she saw Coco with her deep tan. She looked relaxed and said the move had gone well. They were all moved in, and were going to sleep there that night. To make up for being away for two weeks, Coco stayed to help Leslie until eight o'clock that night. Nigel was out when she got back, and hadn't left her a note.

For the next two days, Nigel and Coco hardly saw each other, after having been constantly together on the boat. Leslie had set up a slew of appointments with new clients. Right before their noon meeting on Thursday, Coco realized she had left their color wheel at home.

"Damn, I'll run home and get it. I'll be back in ten minutes," she said and sped out the door, as Leslie thanked her. She let herself into the house, looked in her office on the main floor, which Nigel had designed for her, couldn't find the color wheel, and then remembered that she had left it in their bedroom and sped up the stairs. The door was open, and the cleaning staff they had hired to come in every day hadn't started yet, so she flew through the door and found herself looking at her husband, with his head deep between a woman's legs. The woman started to scream just as Coco saw them. She stood rooted to the floor, unable to believe what she was seeing, or run away. As soon as the woman came, Nigel entered her and they both came again as Coco stood there too horrified to move and whispered, "Oh my God." From somewhere in the distance, Nigel heard her and glanced over his shoulder and the next thing she knew the woman was screaming again. Nigel leapt out of bed, and tried to take the sheet with him to cover his erect penis, while Coco looked him in the eye, shaking from head to foot.

"For God's sake, Coco, why did you come back here?" As though she was the one at fault. She glanced at the bed, and recognized the blond girl from marketing at the magazine. She ran from the bed into Coco's new bathroom, slammed the door shut, and locked it.

"I forgot my color wheel," Coco said, "and you forgot that you're married. For chrissake, we've lived here for three days, and this is what you do?"

"It was an accident . . . I didn't mean it . . . I can explain . . ." He looked pathetic, as he clutched their new sheets around him.

"I want you both out of my house by the time I come home," was all she said, and then she grabbed the color wheel she saw on the desk, ran back down the stairs, and out the door. She was back in Leslie's office after twenty minutes, not ten, and she was deathly pale under her tan, but the client hadn't arrived yet.

"Are you okay?" Leslie asked her, concerned. "You look like you saw a ghost."

"Yes, something like that. I saw an accident on the way back." She didn't know what else to say to explain her disarray. All she could think of was what she'd seen Nigel doing to the girl on the bed. She had a sleazy reputation at the magazine, which was apparently well deserved. But Nigel was no better. She couldn't let herself think about it now. She had to get through the meeting first.

The client arrived two minutes later and stayed until two while they discussed the apartment Leslie had found them. It was perfect for their needs, and they had to decide what color to paint the rooms. Coco sat back in her chair, and let out a breath as soon as they left, as Leslie watched her. She had made sense in the meeting, but she looked sick.

"Coco, what's wrong?" she asked her gently. Coco shook her head, trying not to cry, and then looked at her.

"I found Nigel in bed with another woman when I went home. The slut secretary from marketing that everyone says is a whore. I guess they're right. They were in my bed, going at it when I walked in." It felt better to tell her and get it off her chest.

"Oh my God," Leslie said, horrified.

"Yeah, I think that's what I said too. I had to leave to get back here."

"I'm so, so sorry. What are you going to do?"

"I told him he had to leave before I get back. And I just gave up the mews house yesterday."

"Do you want to stay here?"

"No, I want him to get out," she said fiercely. "I'm not going to let him do this to me." Leslie made her a cup of tea. Coco stayed at the office to avoid Nigel, and she left at six o'clock. Leslie was worried about her.

The house seemed empty when she got home, and then she saw him in her office, waiting for her when she went upstairs. "I told you to be out of here when I got home. If you don't go, I'm calling the police." She stood with her phone poised in her hand, ready to call them, and he stood up. He didn't look menacing, he looked broken, and she didn't care. He was trying to bankrupt her with what he spent, and now he was cheating on her too, in her own bed. He was the biggest mistake she could ever have made. She was clear about it now. There was no doubt in her mind.

"Coco, we have to talk," he said in a pleading tone.

"No, we don't. The only person I'm going to talk to is my attorney. Get out of my house, Nigel." He couldn't get to her in time, and she called the police. They answered right away. She told them there was an intruder trying to break in, and gave them the address and her name. They said they would be there immediately.

"For fuck's sake, why did you do that?" he shouted at her and headed toward the stairs.

"Why did you have to do that in my bed?" she shouted after him, as he ran toward the front door. "I'll have you put in jail if you come near here again." He didn't stop to talk to her and left seconds before the police arrived. When they questioned her, she told them that her estranged husband had tried to break in, and gave them his name and description, and asked for passing calls to drive by the house and watch for him outside. They assured her they would, and when they left, she called Nigel on his cell. "Don't come back here, Nigel. I gave them your name and your description, and told them you were trying to break in."

"Into my own home?" He was shocked. He didn't want a police report against him. Coco had changed. He had finally pushed her over the edge.

"It's not your home, it's mine. And you don't live here anymore." Her voice was hard. She was done.

"Coco, please. It was a stupid thing to do. I'm sorry. Things have been so rough between us for a while, I just slept with her to let off steam. It doesn't mean anything."

"It means a lot to me. And how rough were things for you on the boat? You had to screw her *now*? Three days after we move into this house you forced me to buy?"

"I made a date with her a long time ago, and forgot about it."

"So you figured that as long as she was here, you would screw her in my bed? Like, why waste an opportunity to get laid?" It was sounding worse and worse as he explained. There was nothing he could say to make it right or better. He had gone one giant step too far. Money was bad enough, but cheating on her was a whole different category of offense. She knew she would never trust him again. "Text me where to send your things," she said in a voice of pure fury.

"I don't have anyplace to stay," he whined.

"You should have thought of that this morning."

The girl he'd had sex with was pure trash, and so was he, whatever his fancy lineage. He was no better than the girl was. He was a fortune-hunter of the worst sort, a user, and a cheat.

"Coco, can we get together and talk about this?"

"There's nothing to say. I saw it all."

"I'm sorry . . . I'm sorry . . . I swear I'll never do it again . . ."

"You can do whatever you want," she said, her voice shaking, "I'm finished with you, Nigel. Done." And with that she hung up and burst into tears. She didn't even call Sam that night. She was too upset.

Nigel called her thirty or forty times that night, and she didn't answer. He was afraid to come to the house and get picked up by the police. She lay awake all night, and then finally in the morning she called Sam and told him what had happened. He was horrified at the meanness and bad taste of it. But at least now she knew who she was dealing with. She was furious and hurt all at the same time.

"He charged that enormous yacht to me, and then came home and screwed that sleazy whore in my bed."

"What are you going to do now?"

"Divorce him. I never should have married him. I can't afford him anyway, emotionally or financially. He was so sweet and so charming and seemed so boyish and innocent when I met him. I never should have married him. You were right. I was an idiot." They had been married for eight months. He had cost her millions, and cheated on her in their bed.

"At least you've figured it out. You'll get over it," he said gently. "You've been through a lot worse," he said, thinking of her parents, and she started to cry when she thought about them too.

"This never would have happened if my father were still alive. I wouldn't have married him. I wanted the kind of relationship my parents had. Dad wouldn't have let me marry him." Sam had tried to stop or at least slow her down, but he didn't have the power, and Coco had been dazzled by Nigel. He was so charming at first.

"He's not a good guy. Neither was Ed. You need a good one now," Sam said quietly.

"I just want him out of my life." She called a lawyer she knew that afternoon. He hadn't called her back yet when Nigel showed up on her front doorstep, begging to come in. Her housekeeper was there, so she wasn't afraid, and she went outside to talk to him.

"What do you want?"

"To talk to my wife." He got down on both knees and begged her forgiveness. He looked so ridiculous, but all she could think of was how he looked when he was having sex with the girl from marketing. It was an image she knew she would never get out of her head.

"I'm divorcing you. Go away," she said, walked back into the house, and slammed the door in his face. He stood ringing the door-bell for half an hour. She went upstairs so she didn't have to hear him, and he finally left.

She went to work every day after that, and when the lawyer called back, she made an appointment with him for the following week. She was going to call Ed, but not until after she'd seen the lawyer. She hated admitting to him that her marriage was a disaster.

Nigel sent her flowers, emails, voicemails, and texts. She didn't respond to any of it. When she finally listened to one of his messages, he swore he would never do it again. He kept bombarding her for days that turned into weeks. She had seen the lawyer. He was poised to file for divorce in January. She wasn't eligible to do so before that. They had to be married for a year to divorce. Finally after two months, she took a call from Nigel. She was trying to decide if she should sell the house, or live in it herself. She didn't need a house that size. But she was enjoying working with Leslie, and didn't want to go back to New York.

"Why are you still calling me?" she said when she took Nigel's call. It was mid-November, and it had been six weeks since she'd spoken to him. She missed him, but she missed who she'd thought he was, not who he turned out to be.

"I'm calling you because I love you, and I'm sorry. We're married. Can't you please give it another chance?"

"I don't trust you anymore, Nigel. I never will again. This wasn't a marriage, it was a prison sentence for both of us." And a very expensive one for her.

"The house in Sussex is beautiful. Won't you come and see it with me?"

"No. Is that where you're living?" He didn't answer her, afraid that she would throw him out if he admitted it. He'd been living at the house in Sussex since he'd left. It had never occurred to her that he was there. "You have no business being there. I own that house too." He had no shame. He was still using her, even now.

"You own everything, Coco, including me, heart and soul."

"Apparently, your dick was never part of that deal," she said coldly and he winced. "I can't live with a man I don't trust."

"I swear to you, on my life, I will never cheat on you again."

"I don't believe you," she said sadly. She had made a terrible mistake with him, and she knew that now. She had two houses she didn't want, and would be divorced, because of him.

"What do you have to lose by giving me another chance? If I do something bad again, you won't have to throw me out. I'll go. Please, Coco, can't you be merciful this one time?"

"Did you find a job?" she asked coldly.

"I've been too upset about us to look for work."

"I'm upset too, and I go to work every day."

"You're stronger than I am," he said, sounding lame. "I'm broken over this. I'll never get over it." He was trying everything. "Have mercy on me, Coco, please . . ." He was crying at his end and she actually felt sorry for him, in spite of how angry she still was. "Will you have lunch with me?" She knew she shouldn't, but thought that maybe they could end it on a kinder note. She didn't want to be angry and hate him for the rest of her life. She had been so in love with him, they could at least say goodbye, she reasoned with herself, and finally agreed to have lunch with him at the pub nearby. He sounded deeply grateful and humble when she agreed.

She met him the next day, and he looked terrible. He had lost at least ten pounds, had dark circles under his eyes, and the handsome face looked ravaged. She was the injured party here and she looked better than he did. She could see how sorry he was from the look in his eyes.

She tried to keep the conversation as neutral as she could, and at the end of lunch, he asked if he could come to the house to pick up some of his things. She hadn't known where to send them, and hadn't thrown them away. His computer was still on his desk and he said he needed it for his job search. His CV was on it, and a list of all the people he needed to call for work.

"Fine. Why don't we go now. I don't have to be back at work for half an hour." He followed her back in his car, the green Jaguar, after he paid for lunch. He followed her meekly up the steps, and went straight to his office, while she went to hers and gathered up some things she needed for a meeting that afternoon. He was taking a long time, and when she walked into his office to remind him that she had to leave, he was crying with his head on the desk. It was embarrassing to see him that way, and she went over and patted his shoulder. When she did, he put his arms around her waist and held her as he used to, and something stirred in her that she had hoped was dead. But it wasn't yet. The last embers of their love were dying, but were not completely out. He pulled her onto his lap then, and kissed her, and she let him, and the next thing she knew, he was gently taking her clothes off, and she was aching for him, as she had before. They ended up on the couch in his office, making love, he cried through most of it, and begged her forgiveness, and told her how much he loved her, and afterward, she held him like a child to her breast.

"Swear to me you'll never do anything like it again," she said in a choked voice.

"I swear," he said, and appeared to be sincere. She knew she was taking a terrible chance, but she told him he could come home. She had held out for almost two months, and filled out the papers for a divorce, but she agreed to give him one more chance. He knew she meant it, and he swore again that he would never betray her. He had learned his lesson. She didn't tell Leslie that he was back. When she got home from work that night, he was waiting for her, and still afraid of what he would do now, they made love again.

Chapter 10

Nigel was very careful with her once Coco let him back into the house. He was walking on eggshells, and she was hypervigilant. He took her to see the results at the house in Sussex, and it was as beautiful as he said. They still had to furnish it, but everything was done, and the grounds were larger than she remembered.

It took her two weeks to admit to Leslie that she had let him come back. Leslie looked leery about it, but wished her the best. Her business was growing, and Coco had become an important part of it. Their clients loved her, and Coco had discovered that she had a knack for decorating, like her mother. Leslie said she had real talent, and great follow-through. Every client had been satisfied so far.

Two weeks after he moved back in, Nigel begged her to give a Christmas party, to christen their new home. She still felt tentative with him, and she wasn't feeling festive, but she finally let him talk her into it, as long as they kept it down to fifty or sixty good friends. She didn't want to give a big showy bash. He was disappointed, but he agreed. They chose the guest list carefully. It was made up of the people they were closest to. It grew to seventy-five easily, but Nigel said that some of them wouldn't show up.

She turned twenty-four a few days before the Christmas party, and she didn't want to celebrate her birthday this year either. It was taking her time to feel close to him again, but she was getting there, and was slowly starting to trust him again.

Sam had been worried about her ever since she'd told him that Nigel was back. He thought it was a terrible mistake. In his opinion, Nigel was not going to change.

She called to wish him a happy Chanukah, and he asked her how things were going.

"A little wobbly, but basically okay. I feel like the KGB watching him. I don't know if it will ever be the same again. I guess people go through worse. What about you? Will everyone come home for Chanukah?" They usually did, but she could hear that he was down.

"My mother won't let either of my sisters come, she's so mad at them. Rebecca converted, and Sabra and Liam will be married in April in a Catholic church. So it's just me and Jacob this year, and my parents. They're putting the heat on me pretty heavily about Tamar. We've been dating for a year and a half and they say I'm disrespecting her. They think that I owe it to her to marry her after this long, and I'll humiliate her in the community if I don't. I'm not even sure why I go out with her, except she's a nice girl and a good person. She helps my father with our books. My mother loves her. Tamar wants to have a million babies, and will keep a kosher home. I feel like I'll turn into my parents if I marry her, and she'll become my mother. It's everything I said I didn't want." He sounded tortured over it. "But I keep seeing her because it's easy and she's always there."

"So?" The answer seemed obvious to Coco. He didn't want to marry her and he wasn't in love with her.

"I feel so damn guilty if I don't marry her. She's so willing and accommodating and I've been lazy. I should have stopped dating her a year ago, but I didn't. My mother says they'll be disappointed in me if I don't marry her. Classic Jewish guilt."

"Don't disappoint yourself," Coco said firmly. "That's more important. You have a right to marry who you want."

"I don't want to marry anyone right now. I'm not even sure I've ever been in love."

"Lucky for you," she said, and he laughed. She always made him feel better, even from three thousand miles away.

"My father says that marrying her is the honorable thing to do, after dating her for all this time. They've probably guessed I'm sleeping with her, so I've defiled her."

"It's only a year and a half, not ten for chrissake, and she could have stopped seeing you."

"She's in love with me. And I'm comfortable with her. But is that enough?"

"No, it's not. If you want comfortable, get a dog, or have lunch with your grandmother. Don't you want someone more exciting?"

"Exciting doesn't last. It's not real. You've proven that twice now. And even if Nigel is back, how long do you think it's going to last? Not forever, that's for sure."

"I don't think forever lasts either. It's just a word. But you need to feel a thrill when she walks across the room, you need to feel it in your gut, your heart should melt when you see her."

"Maybe only girls feel those things." He laughed.

"That's bullshit. So do guys."

"I don't know. She's a good person, she'd be a good wife and mother. She'll keep a kosher home, which will make my parents happy."

"And you miserable," she reminded him. "Think of it. You'll never eat bacon and shrimp again." He laughed. "You're too young to settle, and do what your parents want. Sam, think about it. This is *your* life, not theirs."

"It's hers too. And they're nagging me day and night."

"They're brainwashing you to marry the girl *they* want."

"Sometimes that works," he said, sounding depressed about it. "A lot of Jewish families had arranged marriages. My grandparents did. I think they were happy."

"This is the twenty-first century. You can't let them do this to you."

"I'm twenty-five years old. They think I should be married and having kids by now."

"My parents got married at twenty-two. They're the only people I know who pulled it off. Today that doesn't work. Look at the mess I just made, and I was in love with him when we got married."

"But you go for the exciting ones. That's a big mistake. The exciting ones never last. The boring ones probably do. She won't cheat on me. She'll be pregnant all the time."

"Sam, wake up! Don't do something stupid. This is your future you're talking about. Sixty years maybe. Possibly seventy."

"And they're my parents. I'm supposed to honor them too."

"You're breaking my heart."

"Now you sound like my mother. She says that to me twenty times a day."

"Go out and get laid, or drunk or something. Have a ham sandwich." He laughed but she could feel that she was losing the battle. "One of us has to marry the right person. And I think you're it."

"Maybe she is the right person."

"For someone else," Coco said, pleading with him, but his parents had beaten him down, and he sounded confused. They talked for a long time and then he had to go to dinner with them. She wished him a happy Chanukah, and promised to call him in a few days. Her heart was aching for him when they hung up. He deserved so much better than Tamar.

The Christmas party Nigel and Coco gave in their new home was beautiful. They got a Christmas tree and their florist decorated it for them with antique angels. Nigel hired carolers to sing as the guests came in. Now that he was back, he was billing everything to Coco again, which was lucky for him. He'd been down to his last few hundred pounds when she relented and let him come home. The buffet was delicious, with plenty of caviar. People showed up in good spirits, and were vastly impressed by the house. In the end, they had sixty people, which felt right to Coco, although Nigel was disappointed that more people hadn't shown up. But it was snowing and freezing cold, so some guests stayed home, or had other parties to go to.

Coco and Nigel were getting along better than they had in a long time. He was very careful not to upset her. He gave her a gold bracelet for Christmas that he had paid for himself with a credit card.

He hadn't started looking for a job yet, but promised her he would after New Year's. And she promised not to nag him about it until then. They went to midnight mass together on Christmas Eve, and she gave him the espresso machine he had wanted, and an Hermès sweater. They planned a ski weekend for their anniversary in January, and a week before that, something occurred to Coco that she hadn't thought about before. She stopped at the pharmacy on her way to work, bought a test kit, and wanted to do it at the office, so he wouldn't be around. It had just dawned on her that she hadn't had a period since November, before Nigel had moved back in. She didn't know what she wanted while she waited for the test to give her the answer. She didn't feel ready for a baby yet, but maybe that was what they needed now, to stabilize their marriage. It had been a tumultuous year. She was shocked when the test was positive, even though she suspected that it might be. She was happy and terrified all at the same time.

She didn't say anything to Leslie. She wanted Nigel to be the first to know. She knew it was what he wanted, and would bond them to each other for life, a child. It was a sacrifice she was willing to make for him, even if it seemed too soon to her, and she felt too young. She sped home in her car between appointments, and told Leslie she'd be right back. She didn't want to wait until that night to tell him.

She let herself into the house as quietly as she could, and raced upstairs to surprise him. She could hear him in his office, talking to someone, presumably on the phone. She knocked gently on the door and walked in, and a naked blond woman was sitting on the desk, while Nigel made love to her. She was moaning, and so was he, and saying how much he loved her, which was the conversation she had heard from the stairs. He looked at Coco with horror, withdrew immediately, and held his jeans up in front of him. The girl didn't know what had happened, and then turned and saw Coco. It wasn't someone she knew this time, but it didn't matter.

"I can't believe this," Coco said to him, but she did believe it. She had been afraid of exactly this happening again. "I came home to tell you that I'm pregnant, you son of a bitch," she said, picked up a book and threw it at his head, and narrowly missed him.

"Coco, please!" he said with a tortured look.

"Not this time," she said in an icy tone. "You can both get the fuck out of my house. Now!" The girl scurried off to the bathroom with her clothes in her arms, and Nigel stood staring at her.

"Are you really pregnant?" He looked shell-shocked. Again.

"It doesn't matter now. Just go. Both of you. I'll come back with the police if you don't." And he knew she would. Then she turned around and ran down the stairs. She went back to the office and didn't say anything to Leslie, she was too upset. And when she went home at six o'clock, he was gone. He had taken his computer, and some clothes. He knew she meant business. She didn't cry this time. It was over. She was dead inside, except for a baby she didn't want now. And she didn't want him either. He had killed everything she had ever felt for him, and he had made a fool of her again for loving and trusting him.

She lay awake that night, and called the lawyer in the morning, to file the papers. She didn't know what she was going to do about the baby, but she could figure that out in a few days.

Two days after Nigel left, she was sitting, staring out the window at first light, when she heard a text come in. She thought it might be from Nigel, but it wasn't. She hadn't heard from him this time. He didn't know what to say, and was smart enough not to try, and make things worse for himself. The text was from Sam.

"I just got engaged" was all it said, and she was almost as sad for him as she was for herself. It was a dark day for both of them. Her mistake had just ended. And his had just begun. She didn't have the heart to answer and congratulate him. She was always honest with him. She finally texted a single phrase. "Mazel tov." His parents had won. He was throwing his life away with a girl they both knew he didn't love.

The man she had loved and done too much for had thrown her away for another blonde.

Chapter 11

Coco had called her attorney before she did anything else the morning after she found Nigel cheating on her. It had been four months since she had spoken to him and she apologized for the time lapse and not following through before.

"We were trying to work things out again. It's not possible. He cheated on me again. I want to file for divorce."

"Remind me how long you've been married. It wasn't long, as I recall."

"It will be a year next week."

"That's excellent, and works well for us. You have to be married a year to file for divorce, as I told you before. So we'll file next week. All the papers are still in order. I'm glad you've moved on this quickly. Even a year is considered a short-term marriage, and won't impress any judge if your ex-husband makes unreasonable financial demands. And no children." She didn't tell him she was pregnant, in case she decided not to keep it. She hadn't made up her mind yet. "Is there anything else that I should know, that you didn't mention before?" He was matter-of-fact and methodical, which she liked. And she tried to be as well. She had already given him a copy of their marriage contract, and Ed's office number in New York for any financial information he needed.

"I've caught him having sex with other women, twice. Both times in our home," she said tersely. There was a brief silence as he considered that, and wrote it down. "I didn't tell you about the second time before. It happened yesterday."

"We'll file on grounds of adultery then. Do you know the women's names?"

"Only one of them," the girl from *Time* magazine.

"And you're sure you want to file for divorce this time?" he asked her.

"A hundred percent. I gave him another chance. He did it again. I'm not waiting for the third time."

"That sounds like a wise decision," he said dryly. "I doubt that he'll be eligible for spousal support if he asks for it, after less than a year. He's employed?"

"Not at the moment. He lost his job in June."

"There seems to be nothing new to add, except that one detail, since we last spoke. I can get the papers over to you today for you to read and verify. The faster you sign them, the faster I can submit them to the court, which seems like it might be a good thing to do in this case."

"That one detail" was the blonde he'd been having sex with yesterday, she thought as she hung up.

She left the house with a heavy heart, wondering if she should sell it. Even with one baby it would be too big for her, and the house felt cursed. She had never wanted it, and had only bought it to make him happy, which was no longer of interest to her. And there was the house in Sussex. The house in the city had some real value, and had been expensive, but the one in Sussex had been a bargain. She had paid less for it than two weeks on the yacht with ten of his friends. Everything he had done during the year of their marriage had cost her money in large amounts, and allowed him to show off to the people he wanted to impress.

The texts from Nigel started coming once she got to the office. Frantically at first, apologizing and swearing it would never happen again. And with no response from her, they slowed down quickly. Her only text to him stated the name of her lawyer, and to expect to hear from him shortly, and asking for the name of his. She had no other comment on the scene she had walked in on the day before. It hurt less this time. It had been only slightly less dramatic, except for the fact that she was pregnant, and had hoped that he'd be over-joyed, and it might save their marriage. There was nothing left to save now, if there ever had been. She didn't know anymore. Maybe it had only been about money for him, and had been a setup from the first. He was well versed about what she had from her parents, which he knew from their prenup and had probably culled from the press and gotten off the Internet. Fortunately, their numbers weren't accurate, but they were bad enough, and a lure to bad guys like him. It was the flash of men like him that always got to her. The dazzle. Of Ed, and now Nigel. Even her own trustee, appointed by her father, had taken advantage of her. In Ed's case, he had stolen her trust and innocence, Nigel had done the same and upped the stakes by getting her to spend millions for his benefit. At least she had something solid to show for it, and could sell both houses as soon as possible. She didn't want to live in either of them.

The forms for her to check and sign arrived from her lawyer shortly before noon, and she told Leslie what had happened.

"I'm filing for divorce," she said matter-of-factly, as Leslie nodded, shocked and sorry for Coco, but no longer surprised.

"I've known him since we were kids. I didn't think he was capable of something like this." It was highway robbery and manipulation on a grand scale. Coco was young, but she was nobody's fool. She was onto him now. And Nigel knew it too.

He managed to surprise her again a week later, with an email where he mentioned the name of a lawyer he had hired to represent him. He wasn't begging to come back this time. He knew she'd never let him, and was turning his attention to more practical aspects now. She read his most astonishing paragraph twice to make sure she had understood it fully.

"If you really are pregnant, as you said, and didn't just invent that out of whole cloth to hurt me and make the situation worse, bringing up a child is a collaborative venture, and I cannot imagine our being able to cooperate with each other now, given your attitude toward me. I doubt that you would continue with the pregnancy, in these circumstances, but if you do, I would relinquish all parental claim to the result of the pregnancy in exchange for full ownership of our London home. This would be in addition to any financial arrangements and consideration the courts would give me, and not in lieu of." She assumed that his lawyer had helped him with the language. The idea behind it was pure Nigel, and showed her a total lack of caring and morality. He didn't even have the decency to refer to it as a baby. Just reading it disgusted her, and she had no intention of giving him anything, let alone an extremely valuable piece of London real estate that she should be able to sell easily. The house apparently meant more to him than his own child.

The crassness of his suggestion gnawed at her all weekend. She hadn't decided yet if she was going to keep the baby. But if she did, on Sunday night she had an idea of her own. The prospect of his giving up all parental rights showed his total lack of feeling for her and the baby, but was not entirely a bad suggestion, once you got past the heartlessness behind it. If she kept the pregnancy, buying off his parental rights would avoid years of battles over joint custody, disagreements over how to bring up the child, and visitation, and what the child would be exposed to when with him, if he ever saw it. And she was not about to sacrifice a house worth millions to him. But if she kept the baby, she would be more than willing to give up the Sussex property, which had cost her very little and she had no real use for. She didn't intend to give weekend house parties without Nigel, and it would be an excellent trade if he'd accept it, to buy their child's freedom from him and her own, to raise a child in peace.

She wrote him back, suggesting the Sussex property in lieu of the London house, if she continued the pregnancy, and got no immediate answer, and advised her attorney of the name of his. The more she thought about it, the more she liked his proposition. Parenting was a two-person endeavor, but not with a man like Nigel. The child, if it was ever born, would be better off without him. His value system, and morals on every front, were deplorable. In Coco's opinion, he was a disgusting human being, if one could even call him that, after all he'd done. Knowing him, she was sure he would try to justify his actions, buying houses and chartering yachts, as a way of "improving her life" and "putting her inheritance to good use," which she knew now had nothing to do with her. It was all about him, and he had used her to impress the friends in his social circle, and elevate his own status with them. She was just taken along for the ride, to pay the bills, which she had done willingly, because she loved him. It all seemed like a cruel joke now, and a terrible trick he had played on her for his own gain.

It took Nigel two days to respond to her email, and much to her amazement, he accepted her offer to trade the Sussex property instead of the London house for all parental rights to their child. He was smart enough to take the lesser offer when he didn't have a winning hand. Coco thought his idea would benefit both of them, and even the baby, to keep it out of Nigel's clutches, and she forwarded the email exchange to her attorney. He called her as soon as he got it.

"You didn't mention that you're pregnant," he said in a serious voice. "That could be complicated, although the exchange that he's suggesting would certainly simplify it. We'll have to choose the language very carefully, to make it palatable to the court. A judge might feel that he was protecting the child's rights, by not depriving him or her of a father. You'd be satisfied with that exchange, though, for your property in Sussex?"

"Yes, I would. Very much so. I'd rather lose the money I spent on it, and have him out of our lives."

"When is the baby due?" he asked cautiously. The exchange they had unofficially agreed to, and come up with between them, was one he had never done before, but even he agreed it had its merits.

"I'm not sure," Coco said in answer to his question. "Probably next summer, if I have it. I haven't decided yet." He understood the option she was referring to, and refrained from comment.

The following week, Nigel's attorney communicated the rest of what he wanted from her, in light of her personal fortune. Nigel was trying to annul their prenuptial contract, claiming that he had not been represented by an attorney, which had been his choice at the time. He had simply signed it and handed it back to her. Now he was claiming that he hadn't understood what he was signing and no one had explained it to him. He wanted a five-million-dollar settlement as consolation for the pain and suffering and trauma of the divorce, another million in damages, citing his being fired as her fault, because she had kept him so busy supervising the work on the houses and their demanding social life. He wanted spousal support of three million dollars a year for ten years, to help him get on his feet, and to live in the style to which she had accustomed him. And another million for his summer vacation, using the yacht they had chartered as the model for it. In addition to the Sussex property, as compensation for losing his home in the city, on the terms that they had agreed to. In its totality, he was asking for a thirty-seven-million-dollar divorce, plus Sussex, for eleven months of being married to her. It amounted roughly to a forty-million-dollar divorce for breaking her heart and eleven months of her time. Ed Easton had been an amateur compared to him.

"He has an ambitious attorney," hers said in a cool tone. They had said that given the size of her fortune, it was a drop in the bucket to her, and a negligible amount in proportion to what she had. "He puts a high value on himself, doesn't he?" He already couldn't stand the guy, just reading his demands. He stayed neutral in the cases he handled as a rule, but Nigel's proposals were so outrageous that her lawyer, Harold Humphreys, felt protective of her. Nigel's intentions were plainly transparent. It was interesting that she had managed to hold down a job during the entire time, despite two house remodels, a full social life, and even a pregnancy, and he couldn't, and had made no effort to find one after he was fired. "I think a judge will take a very dim view of this, Miss Martin." She had called him using her maiden name, and not her married one. She wanted nothing more to do with anything of Nigel's, not even his name. "Judges are human too, and work for a living. They have families to support, and the same expenses the rest of us do. For him to ask for support in these amounts, damages, and compensation, no matter what your parents left you, will infuriate any judge after an eleven-month marriage. You could even ask for an annulment on the basis of fraud, but it might take longer. I think you'll be best served by being rid of him as quickly as possible, for the least amount of money."

"Thank you, I'd like that."

"I'll get the ball rolling immediately."

She hadn't heard a word from Nigel since his email about the Sussex property, and she suspected she wouldn't. She could just imagine Nigel and his lawyer going over the numbers and trying to figure out how much they could get away with. What they had come up with was shocking, and according to Harold Humphreys, offensive. He said that with luck, the marriage should be dissolved within six months. Their coming to an agreement would speed it along. The lawyer suspected that what Nigel wanted most on the list was the Sussex property. And as much money as he could get. The issue of parental rights could be more complicated, if he didn't agree to the Sussex property, or reneged on the arrangement.

"I'd like that part of it settled before the baby's born," Coco said. But if she was two months pregnant, she'd be divorced a month before the baby was born.

"I'll do my best," he promised her. She knew she had some battles ahead with Nigel, and probably very nasty ones, and there was always the danger that it would leak to the press, particularly with those amounts, but she thought that her lawyer was the right man for the job, and Nigel's had overshot the mark, possibly to his client's detriment. Nigel had probably spurred him on in his unlimited greed and total lack of remorse.

After the first exchange between the lawyers, and several calls between her attorney and her trustee, Coco did what she'd been planning to do all week. She packed up every last shred of Nigel's belongings, some personal files he had, his gym equipment, his clothes, the few things he had brought from his apartment. She boxed it up, hired a delivery service, and sent it all to her house in Sussex, where she knew he was living, until further notice. If they didn't make the agreement he had suggested, she intended to evict him and put it up for sale. She didn't want the headache of a country estate and didn't need it. She hadn't made a decision about the city house yet, and needed to think about what to do about the baby first, before she dealt with real estate. There was so much to think about. She returned his grandmother's ring to her attorney to turn over to Nigel's.

She didn't miss their social life at all. She had stayed off that circuit since his first catastrophic indiscretion in September, and she had no desire to see any of his friends again. She was out of his life for good, and wanted to stay that way. Her only close friend in London was Leslie, and Sam in New York. She had lost touch with her school friends in New York when her parents died, and the last of them when she moved to London. The people she knew at Columbia had all graduated after she dropped out, and were scattered everywhere by now. She had meant to stay in touch with some of them, but hadn't. Her life had changed too much after her parents' deaths, when she'd moved to London for *Time,* and married Nigel. The currents of life had swept her along in one direction, and them in others.

It took her a week after she walked in on Nigel for the second time to call Sam. At first she was too upset and embarrassed by what had happened, again. She felt stupid for having given him a second chance, and it was all so sordid. Other people learned about cheating partners from others, or suspected an affair from lipstick on their husband's collar. Instead she had had the privilege of walking in on him having sex with cheap women, twice, and the humiliation it had caused. She hated to tell Sam about it, but they hadn't spoken since he got engaged, and she didn't want him to think she disapproved of his engagement, although she did. She felt sorry for him and thought he was making a mistake, but she wanted to be supportive. He had sent her several texts asking if she was okay. She had responded that she was, which wasn't entirely true. She had started getting morning sickness after her email exchange with Nigel about relinquishing his parental rights. She wasn't sure if it was physical, or her upset over filing for the divorce. But either way, she threw up at least once every morning, and several times at night. It made eating anything a chore, and from both circumstances, she was losing weight, and had lost ten pounds. Already thin to begin with, she was looking gaunt, and Leslie was concerned about her. She hated what she was going through, and knew nothing about the pregnancy. If she kept it, Coco didn't intend to tell anyone for a long time, until it showed. She needed time to adjust to it herself, and didn't want advice or opinions, except her own.

She had gone to her doctor, who confirmed the pregnancy with a blood test. They had discussed the possibility of an abortion. The baby was due in August, her doctor told her, and Coco had to decide what she was going to do. They did a routine ultrasound, saw that the fetus's heart was beating nicely, and seeing the baby on the screen made the decision harder than she'd thought. She felt too young for the responsibilities of motherhood at twenty-four, but that would have been true if her marriage was still intact, and she would have had it then. Nigel giving up his parental rights would make it both easier and more difficult. And like everything else in her life for the past two and a half years, she would have to face it alone. Sam had his own problems now, she didn't expect him to be constantly present to help shoulder hers.

When she called him, he sounded busy, but relieved to hear from her.

"You're not pissed at me?" he asked her, sounding anxious. "I know you didn't think I should get engaged to Tamar."

"I just don't want to see you settle. How are you feeling about it now?"

"About the same. I think I owed it to her after all this time. It was the right thing to do." For everyone but him, Coco knew.

"A year and a half isn't an eternity, Sam. You didn't keep her chained up in the garage. She didn't have to keep dating you. It must have been working for her."

"She kept thinking I was going to propose, and I took my time." He felt guilty about that too. It was why his parents had insisted that he was duty-bound to marry her, which sounded to Coco like a poor reason to get married. Duty over love. Sam had bought into it, not wanting to disappoint them as his sisters had. But these were modern times. It wouldn't have ruined her if he didn't marry her, and she wasn't pregnant. But he was always willing to take the weight of the world on his shoulders, and do the right thing, even if he sacrificed himself. "Tamar is all excited planning the wedding now. It's nice to see her happy." Coco would have preferred to see him happy, and thrilled about who he was marrying, instead of resigned. Doing the right thing was more important to him than marrying the right girl, which seemed crazy to her. But a lot of what she'd done had been crazy too, like marrying Nigel too fast. "We're getting married at the end of June. I expect you to be there," he said seriously, and she did a rapid calculation and knew she couldn't. She'd be six weeks away from giving birth by then, if she kept the pregnancy, and wouldn't be allowed to fly.

"I might not be able to make it then," she said hesitantly, dreading telling him, in the circumstances she was in. She knew he wouldn't approve.

"You can't possibly know that now. Do you have some other wedding to go to?" It was the only reason he could think of. Coco being pregnant hadn't crossed his mind.

"No, not really." And then she took a breath and leapt in. "I'm pregnant. I don't know what I'm going to do about it, but I am."

"Isn't that good news?" It didn't sound like it to him. "Nigel must be thrilled. Now he can start filling all those bedrooms with babies. It was all he could talk about when I saw the house." And then he thought of something else. "Is there something wrong with the pregnancy?"

"No, with the father. I walked in on him again, having one of his charming little escapades, with a blonde I didn't know this time. Porno live. On his desk, at least not in my bed again." She tried to keep it light, but they both knew it was anything but.

"Oh God, Coco. How did that play out?"

"Pretty badly. I threw him out, and I'm filing for divorce, for real this time. No hall passes for cheaters. I'm done, and he knows it."

"Does he know about the pregnancy?"

"Ironically, I went home to tell him, which is how I walked in on them. And, interesting, he's trying to sell me his parental rights in exchange for the house in Sussex, and I'm willing to make the deal. In fact, I want to, to get him out of my life. He wanted the city house, but I wouldn't give it to him, so I can sell it myself, and get some money back. But he'll settle for the house in Sussex, which was originally his idea, not mine. And he wants another thirty-seven million in 'damages' and support."

"Damages for what? Is he insane?"

"No, I think he's pretty lucid. My lawyer says he won't get it, but he might get something, in addition to Sussex. So that's why I haven't called you. I've been trying to sort this mess out. It had just happened two days before you got engaged."

"I thought something might be wrong at first, but I told myself I was paranoid, and decided you were pissed."

"Of course I'm not. And I'm sorry I can't come to the wedding if I have the baby." She was genuinely sad about it, and not being there for him, if he was really going to do it. She wanted to be there to support him.

"What do you think you'll do about the pregnancy?"

"I'm not sure. I have to figure it out soon. I don't feel right doing anything about it. But I'm not so sure I can do a good job of being a parent alone, or if I want to take that on," she said honestly.

"You can do anything you want," he reminded her. "You're the strongest human being I know, man or woman. I wish I had your balls."

"You do, you just don't know it," she said gently. "You're such a good person, you always want to do the right thing for everyone. Sometimes being strong is not doing it, and taking care of yourself."

"I wish I felt I had the right to do that. I don't want to let Tamar down, or my parents. Maybe I'd never meet another girl who would be the right wife for me anyway. She's the perfect traditional choice they want for me," he said, sounding discouraged.

"Is that what *you* want, Sam? Tradition? Or something more exciting that suits you better?"

"Exciting is your downfall, Coco. Ed is exciting. So is Nigel in a way, in his world. That's all flash with no substance."

"And Tamar is substance without flash," she finished for him.

"I don't want an exciting marriage. I want a peaceful one. And so will you one day."

"I thought Nigel had substance," she defended herself. "I thought he was a good guy."

"You didn't know him long enough to tell. And Ed was cheating on his wife, which should have disqualified him. It's the flash, Coco. Those damn exciting guys. It screws you every time."

"I'll try to find some really dull guy next time." She wasn't entirely kidding. "The next flashy guy who shows up, or comes out of the mists, I'm going to run like hell."

"I hope so. Are you thinking of coming back to New York if you're pregnant?"

"I don't think so. I love my job here. It's really fun, and Leslie is terrific to work for. I'm learning a lot about interior design, real estate, all kinds of stuff." Sam could hear her getting farther and farther away from going back to school. He doubted now that she'd ever go back for her degree, especially if she had a baby. That would keep her busy for years, particularly if she was alone. But it might make her happy too, as consolation for losing her parents. It might be just what she needed, but he didn't want to interfere. The decision had to be entirely up to her.

He was sure he'd be having babies soon too. Tamar wanted them immediately, as soon as they got married. It unnerved him to think about it. He could feel his youth flying out the window for good, at twenty-five. He had hoped to avoid fatherhood for several more years, but it didn't look like that was going to happen. Tamar's parents already thought she was late getting started at twenty-three, and were greatly relieved by their engagement.

Knowing he was getting married in June, Sam felt as though he had five months left to live and breathe without the responsibilities of marriage. But he had the consolation of knowing he was doing the right thing to honor his family and future wife. It broke Coco's heart to think of it. He wasn't happy for Coco either, after all that had happened to her, and now she had to face motherhood alone, if she went forward with the pregnancy.

"We're in a fine mess, both of us," Coco said to him, and he laughed. She used to say that to him in school, as children, when they got in trouble together.

"I guess so. Hopefully, it will turn out right in the end. Don't let that bastard get a penny out of you. He doesn't deserve even the property in Sussex. It's amazing how guys like that always get some benefit from their misdeeds."

"I believe their karma gets them in the end," Coco said philosophically. But for the moment, it was getting both of them.

Chapter 12

T he exchanges between Coco's attorney and Nigel's got increasingly heated as they tried to come to some agreement. Nigel's aspirations were completely unrealistic, but he wasn't giving an inch. He was resting on the argument that he didn't have legal representation for their marriage contract, and didn't know what he'd signed. She wondered if that was why he hadn't shown it to an attorney, and knew he could use it as a loophole to try and invalidate the contract later. Anything was possible with him. She realized now how calculating he was. The only part of their exchange he had agreed to so far was the transfer of the Sussex property to him, for relinquishing the parental rights he didn't want anyway. It was no sacrifice for him. He acted as though Coco were pregnant by someone else, which they both knew she wasn't. He had no feelings whatsoever for their baby, and seemed to view it as some kind of encumbrance he couldn't wait to get rid of now that they would no longer be married. The prospect of sharing custody or the responsibilities of visitation held no allure for him at all. The baby he had claimed he wanted was of no interest to him, only Coco's money. She'd had several conversations with Ed about the proceedings, and he was satisfied with her lawyer. He was willing to fight hard to protect her inheritance from Nigel. Ed was standing by to assist in any way he could. He was a worm of a human being, but was finally proving to be a decent trustee.

Nigel's callousness finally tipped the scale for Coco. She had had doting parents until they'd died. The fact that her baby's father cared nothing about it seemed so shocking and unfair to her that it created a stronger bond to the baby on her part. She wanted to protect it, and decided to continue the pregnancy. The baby was due in August, and so far everything was fine, and when it was born, it would be as though its father had died or never existed. Coco would be the only parent her baby had, which made her decide to redouble her efforts to love it, and welcome it into her life.

For the time being, she was staying in the new house. It would be a good place to come home to, big enough for a baby nurse at first, and eventually a nanny to live there with her and help her, and take care of the baby when she went to work.

As she passed the three-month mark in her pregnancy, and the exchanges about the divorce settled down to a dull roar, she began to feel physically better, and was able to work harder again and longer hours. She loved her job, working with Leslie in the business they had created. They had to face new challenges with every client, be creative and innovative, find them the right location which suited them, and their family, in their new city, near schools in some cases, with and without gardens, big enough or small enough. In most cases, Coco and Leslie got to do the decorating, or staging if furniture and art had to be rented. Each client's needs and requirements were different, and they had to reinvent what they created every time. Coco loved it, and she and Leslie were thriving, with a constant flow of new clients, each satisfied person recommending them to someone else.

Leslie was swamped in February, when she walked over to Coco's desk with a new file.

"I hate to do this to you, Coco. I know you don't have a minute to breathe as it is, but can you take this one on for me? New client, personal recommendation from a previous client. VIP, famous American author. He's coming to London to work on the movie of one of his books. He wants the place for a year, and isn't bringing a stick of furniture. Hates contemporary art, seems to hate people, and loves dogs. You'll love this. He has a hundred-and-eighty-pound bull mastiff. Landlords are going to love that."

"Oh, an easy one." Coco laughed, as she took the file from her. "Who is he? Have I heard of him?"

"Only if you've ever read a book. Ian Kingston."

Coco's eyes opened wide. "Wow! The big guns."

"The good news is that he doesn't care how much he spends, the producers are paying for it. Any price. An apartment or house. But it has to be quiet. He wants to do some writing while he's here. He's working on a new book."

"Any other particulars?"

"I would say something comfortable, male, quiet obviously, maybe near a park for the dog. They didn't say it, but he sounds difficult. The producers called me. Kingston doesn't want to be involved, but he expects us to get it right without even talking to him beforehand."

"Christ, we have to be psychic with clients like that."

"That's your forte," Leslie complimented her, "you always seem to know what they really want and aren't telling us. Oh, and he wants a good kitchen. He likes to cook."

"He sounds interesting."

"And difficult. Spoiled, I suspect. He also wants a gym somewhere in the neighborhood. He's forty-one."

"Married? Girlfriend? Gay? Kids?" Coco knew all the right questions to ask now.

"They didn't say. He sounds like something of a loner." Leslie looked at the profile again, and another item caught her eye. "No kids in the building. Too noisy. He claims his dog never barks and sleeps all the time." Coco nodded, and had jotted down some notes. The first thing she had to do was call realtors and find a location. A year would be easier than a few months. And house or apartment was good too. He didn't seem to care how many rooms, as long as there was a good room for him to write, and a bedroom for him. The fancy kitchen might be harder.

After a week of endless calls to all her contacts, Coco had six places to see on a Friday. She had the authority to rent a place at her own discretion, which was an awesome responsibility.

She was meeting with three different realtors, one of whom she preferred. She had never lied to her, which many did, claiming attributes the apartment didn't have and hiding flaws.

None of the places she saw felt right, until the last one. It was in a quiet residential street near a park. The house was owned, as an investment, by a Swiss couple who almost never came to London, and had kept the two top floors for themselves, and occasionally lent it to their son, who was a banker. They rented out the two lower floors, if they liked the tenant. The house was relatively small and well maintained. They had people who came regularly to check on it. There was a two-car garage no one used, and the entire apartment was sunny and faced south. On the main floor were a living and dining room of modest proportions, and a sizeable kitchen with state-of-the-art equipment.

"Their current tenant is a chef from Rome. He's the star chef at Harry's Bar. His father died, and he went home to run the family restaurant for a year for his mother. The kitchen equipment and all the furniture belong to him. He's not letting the place go, but they're allowing him to sublet it." The kitchen definitely checked out for an amateur chef. There was a large dining table in it, so the tenant could use the dining room or kitchen to entertain. The dining room was wood-paneled and more formal, and both the living room and dining room had fireplaces.

On the second floor were a big bedroom, a small guest room, and a den which could be used as an office. It looked like the perfect lair for a writer. It had a warm, inviting feeling, with a fireplace and wood paneling. The décor was masculine, with big comfortable leather chairs and dark Persian rugs. There was a big well-appointed bathroom with shower and bath, another one with only a shower in the guest room, and a powder room downstairs for guests.

"Wow," Coco said, looking at her, "it's perfect. I'll take it. I haven't met the client, but it matches his profile perfectly."

"It helps that the subletting tenant is a guy. Everything is the right proportion for a man to feel comfortable here and not confined." She had done her job well, and Coco was thrilled.

"Is there a gym nearby?"

"Two blocks away. It's expensive and fairly exclusive, but if the production company is paying, as you said, they may not care."

"Perfect," Coco said again. "I'll take it."

"First month's rent, one-year lease, security deposit. They want five thousand in security because of the dog, in case he does any damage." The rent wasn't even too high considering how nice the space was. "And the chef who lives here wants any of the pans replaced if the tenant damages them."

"We can take care of that when he leaves," Coco said, and for once she didn't need to have the place painted, carpeted, curtains made, or find decent not-too-expensive art to put on the walls. It was all there. "When can he move in?"

"Immediately. The Roman chef left a week ago. They already had the place thoroughly cleaned. And china and linens are included of course, since it's a furnished rental. I checked and they have very nice sheets."

Coco signed the check for the rent and deposit on the office account, as Leslie allowed her to do. The production company was going to sign the lease, and she looked delighted when she got back to the office.

"We really lucked out on this one. It's everything he wanted and more, including the fancy kitchen. A Roman chef lives there and went back to Rome for a year. Ian Kingston is going to love it. If he doesn't move in, I will, and he can have my house. It's really a great setup, and there's a wonderful den where he can write. I can't wait till he sees it."

"We may never hear from him," Leslie said, "since the production company is the client. But they'll be happy too."

"Do you know when he's arriving?"

"They said April first, but they said he might arrive in March if we had something for him by then."

"He can come tomorrow if he wants. It's all his."

She handed the file back to Leslie with all her notes, and went back to the file of another client they hadn't found a place for yet, an American family arriving with six kids under the age of ten. They needed a big house, and landlords weren't thrilled to have a lot of children. Leslie had suggested a house to them, rather than an apartment where the neighbors would be complaining about noise all the time. And they had a black Lab. Their work was teaching them both a lot about people, relationships, and how some people wanted to live.

In March, Coco went to court for the divorce for the first time. It was a preliminary hearing, to hear what each party wanted. They got a female judge, which Coco's attorney said could go either way. Some women judges were tougher than men, others seemed more sympathetic to their own sex. The one they were assigned had already reviewed the case.

The judge, in her navy blue robe, looked directly at Coco when it was her turn. "Are you comfortable with this arrangement, trading a country property for your ex-husband's parental rights? I gather he doesn't want to be involved with the child," she said with a look of disapproval.

"Apparently not, Your Honor," Coco said politely.

"Who owns the house? In other words, who paid for it?"

"I did, Your Honor."

"It's free and clear?"

"Completely."

"It's a very unusual request, but I'm going to grant it. You're sure you can manage alone?" She had noticed Coco's age, but she looked mature and sensible when she appeared in court. She wasn't some wild thing with piercings all over her face. She looked like a grown-up, with her hair pulled back, in a dark gray suit and high heels.

"I believe I can manage, Your Honor."

"Are your parents going to help you? Are they here?" She could hear that Coco was American.

"No, they're deceased. They died almost three years ago. But I'll be fine." Coco looked calm and capable when she spoke.

"You're employed?" The judge looked over her glasses at her, observing her keenly.

"Yes, I work in the relocation business, finding and setting up homes for executives and families moving here, usually from other countries, for determinate stays. Corporate executives, some diplomats, researchers, writers, movie producers." She smiled at Coco's description and thought she looked like an enterprising girl, despite her age. Her parents being deceased also explained the kind of numbers her ex-husband was bandying around, if she had inherited money from them.

"I'm going to confirm the relinquishment of parental rights, and make it official. You'll have to transfer the deed of the property to your ex-husband's name. And I am restoring your maiden name, as you requested. As for the rest of this . . ." she said, picking up the file with a frown and glancing at both attorneys. Nigel had opted not to come to court, and let his attorney represent him. He looked like what Coco's father would have called a shyster lawyer, in a shiny too-blue suit. "Gentlemen," she said to the attorneys, "are we talking about pounds or dollars here, or yen, or some currency I don't know of? The couple in question were married for eleven months. Mr.

Halsey-Smythe was employed until eight months ago, and he's an able-bodied man of thirty-four with a university degree. I'm sure he'll be employed again shortly. I see that we're referring to both dollars and pounds here. And that there is a premarital contract in force that Mr. Halsey-Smythe signed and is contesting now," she said with a frown and a sour look.

"Miss Martin's inheritance is invested in the United States, Your Honor. From her deceased parents," her attorney stressed, hoping to arouse the judge's sympathy.

"She should leave it there. Three million dollars a year in spousal support for a healthy man in his thirties for ten years, after an eleven-month marriage, is beyond excessive. And I see no reason to award him a million dollars in damages for losing a job that was paying him sixty thousand a year. As for the five million he wants for pain and suffering, since Miss Martin is being left pregnant and abandoned, whatever her resources, I think the five million for pain and suffering should go to her." Nigel's lawyer in the shiny suit looked instantly panicked, stood up without permission to do so, and addressed the judge.

"Mr. Halsey-Smythe doesn't have the funds to pay her damages, Your Honor."

"Thank you for the information. Please sit down. I am therefore throwing out Mr. Halsey-Smythe's petition for a million dollars in damages and five million for his pain and suffering. And I would like to know what one does on a million-dollar vacation? That would be fascinating. I believe he can manage without that too. In the separate agreement he is being given a very fine, newly remodeled country estate, with extensive grounds and four usable houses on it, accord-ing to the documents submitted to the court. That is more than adequate compensation. And I am reducing his request for ten years of spousal support at three million dollars a year, to eleven months, the length of the marriage, at five thousand dollars a month, which is the salary he was making, which comes to fifty-five thousand dollars. I think he should be very pleased with his new house. I will confirm these orders, sign them, and return them to both parties. If there are further matters to be resolved, you may address them to me for a future hearing. I see that Mr. Halsey-Smythe is not contesting the grounds of adultery, so I am granting both parties a decree nisi today, because the court sees no reason why you can't divorce. Six weeks and one day from today, which will be May first, you may apply for a decree absolute. When both parties receive the decree absolute, probably in July, you are divorced, no longer married, and are free to marry again if you wish." She rapped her gavel then, and Coco and her attorney left the courtroom smiling broadly, after thanking the judge. Nigel's attorney scurried out of the courtroom, presumably to call him. It had been a major victory for her. She had lost a house, but she had traded it willingly for freedom for her child, to be rid of a father like Nigel, who probably would have ultimately attempted to bilk money from his child. And the judge was right. He should have been very grateful for the Sussex house, which he didn't deserve. He was walking away with a prize, and Coco with a baby. She felt more and more protective toward it every day.

And at the next doctor's visit, after the court hearing, they told her it was a girl. She was going to name her Bethanie, after her mother. The baby had some reality to her, now that Coco knew her sex. She was genuinely excited about it. She was four months pregnant, and it was beginning to show, though only slightly.

She had called Sam to tell him about the results in court, and he was extremely pleased for her. Justice had been served, although it still irked him that Nigel was getting a beautiful country property Coco had paid for, and he didn't deserve. But she had bought her baby's freedom from a bad man. She was better off without a father, as the judge apparently concurred.

Leslie and Coco had been told that Ian Kingston had moved into his new London home in mid-March. They heard no complaints and no compliments, and assumed that meant he was satisfied. So they were surprised to hear from him in the first week of April. He called and asked if he could drop by and Leslie agreed. She forgot to tell Coco, and two days later he showed up. He was tall, slim, had hair as dark as Coco's, dark smoldering eyes, was wearing jeans, a white T-shirt, a black leather jacket, and motorcycle boots. He had just bought a vintage Ducati motorcycle in Italy and had ridden it back to London. He looked like the perfect bad boy, with a warm, slightly crooked smile and perfect teeth. Coco didn't know who he was when he walked in, but Leslie recognized him immediately and got up to greet him. He thanked her for the perfect home, and said he wanted a ten-year extension. She laughed and introduced him to Coco, who had been trying not to stare at him. He was fatally handsome. Leslie credited Coco with finding the place for him.

"I've been sending photographs of the kitchen to my architect in New York," he said to her. "I want him to duplicate it exactly. I looked up the chef who lives there when I was in Rome last week. He's a terrific guy. I had dinner at his family restaurant, and warned him that he may end up homeless if I refuse to move." Leslie and Coco were both pleased to know he was so happy. He said they were starting to film the movie of his book in a few days, and it was chaos on the set. But once things settled down, he could go back to writing the new book he had already started.

He didn't stay long, but his visit made a powerful impression on both women. He was one of the top two or three writers in the States. His huge success had given him movie star status, and his looks didn't hurt. He was sexy more than handsome, and there was an aloofness to him which made him seem just out of reach. He looked like a storm cloud, and then he smiled and the ice around him melted.

"Wow, he's a looker, isn't he?" Leslie said after he left and Coco agreed. Women couldn't help but be affected by him. He was a powerful presence.

"Did you see the way he looked at you?" Leslie asked Coco. "He couldn't take his eyes off you." She would have been jealous of Coco if she didn't like her so much. She worked so hard that one forgot how beautiful she was, or became inured to it, since she was oblivious to it herself and never played on her looks.

"He looked at you exactly the same way," Coco insisted.

"No, he didn't." Leslie smiled. "Guys like him always go after younger women. I'm nearly his age." She was pretty, but nothing like Coco, who was stunningly lovely and unconsciously sexy. It didn't bother Leslie. She was finally recovering from her own divorce and dating a new man, who was crazy about her, and she liked him a lot. She had an easy, uncomplicated nature, and was not given to jealousy. They were work partners and friends and not in competition with each other.

Coco was surprised when Ian Kingston called her later that afternoon.

"I wanted to thank you again for finding me the perfect home," he said in a deep voice that added to his mystique. "Can I buy you a drink sometime?"

"Sure," she said casually. She didn't imagine for a minute that he was attracted to her. She wasn't in his league. He was much too glamorous, very famous, and could go out with anyone he wanted. She was five months pregnant now, so he thought she was either fat, or off-limits and probably married. Leslie had read a lot about him, since she loved his books, and she said he was omnivorous and dated everything from teenagers to sixty-year-old movie stars, who were twenty years older than he was. But most of the time, he dated beautiful young girls like Coco.

"How about tomorrow?" he suggested, and they agreed to meet at a trendy bar in Notting Hill that Coco had heard about and never been to. Writers, models, photographers, and movie stars went there.

She told Leslie about it the next day. She was impressed and raised an eyebrow to tease her.

"Hardly," Coco said, patting her slightly protruding belly. She had worn black jeans, and a pink sweater, and her own motorcycle boots that she had brought with her but hadn't worn since college. She had dressed like an adult for Nigel, in fancy cocktail dresses when they went out. She could be more casual now, which suited her better and was more familiar. It was a relief not to be at parties all the time, or a houseguest somewhere every weekend.

She had read in the gossip columns that Nigel was entertaining in his fabulous new country estate in Sussex, and invitations to spend a weekend there were in high demand. She wondered how he was paying for it on his five-thousand-dollar-a-month spousal support the judge had awarded him instead of three million a year.

She met Ian at the bar in Notting Hill on Friday night at seven. The place was jammed with lots of people from the neighborhood, and a smattering of models and well-known trendies in jeans and T-shirts. He was waiting at the bar for her when she arrived, and she walked over to him with a smile. Her sweater was loose enough that her pregnancy barely showed, and he didn't seem to notice, and probably didn't care. It was just a courtesy drink, but she thought it was a nice gesture on his part to thank her.

"Is that your dog outside?" she asked him, after they ordered beers. Her doctor said she could have two a week and an occasional glass of wine. They were more relaxed about pregnant women drinking moderately in Europe. She had seen a huge cinnamon-colored bull mastiff sitting politely next to the entrance. He was massive and no one was going to bother him.

"That's Bruce. He likes it here. He's my best friend. He's my alter ego. I'm not so good with people," he confessed, with his dazzling smile. "Most writers aren't. That's why they become writers. Because they're afraid to talk to people, so they write. We're born observers, but poor participators." It was an interesting analysis of the breed. His mind was quick and sharp, and she suspected that his tongue could be as well. She could easily imagine him getting angry. He exuded brooding inner tension, and then he smiled and the sun came out. He made you want to work for one of those smiles, like winning a trophy for a game well played. "How did you wind up in London? Did you grow up here?" he asked her.

"The reason I'm here is boring and complicated," she said quietly.

"Like life." He nodded.

"I dropped out of school in New York, Columbia, journalism major, got an internship at *Time* over here, worked there for about eight months, and got a job offer from Leslie, who was my boss at *Time* and started the relocation business, so here I am."

"I have a feeling it's more complicated than that," he said, pointing to her belly. He had noticed.

"Yes, it is. I thought I'd spare you the long version. Bad romance in New York, with a married man, after I dropped out of school. I was an idiot. Lesson learned, so I got that out of the way. Fell for someone else when I got here, got married too quickly. It lasted for eleven months, now I'm getting divorced. And I'm having a baby. He gave up his rights, so my daughter and I will be on our own, which is fine." At least she hoped it would be. She wasn't as confident as she appeared, but she didn't know him.

"Well, it sounds like you got all your big mistakes out of the way quickly. Married man, bad guy. I'm sure the next one will be a good one."

"I'm not looking. I'm taking a breather."

"Is your family in New York?" She hesitated at the question, and he noticed that too. He was an observer of people and the human condition, and good at it. It was what he did for a living. "Bad question? Didn't like your husband? Angry about the baby?"

"No, they died almost three years ago. In the attack in Cannes. Two of the eleven Americans who were killed."

"Oh Jesus, I'm sorry." He winced. "Terrible question. Writers always think they can ask whatever they want to get to the truth. It must have been awful for you when it happened?"

"We were very close. They were wonderful." She managed not to cry when she said it. She was better at that these days. Time had helped, although she still missed them every day.

"I lost my parents young too. You grow up fast after that. My mother was fantastic, a saint, and my father was a devil. He was a drunk, and violent. He killed my mother and then shot himself. I was seventeen, in high school. I dropped out too, hitchhiked my way around Europe, wound up in Turkey, and then in North Africa, Morocco, Tangiers, Libya for a while, then lived in Paris, and eventually went back to New York, when my first book was published. I wrote it at eighteen, dragged it around in my backpack for a couple of years, finally sent it to a publisher, and presto magic, became a writer.

"I come to London a lot. I like it here. I eventually wind up back in New York for a while, and then leave again. I find it hard to stay in one place, and stay connected. I disappear when I write, which most people find difficult, particularly women. I've been married twice, to two very nice women I made miserably unhappy, but they seem to have forgiven me, since they're better people than I am. I spend a lot of time with Bruce. He understands me. I don't have kids. I'd be afraid to turn out like my father. I like being alone, until I get tired of it, and then I surface, and discover that everyone is pissed at me because I disappeared." He smiled, without remorse. He was warning her of just how difficult he was. He was more than complicated, but utterly fascinating. "I hate the idea of being responsible for another human being, and I'm allergic to commitment of any kind. So at the risk of sounding rude, if you're looking for a father for your baby, it won't be me. I get hives thinking about it. But I think you're terrific, and I'd like to spend time with you, if you don't mind my disappearing act, and don't count on me. I believe in truth in labeling. I'm a nice guy, but I'm an asshole too, as my ex-wives would be happy to tell you, but they love me anyway. I love them too. We're very devoted to each other." She laughed. He was certainly an honest person, and a little bit odd, or even a lot, and didn't pretend to be anything other than what he was. As he finished his full disclosure, two women came up to him and asked for an autograph. He was polite to them but not warm. He looked at Coco intensely after they left. "And I'm not good with strangers," he added. "I find being famous a pain in the ass. Sometimes I pretend I'm not me."

"I'm not looking for a father for my baby," she told him just as bluntly. "She was an accident, and the day I found out and rushed home to tell my husband, I found him having sex with someone else, for the second time in four months. So that was the end of it. He suggested giving up his parental rights, which sounded good to me. I traded him a country estate for her. I think it was a good trade. I'm planning to do this on my own. I think I can manage it."

"He sounds like a real asshole," Ian said sympathetically, "not a lovable one like me." She laughed. She could easily imagine him being difficult, and even disappearing. His father murdering his mother had to have left him with some serious damage. He had put it to good use in his books, which were extremely violent, but sensitive too. He had an uncanny understanding of people, and clearly had his own demons. "I think we've gotten the introductions pretty well covered." He smiled at her. "Would you like to have dinner with me? I'm not a vegetarian, or a vegan, and I like fast food, the greasier the better. I love cheeseburgers."

"So do I." She smiled at him. She was enjoying his company, and his frank, outrageous brand of honesty and revelation about himself. He was the modern day James Dean, angry, brooding, and even at forty-one, much more handsome.

"How old are you, by the way? Will I get arrested having dinner with you?" She looked very young to him.

"I'm twenty-four," she said casually.

"That works. I'm only old enough to be your father, not your grandfather." Nigel had been ten years older than she was. Older men didn't scare her. In fact, she liked them, and sometimes thought she had more in common with them, except for Sam, who was her family and wise for his years, as she was. Even Ed had seemed immature to her at times, and irresponsible. "Where should we go to dinner? I know a hamburger joint nearby. The burgers are pretty good."

It turned out to be an American style diner she'd never heard of, and the burgers were delicious. She had come in a cab, and they walked to the restaurant, with Bruce loping along beside Ian.

They had a great time talking over dinner, about Marrakesh and Tangiers, and some of his other travels. He had loved Turkey too. He admitted that it was hard to settle down in the States after that.

"I'm a nomad. But I have to say the tent you found for me is the nicest one I've ever had. The guy who lives there is great. It was fun looking him up in Rome and having dinner in his restaurant. He's cool." And so was Ian. Almost too cool. She thoroughly enjoyed her evening with him.

He sent her home in a cab, as she mulled over the evening, and called her two days later.

"Are you ready for another burger? They've been driving me crazy on the set, with a bunch of divas. I need to talk to a sane person. You're the only one I know here."

"I'm flattered. I'd love it." They went to his house afterward, and it looked even better with some of his own things spread around here and there. Their age difference didn't bother her, and he was fascinating to talk to. His mind raced at a million miles an hour, and she was breathless listening to him.

They started seeing each other two or three times a week after that, for coffee or a drink, or dinner. He cooked her a Moroccan meal at his house one night, and it was exquisite, lamb and couscous with delicate spices. She noticed that he drank very little, which surprised her. He went to the gym at five o'clock every morning, and was in remarkable shape.

The first time he kissed her in May, she was six months pregnant, and he didn't seem to care. She was self-conscious about it, and he said he thought she was beautiful, and the baby didn't bother him, as long as he didn't have to bring it up or deal with it as a teenager, which made her laugh. Their lovemaking was as easy and natural as though they had always been together. She spent several nights with him, and then he came to her house, and was stunned by how huge it was.

"Was this place your husband's idea?" he asked her and she nodded. "I thought so. It doesn't look like you. This house is going to give you a lot of trouble," he warned her. "It's going to attract all the wrong guys like bees to honey. It screams money. You should tell them you're housesitting. If they know it's yours, you're going to have every fortune hunter in London on your doorstep."

"I know. I married one of them," she said simply.

She didn't have to worry about it with Ian. He was one of the most successful writers in the world. And she loved being with him. She kept reminding herself not to fall in love with him, or she'd get hurt. He didn't promise her any kind of future or even suggest it. He lived in the moment, but he was so sexy and smart and easy to be with. She was falling in love with his mind, and he was happy with her.

In June, he warned her that he was going to start writing and he would disappear for a while. Things had calmed down on the movie

set. He didn't know when he'd surface again, and told her that sometimes it took months. He could never predict it. He was at the mercy
of the book he was writing.

"At least I warn people now. I used to just disappear and surface
six months later, and everyone was pissed."

"I'll miss you," she said softly, and he wagged a finger at her.

"Don't. I'll miss you too, but that's not what I'm about. I come and
go, that's who I am. Like birds, or the seasons, or a stray cat who
shows up, hangs around for a while, and then disappears. I'll probably miss you more than you miss me. I get addicted to people, and
then I need to break the habit. And the writing always comes first
with me. It has to, or I wouldn't be good at it."

She saw him one more time after that, and then he was gone.
She'd had two wonderful months with him, and realized that it might
be all she'd ever get. She might never hear from him again. But he
had been one of those incredible comets flashing through the sky in
a shower of stars. Just being with him was exciting.

She told Sam about him when she called him before his wedding.

"There you go again. Coco, please don't get hooked on this guy. He
told you he's not reliable. Believe him. I love his books too, but he
has to be a little whacko to write like that."

"He's not whacko. He's brilliant," she defended him.

"That's the point. He's the flash again. You have to give that up,
and find a real one."

"He's about as real as it gets."

"No, he's not. That's not real. It's excitement again. Real is something very quiet that you can come home to at night, and know will
still be there. Ian Kingston is never going to be there for you. He told
you that in the beginning."

"Yes, he did," she admitted. "Is that what you have with Tamar?" Something quiet that would always be there. Maybe he was right.

"Yeah, I guess so. I know she's always going to be there for me. I won't have nights with her like you've had with Ian Kingston. But she won't disappoint me either."

"How can you be sure?"

"You never are in life. But with the wild ones, the flashy ones, you know they're going to burn themselves out and disappear in the heavens somewhere. They can't help it, and they burn you in the process. That's who they are. I know how appealing they must be. But one day you reach for them, and your hands are empty. You need someone with you, Coco, especially now with the baby. But you've got me." He was getting married in a week. And now he would belong to Tamar too. Coco wasn't sure she liked that.

"Are you sure you want to do this?" she asked him again.

"Yes. I'm okay about it now."

"Is that enough? Okay?"

"It has to be. It's where my life is." Working in his father's business, marrying a plain, reliable woman who was the kind of woman his parents wanted him to marry. Coco wanted more for him, but Sam didn't. Maybe Sam was right. Maybe reaching for the flash of brilliance in the sky, she'd have glorious moments he would never know that brought her soul alive, but in the end she'd always come up empty-handed. And Ian was the flash, more than any man she'd ever known.

Chapter 13

Coco was seven months pregnant when Ian disappeared to write, in June. She missed him a lot at first. They had spent so much time together, but then she got used to it. She got busy preparing for the baby. She was nervous about the delivery, without her mother or any female relatives to get her through it.

And in July, as the judge had said, she got her decree absolute in the mail, and she was divorced. The marriage to Nigel was over. It was a painful chapter in her life, and she had nothing to show for it except a house in London and the baby. His parental rights had been terminated along with the marriage, in exchange for the estate in Sussex.

The last weeks of her pregnancy were the hardest. There was a heat wave in London, and she felt like a beached whale. She never heard from Nigel, and didn't want to. He had no part in the baby's life now, or her future. She wondered if Ian would check in with her before the baby was born, but he didn't. He was lost in his own world somewhere. She talked to Sam a lot at the end, and showed him her enormous belly on FaceTime. It looked like she had a beach ball under her dress, and she couldn't imagine how she was going to push the baby out. It seemed like an impossible feat. She admitted to Sam that she was scared. He was sorry he wasn't there with her.

A week before her due date, he told her that Tamar was two months pregnant.

"Wow, that was fast!" Coco commented. They'd been married for two months.

"She got pregnant on our wedding night." She was twenty-three. Sam was respectful and protective of her. She was his wife now, and soon to be the mother of his child. He admitted to Coco that being a father scared him. It was so much responsibility. He had a wife and would have a child soon. Tamar had been sick from the beginning. He felt sorry for her. Coco promised to call Sam as soon as she went into labor.

Leslie had offered to drive her to the hospital, but she wasn't going to stay with her. Coco was going to manage it alone with the midwife and the labor nurses. She felt awkward having Leslie watch her deliver. She would have liked to have her mother there. She didn't know what to expect. She didn't know anyone who'd ever had a baby, and could tell her the truth. She only knew what she'd read in books, which scared her more. She took some birthing classes, but she felt unprepared anyway.

Conveniently, she went into labor at the office. She had worked until the last day. She didn't know what it was at first, and thought it was something she'd eaten, and then the cramps turned into contractions by lunchtime. She didn't want to go home and be alone, so she just stayed there, and by four o'clock, the pains were strong, and she called the midwife, who told her to come in to be checked.

"Okay, you're on," she said to Leslie, holding on to her desk as another contraction started. "My midwife said to come to the hospital now," she said through clenched teeth. She hadn't complained about it all day, and Leslie was shocked.

"Are you having it now?"

"Not this minute, but soon, I hope," Coco said to her. "We have to pick my bag up on the way."

They walked out to Leslie's car, and she ran inside to get Coco's bag at her house, and they were at the hospital twenty minutes later. By then the pains had gotten a lot worse. A nurse came out to the car, and put Coco in a wheelchair.

"Good luck!" Leslie said, as they rolled her away, and Coco waved. "You'll be a mum the next time I see you!" Leslie called after her, and felt sad for her that she was going to be alone without her mother, or the baby's father. Coco had been very clear that she didn't want her to stay. This was something she felt she had to do alone. Leslie didn't want to insist and embarrass her. She went back to the office and puttered around, worrying about her, and waiting for Coco to call her after the baby was delivered.

A nurse helped Coco undress, and assisted her onto the bed, while they waited for the midwife. The pains had gotten a lot stronger, and her water broke as soon as she lay down on the bed, and then the contractions got rapidly worse. She called Sam while she still could, and they talked on FaceTime.

"How is it?" he asked her, watching her face and worried. He wished he was there with her since no one else was.

"Shit, it's awful," she said, grimacing.

"It'll be over soon, and then you'll see her." He didn't know what else to say to her, and then the midwife came, and they hung up, and she didn't call him again. She couldn't. Everything was happening too fast. She was seven centimeters dilated, and an anesthesiologist came to give her the epidural she had wanted. She cried while she squeezed the nurse's hand. She felt like she was on an express train, and noticed that it was dark outside. It was nighttime, and she wondered how long she'd been there. She had lost track of time with the pain.

The contractions slowed down once she had the epidural, she dozed for a few minutes and then everything speeded up again. A nurse was with her, and the midwife told her to push. They lightened the dose in the epidural and the pain was unbearable, so they made it stronger again. Someone said she had been pushing for two hours, and it felt like an entire lifetime. She had to push more and harder. There were two nurses in the room then, holding her legs, and she pushed and pushed until she couldn't anymore, and then she felt pressure like she'd never felt before and everyone was telling her to push harder, and then she heard a wail, and looked down and saw her baby, and Coco was crying and laughing as she looked at her.

She was so beautiful. She looked like Coco's mother, and Coco suddenly felt as though her mother was in the room with her. She glanced at the window and the sun was coming up. It was six in the morning, and someone said that it had taken only fourteen hours, which was great and really fast for a first baby. Coco groaned. The baby was at her breast by then, looking up at her mother. They said she was small, only six pounds, but it hadn't felt like she was small. It felt like an elephant was pushing through her. She wondered how something so little could hurt so much. But as she lay there holding Bethanie, it all seemed worth it. That little precious face looking up at her, and tiny toes and fingers. She wanted to call Sam and show the baby to him, but she was shaking too hard to call him, as they put a warm blanket on her, and took the baby to the nursery to clean her up. It was over. She had done it. She had finally arrived, and as Leslie had said, she was a mother now. It all seemed so miraculous and mysterious. They gave her a shot for the pain so she could sleep, and as she drifted off, she knew that when she woke up, she and Bethanie would start their journey together.

Leslie came to see her and the baby that afternoon, and she could see on Coco's face how hard it had been. But she could also see how happy she was, and the baby was beautiful and looked just like her.

She had called Sam by then, and showed him the sleeping baby with the tiny rosebud face.

"How was it?" he asked, relieved that they were both okay.

"Hard. It felt like it took forever. But it's worth it. She looks so sweet." It touched him seeing the baby, and seeing Coco, even with dark circles under her eyes. She was so proud of her daughter, and he was proud of her.

"I can't wait to meet her," Sam said. Leslie had arrived then, and Coco promised to call Sam back.

They went home the next day, and Coco had everything ready in the nursery, and a basket for her set up in her room. She had no one to help her and didn't want help. She wanted to live every moment of the experience. A nurse came to check on them at home the next day, and said they were doing fine.

Coco stayed home with the baby for two weeks, and then brought

Bethanie to visit in the office. She had arranged for someone to come to the house and stay with the baby as soon as she went back to work.

Leslie startled her with a proposition then. She needed some funding to help the business grow and to hire more assistants, and she loved working with Coco. She asked if she wanted to become a partner and invest in the business and Coco loved the idea. They talked about it again on the phone that night, when the baby was sleeping. She loved the prospect of being part owner of the business, and she and Leslie worked well together.

When Coco went to sleep that night, she had a new business, and a new daughter. It seemed like a lot. She felt blessed alone in her big house. She looked down at Bethanie sound asleep in her basket, checked on her one last time, and knew that all was well in her world. She hadn't thought of Nigel the whole time she had given birth to her. He didn't exist for her anymore, and never would for Bethanie. Coco knew that would be enough for both of them. She smiled as she looked at Bethanie in her basket, and for the first time, realized how much her parents had loved her. As much as the heavens had stars. It was the one gift Nigel had given her that mattered, and for an instant she was grateful to him and then resolutely put him out of her mind forever. He had served a purpose in her life after all.

Chapter 14

Ian surfaced in October, four months after he had disappeared, and returned pleased with the first draft of his new book, and delighted to see Coco again.

She showed him her creation too. Bethanie sound asleep in her crib, eight weeks old.

"She's very pretty," he said, fascinated by her. "She looks like you."

"And like my mother too." She wasn't imagining it. Sam had even seen it on FaceTime.

Coco was back at the office full-time again by then, and an equal partner in the business. She had a nanny for Bethanie in the daytime and took care of her herself at night. She loved the time she spent with her.

They had the funding they needed now to advertise their business and hire more people. They were talking about moving to a bigger space than Leslie's dining room.

Ian told her all about his book when he took her out to dinner. She got the nanny to stay late.

"I missed you," he said, with a look of surprise.

"I missed you too."

"How was it having the baby? Did it go okay? I was worried about you." But not enough so to call her, which went against the grain with him, and would have implied commitment, which he didn't want.

"It was scary and hard and gorgeous at the end. It hurts a lot, worse than I thought it would."

"You'll know for next time." He smiled at her.

"I don't want a next time unless I do it right with the right person. I don't think you're meant to go through stuff like this alone," she said pensively. The whole experience had impressed her, and she was grateful that he was back. He admitted that he liked the house so much that he had been in London the whole time, but he still hadn't called her. It was who he was and nothing was ever going to change him. She knew that.

"Maybe you're not supposed to do it alone, but you did it, Coco, and it looks like you did a great job."

They started seeing each other as much as they had before. He stayed at her house now, since she had to be there for the baby. He wasn't around for her at important times, but he had an easy way of sliding into her life that worked for them both. He filled an empty space in her world, and fit right into it like the missing piece in a puzzle. She didn't expect more of him than he was able to offer. She had no idea how long it would last, or when he'd disappear again, but for now, it was all she needed and had room for in her life too. His dog, Bruce, slept in the kitchen at night, and was happy to see them in the morning.

*   *   *

A month after Ian came back, Sam called her in the middle of the
night for her. He was sobbing and at first she couldn't understand
him. His father had died during dinner of a heart attack. His mother
was devastated, as were his siblings. No one had expected it and they
were all turning to him. And he was heartbroken too. Now everything rested on his shoulders. The business, the family, his wife, a
baby soon. It was overwhelming.

They talked until he calmed down, and she told him she would
take the first plane out the next day. She had to bring the baby with
her. She was only three months old, and Coco had gotten a passport
for her, just a few weeks before, in case they ever went to New York.

"Are you really coming?" he asked, touched by the gesture. He had
always been there for her too.

"Of course I'm coming. You were there for me when my parents
died, weren't you?" He had stayed with her for months, and visited
her every day after that.

"We'll be sitting shiva for the next week," he explained.

"That's when people come to visit, isn't it?"

"And pray."

"Will your mom let me come to that?"

"I'm the head of the family now. I make the rules," he said somberly. He was so young. They both were, and had to take the reins so
early. She knew how much his family expected of him, somehow it
didn't seem fair.

"I'll text you when I know when I'm arriving. I'll call you when I
get to the apartment." She called the housekeeper then, since it was
dinnertime in New York. Theresa still maintained her parents' apart-

ment. Coco asked her if she would babysit for Bethanie for her, and Theresa was thrilled. She couldn't wait to see them both. Coco had sent her a photo of the baby when she was born.

Ian had spent the night with her, but she didn't go back to bed after Sam's call. Instead, she packed quietly in her dressing room. She took several black dresses, and a nice one for the funeral, and she packed for the baby too. She called the airline, and there was a flight to New York at noon. She had to be at the airport to check in at ten, and leave her house at nine.

She slipped back into bed with Ian then, and he woke up at five, as he always did to go to the gym. She told him she was leaving for New York that morning. She told him about Sam's father. "I'll be back in a few days."

"I'll be here, waiting for you." He smiled at her, and pulled her into his arms before they got up. "I'm sorry you have to do that." He knew it would be painful for her and bring back hard memories.

"He's always been there for me. I can't miss it. And Sam's going to have so much responsibility on his shoulders now."

"Just like you," he said sympathetically, and then they got out of bed, and she went to make him the tea he liked. She kept a stock of it at her house for whenever he spent the night.

"You're a good friend," he said, as she poured coffee for herself. The baby was still asleep. She had just stopped nursing her. She and Ian were at ease with each other, as they sat at the kitchen table, waking up.

Ian kissed her when he left, and she heard him drive away on his motorcycle, slow enough for Bruce to follow him the short distance to his house. It was going to be a sad few days for her in New York. Then Bethanie started to cry, and she had to feed her and dress both of them, in time to leave for the airport. She was juggling the diaper bag, her purse, the baby, a stroller, a car seat, and a suitcase when she got in the cab. It was the first time she had traveled with Bethanie. She felt like an octopus trying to keep track of it all.

She managed to keep the baby entertained before they boarded the flight, and they both slept for half the trip. Then the baby cried for a while, and Coco apologized to the passengers around her. She got a porter at JFK, and managed to get through customs with the baby, the stroller, and all their bags, got a cab, and headed to her parents' apartment in the city. She hadn't been there in two and a half years. She had gotten married and divorced and had become a mother since she'd left. So much had changed in her life. And now Sam's was about to change too.

Theresa was waiting for them when she got to the apartment. With the time change, it was four-thirty in the afternoon in New York, and nine-thirty at night for them on London time. Theresa couldn't believe how beautiful the baby was, and said she looked just like her grandmother. There was something comforting about that too, as though her mother lived on in her daughter.

She handed the baby over to Theresa, and told her when to feed her from the stock of formula she had brought. She dressed quickly to go to Sam's apartment.

When she got to Sam's in a plain black wool dress and wool coat and flat shoes, there were about two dozen visitors milling around the apartment, and the family was seated around the dining table, speaking in soft voices, as people came to greet them. They had buried Sam's father that morning, according to Jewish law.

Coco went to speak to Sam's mother first, and she hugged Coco, and thanked her for coming.

"She came from London, Mom," Sam said, suddenly standing next to her, and Coco looked up at him and smiled and hugged him too. Coco noticed immediately that neither of Sam's sisters was there, and remembered that their mother had forbidden them to come to Chanukah, since both of them were converts to Christianity now. Sam's brother was wearing a yarmulke and a big black hat, like the one the rabbi was wearing. Sam's little brother was seventeen now, nearly eighteen.

Coco followed Sam out to the kitchen, where massive amounts of food were being prepared and put on trays, all of it kosher.

"No BLTs?" Coco whispered to him and he laughed.

"Ssshhhh . . . my mother can hear through stone walls." As he said it, an attractive blond girl approached them, wearing no makeup and visibly pregnant. Coco knew instantly it was Tamar from the way she looked at Sam, and she thought the young woman's hair looked stiff and odd, and she realized that she was wearing a wig, like the other Orthodox women. His mother's was stylish and she had it done by her hairdresser. Tamar's was unflattering and more obviously a wig, and it shocked her. It made her realize how different Sam's life was now. He was steeped in Orthodox Judaism, with his mother, brother, and wife all Orthodox, even more so since his sisters had defected. His father had been the least Orthodox of all. She knew Sam had dreamed of being in a Reform synagogue when he was younger, or none at all. He had never been religious. She saw that he was wearing a black velvet yarmulke while they sat shiva for the next week.

He put an arm around Tamar when she came to stand next to him. She looked shyly at Coco in her chic black dress. Coco was as thin as she had been before the baby. Sam introduced them since they had never met before.

"Hello, Tamar, how are you feeling?" she asked, referring to the pregnancy. She felt guilty, knowing how ardently she had tried to dissuade Sam from marrying Tamar, and she didn't feel any differently seeing her now. She didn't seem like the right match for him, with her strict Orthodox traditions he didn't believe in, and the ugly wig, which didn't look natural. She wondered if Sam's daughters would have to wear them too, if they had any. And the boys yarmulkes. She was sure they would. According to Sam, Tamar kept a strict home. Like only the most religious Orthodox women, Tamar shaved her head and only took her wig off at night when she went to bed and then covered her head with a scarf. Only Sam was allowed to see her without the wig, for modesty. She wondered if Sam wore a yarmulke all the time now to please his wife, and hadn't told Coco.

"I feel better now," Tamar answered Coco in a small voice. "I was pretty sick in the beginning, though." She was five months pregnant, and was wearing a shapeless black dress that was too long for her. Everything about her seemed so colorless and dull. There was nothing exciting about her, but that was what Sam said he wanted. Stability, someone solid.

On his own, Sam was so much more sophisticated and worldly, and modern, but not with Tamar at his side. All Coco could see now as she looked at him was that he was trapped, stifled by traditions he didn't like, surrounded by people who wanted to hold him back, and married to a woman who wanted to surround him with children he wasn't ready for. She wanted to grab Sam by the hand and run out the door with him to freedom. He had given it up to marry Tamar because she was a "nice person." That didn't seem like enough. His sacrifice seemed larger than life to Coco, personified by his drab wife.

Coco stayed for two hours, talking quietly to Sam, and then said goodbye to Mrs. Stein. Tamar was sitting next to her. She looked like her daughter as they sat there. There was a small amount of sweet kosher wine being served, and everyone at the table had a glass. She and Sam had gotten drunk on a bottle of Manischewitz once, at fifteen. He stole it after Shabbat, and walked to her house carrying it in his jacket. It tasted like grape juice to Coco, and she drank too much of it and Sam had to sneak her into the apartment without her parents seeing them.

Sam rode down in the elevator with her to get her a cab, and they stood on the sidewalk talking for a few minutes. The memorial at the synagogue was the next morning.

"Does she wear a wig all the time?" Coco asked him, curious, and he nodded.

"Except in bed with me. It's considered modest. No one is supposed to see her hair except me. She's very religious so she shaves her head, and she wears a scarf in bed. I'm used to it now." One could get used to anything, Coco thought, but traditions that made young women look old and dreary seemed so unnecessary. There certainly was no glamour in Sam's life, and very little beauty. They knew now that they were having a boy, which in some ways was a relief. Everyone was happy for them.

"Maybe our kids will get married someday." Coco smiled at him as they stood on the sidewalk in the chill November air. He wasn't wearing a topcoat over his suit.

"It's going to be strange not seeing my father every day at the office," Sam said with sadness in his voice. "Who will I fight with at work?" There were tears in his eyes, and they spilled onto his cheeks as she took him into her arms and held him.

"You'll get used to it. I promise. I felt that way about Mom and Dad at first, and then one day they just feel like they're part of you, and they're inside you and not outside." He nodded, hoping she was right. "What will the service be like tomorrow?"

"Long. The women and men don't sit together. They sit separately in shul. Men and women didn't dance together at our wedding. I wanted to, and our families wouldn't allow it. There was supposed to be a divider, but Tamar's family insisted on separate rooms for the men and women for dancing."

"Don't you ever get tired of all this?" she asked him. "Of everyone making the rules for you?" Her mother's words were still echoing in her head too.

"All the time, but this is how it has to be. It's what is expected of me and what I signed on for. It's familiar to me, Coco. It doesn't shock me the way it does you." But it still shocked her, and his family seemed much more strict and religious now than when they'd gone to grade school together, or maybe she just hadn't noticed. Sam had said that his father occasionally ate non-kosher things too, but never told Sam's mother. And now he was gone, and the poor woman was going to be alone. At least Sam had Tamar and they would have a family, and a baby to compensate for the loss.

"Has Ian surfaced again?" he asked her. He was impressed that she was dating him, although he was another flash guy who was never going to be there for her and said so.

"He came back a few weeks ago. He was in London the whole time and never called me," she said wistfully. "He was writing."

"He's never going to be what you want, Coco. Be careful that he doesn't take up space and keep you from meeting anyone real who might be there full-time. Relationships like that are dangerous. They feed you enough to keep you satisfied and closed off to other people, when they're not really there in the way you want them to be. They take up real estate without being candidates for a life together."

"That describes it perfectly. But I don't want anyone else right now anyway."

"You never will if you create a world specially designed for him, tailor-made."

"He's brilliant, Sam."

"I know he is, but he's not eligible for real life. He doesn't want that." She nodded. Ian said it himself, but his mind was so intoxicating and addictive to be around. She was hooked, and she didn't care how little of him she got. It was always enough, and so much better and more interesting than what she'd have gotten from anyone else.

He hailed a cab for her then, to cross the park to her parents' apartment. She and Sam used to try to signal each other with mirrors catching the sunlight, but it had never worked, they were too far apart on opposite sides of the park. She had always been afraid that they'd burn Central Park down if the mirrors had worked.

"See you tomorrow," he said, as she got into the cab and looked back at him with a smile. "Thank you for coming from London."

"I'd come from the moon if you needed me," she reminded him. She wondered on the way home what their life would have been like if they had wound up together. Silly and fun, and crazy and smart. But it never could have happened. His mother would have killed her. No Christian girl was going to get her son. The idea of romance had never occurred to either one of them. They loved being best friends.

*   *   *

The memorial service was at Congregation Ohab Zedek on the Upper West Side the next day. It was as long as Sam had said it would be. The cantor sang beautifully, and the congregants knew all the prayers. She stood quietly remembering his father, and her parents, and hoped they were in a better place where hearts didn't get broken and people who loved each other didn't lose each other, and no one got disappointed. She hoped that Bethanie and Sam's son would make it a better world one day that was a little closer to Heaven than what they had now.

Coco spent four days in New York, and didn't visit his apartment again. She didn't want to wear out her welcome with his mother, or crowd Tamar, who looked nervous when Coco was around.

She and Sam met for a walk along Central Park West the night before she left. There was no reason for her to stay, and it made her too sad being at the apartment. It seemed so empty now, with both of her parents gone. London was a clean slate for her. It was easier.

"Do you think you'll ever go back to school?" he asked her.

"I don't know. I don't know that I need to. I'm enjoying the business with Leslie and it's doing well. I can't see myself in journalism anymore."

"I can't see myself in accounting anymore either. But it's my show now."

"Maybe you can make the changes you wanted to, and he wouldn't let you."

"That's what I'm hoping. Tamar said she'd help me, but she'll be busy with the baby. My mom said she'd babysit. Sabra is having a baby too, but my mom wants nothing to do with them. She's a stubborn woman. Rebecca is thinking about becoming a nun. That even shocked me. She's more religious than my mother. I think my whole family is a little crazy," he said, grinning. "I don't think my mother would survive having a daughter who's a nun."

"There were some very interesting Jewish activists who became nuns in World War II, like Saint Edith Stein. I was always fascinated by her. She saved a lot of people and died in Auschwitz. I thought she was much more worthy than the traditional saints. I read a book about her."

"At least you didn't become a nun." He smiled at her.

"Maybe I should when Bethanie grows up. I can't see myself in a traditional couple anymore. The ones you tell me I should be with bore me, and the intriguing, unusual guys, the flash, as you put it, burn you every time."

"Just make sure that Ian Kingston doesn't burn you. I worry about that. He's damaged and dangerous."

"Maybe that's what makes him so interesting. Maybe I'm like that now too, after my parents, and Nigel, and having Bethanie on my own. I'm not exactly traditional anymore either."

"You're reliable. I know I can always count on you. You're just traditional enough for the right man. A little eccentricity adds some spice to life." She couldn't see how Tamar added spice to his. She was as spicy as rice pudding. But it was what he had chosen, and it was too late to challenge it now. She was a bright girl, she just had no personality and no style and he did. In biblical terms, Coco thought he was hiding his light under a bushel. And Tamar was the bushel.

But it was no longer up to Coco to question it, with a baby on the way. He thanked her again for coming all the way from London.

"Maybe I'll come back and visit when you have the baby. I can't wait to see him," she said, and they hugged when she left him, and she waved from the cab as they drove away.

She was awake for most of that night in her parents' apartment, thinking about them, and looking at old pictures that were still in frames around the apartment. She put several of them in her suitcase to take with her. She didn't know why, but when she left for London the next morning, with her baby, she had the feeling that she wouldn't be back again, or not for a long time. She had finally accepted that her parents weren't coming back again. They were gone. In a strange way it made her feel free.

Chapter 15

W hen Coco got back to London, Ian was eager to see her. He came over that night, and they made love for hours after Bethanie fell asleep. She was a good sleeper, and slept through most of the night. Coco loved being with her, and in spite of his claims of not liking children, Ian had fun with her too. He spoke to her as though she was a very small adult who did not speak the language but understood every word he was saying to her.

He explained to her all about green tea and chandeliers, French wall sconces, and Chinese art, French cuisine versus pasta, and the value of the metric system. Sometimes she just stared at him, and gave a big belly laugh as though he was ridiculous, or highly amusing. Coco fully expected her to answer him one day with her own monologue.

Ian spent Coco's twenty-fifth birthday with her, and cooked her a magnificent dinner at his place and served Chateau Margaux with the meal, and Chateau d'Yquem with dessert. They'd left Bethanie with the nanny and gone away for a few romantic weekends, particularly one in Venice, where they went from one church to the next until their heads were reeling. He seemed to know all of them and every detail of their history. She learned more from him than she had in her art history classes at Columbia.

They spent Christmas together since neither of them had anyone else to be with, and in January he disappeared again for two months to do some writing. She concentrated on Bethanie. The business kept her busy too. She knew that Ian would turn up before long, which he did, like the swallows returning in spring. He came and went, but the aura he left behind was so rich that she had no hunger for anyone else when she wasn't with him. That was what Sam had warned her about. She was so well sated by Ian that she had no need for anyone else in his absence and no one could compare to him. He was unique and brilliant and a fabulous lover, and even three months wasn't too long to wait for him. She didn't pine for him. She hibernated, gathering strength and knowledge to share with him when he returned to fill her soul and her mind again.

Sam and Tamar's son was born in March, two weeks late, and poor Tamar labored for two days. She had complications after the birth, and Sam took care of both of them, and fell in love with the baby boy they named Nathan. His middle name was Isaac, for Sam's father, according to Jewish tradition, using the name of a deceased family member.

Coco went to Saint Petersburg in Russia with Ian in the spring when he surfaced again, and he had started giving her his manuscripts to read when he returned with the first draft. It was extraordinary sharing the process with him. He valued her opinion, and she was judicious and sparing with the comments she made. He was a masterful writer and it was an honor to read his new work.

Without their noticing it, the time passed, and the years grew like a string of beads. Ian went to New York on business to see his publisher, and she went with him to see Sam, and eventually their second baby, Hannah. And then Ruth was born ten months later. Tamar was still helping him with the business but was too busy most of the time, and she got pregnant with their fourth baby just as quickly, another boy. Sam had changed his father's business considerably and it wasn't just an accounting firm now. He was a tax advisor to some hard-hitting clients, frequently referred by estate attorneys who respected him. His mother objected strenuously to any changes he made, and Tamar wasn't sure of them either, but Sam had started to enjoy what he was doing when it became his business and he could mold it the way he wanted. It was his consolation prize for losing his father.

There was never any question of Coco and Ian becoming an official couple, but they always stayed together when he wasn't on one of his sabbaticals. He stayed at her house now, with his dog. Bruce lived in the kitchen or in the room Ian used as an office. Ian had had to give his sublet back to the Roman chef when he came to reclaim it. Ian had his own office in her house now, and he came and went as he chose without comment from her.

They had been together for four years. Coco was twenty-eight, and Ian forty-five, and he stood in as a benevolent uncle to Bethanie. They still had long conversations over breakfast every day before she went to school. She called him Mr. Ian, as he had told her to, which was a joke between them, since he didn't want to be her stand-in father, although in many ways he was, whether he admitted it or not.

And Leslie and Coco had a chic office in Knightsbridge now, and ran a very successful business.

Ian and Coco were just back from a weekend in Prague, and Coco found Bethanie listless when she got home. She was running a fever. She thought it was the flu, gave her some medicine to bring the fever down, but she was worse the next day. She called the pediatrician, and it persisted for a week. The doctor suggested Coco bring her in, and maybe run a few tests. It could be strep, mononucleosis, or a number of other things, or just a nasty virus. Coco drove her to the doctor on the fifth day. They did a blood draw. Coco took her for some ice cream and a balloon afterward, and Bethanie didn't want to get out of the car.

Ian reassured Coco that night, but she didn't like the way Bethanie looked. She worried about things like meningitis, but her pediatrician had reassured her that she'd be much sicker if she had that, or even dead by then, which sent chills down Coco's spine.

"I'm sure it's nothing," Ian said when they went to bed that night, and in the morning there was no change. It was unnerving waiting for the test results. The doctor called when Coco was about to leave for work on Monday. She had a meeting and the nanny was there to be with Bethanie, who had stayed home from school again.

The doctor sounded concerned when Coco answered the phone. "I don't have good news," she said. "Something turned up in the blood-work that I didn't expect."

"Meningitis?" Coco sounded panicked. Ian wasn't back from the gym yet. He had errands to do that morning.

"No. She has too many white blood cells and too few red blood cells. She could be showing the early signs of leukemia." She said the words and Coco felt them like a knife piercing her heart. Bethanie had had a checkup recently with no sign of it. "I'd like to get her in to see an oncologist today if possible. We should get on this quickly." Coco felt like she was going to faint and had to sit down.

"Oh my God. How could that happen?"

"It does. It's the second case I've seen recently. I'll call you back after I speak to the oncologist and find out when he can see you."

She called back half an hour later. "He said to bring her in now. Can you do that?"

"Of course." The doctor gave her the address, and she picked Bethanie up in her pajamas, put a coat over them, and settled her in the car, in her car seat. She left the house in less than ten minutes, and Coco called Leslie to say she wasn't coming in.

They were at the doctor fifteen minutes later. Coco carried Bethanie inside and set her down gently in the waiting room. She was afraid of another blood draw, and Bethanie started to cry as soon as Coco set her down. A nurse distracted her with a balloon and a toy, and they waited to see the oncologist, who examined Bethanie, and looked at the tests the pediatrician had sent him. He met with Coco in his office, while the nurse played with Bethanie in the exam room, but all she wanted to do was lie down and clutch the blanket she had brought with her.

Coco looked at the doctor across his desk. "How bad is it?" Bethanie was the love of her life, and the only family she had. The doctor could see all of it in Coco's eyes.

"It's not good. I don't like it. I never do. I'd like to get a spinal tap and a bone marrow biopsy. That should tell us the whole story. If it is leukemia, we have good results with children Bethanie's age, depending on what kind it is."

Coco felt sick as she listened, and he sent them directly to the hospital. Two hours later, both tests were administered with Bethanie under anesthesia. It was Coco's worst nightmare come true. She called Ian at the house, and he was waiting for them when they got home, looking shell-shocked. He looked worse than Coco.

The oncologist called her back the next day, after the longest night of Coco's life. She had acute myelogenous leukemia, AML, supposedly the easiest to cure, and she needed to start chemotherapy as soon as possible. "We caught it early," he reassured her. "I'd like to get her started on chemo by the end of this week." Coco couldn't believe what she was hearing. Her perfect little girl who laughed and played all the time had leukemia, and if they didn't win the fight, she could die. She couldn't bear the thought of it. She asked him a blunt question then.

"How good is treatment here? Should I take her back to the States?"

"You could," he said, without taking offense. It was a reasonable question, since they had the option to do that, as Americans.

"They do great work with kids in Boston, and so does Sloan Kettering in New York. The French are very strong too, better than we are in some areas."

"Can we wait till tomorrow to make a decision?" she asked him, and he nodded. "I'd like to call some people in New York. I'll call you back tomorrow."

"You have some time. We can't drag our feet, but you certainly have the time to explore your options. Call me anytime." He gave her his cellphone number, and she thanked him and hung up. Her head was spinning, Ian was at the gym, and she called Sam as soon as she hung up. She sounded terrible when he answered. Her voice was shaking and she sounded sick.

"What's wrong?" He was still her go-to person for every disaster that happened to her. She closed her office door before she answered him, and then started to cry at last.

"Bethanie has leukemia. They ran tests on her. I just got the results. She has something called AML. They said she needs chemo. Do you know any outstanding pediatric oncologists in New York?" She expected him to say he'd research it, and she knew he would. She didn't expect the answer she got.

"Yes, I do. Don't do anything until I talk to him. What's your doctor's name?" She gave him the name of the oncologist so Sam could check him out. "I have a client, I do his taxes. He's supposedly the best in New York. I'll find out if he can see you, or recommend a doctor to consult with your oncologist there. I'll call you back as soon as I get him." She waited in her office with her head in her hands. Sam called her back ten minutes later. "He said the guy you saw is very good, one of the best, but he'd prefer for you to bring her to New York for an evaluation. Then you can decide if you want to proceed with treatment in New York, or go back to London. Coco, I would put my children's lives in this guy's hands. I trust everything he says. He's a star in his field." That was good enough for her. "He can see you day after tomorrow."

"I'll fly in tomorrow," she said, her mind going in a thousand directions at once.

"He wants you to email him the results of all the bloodwork they did, and the diagnosis. That way his team and he can consult on it before you get here."

"I'll take care of it."

"I'll text you his email address and name. He's not the warmest guy, just to warn you, but he's the best there is."

"I don't care if he's Frankenstein's nephew, if he can cure her." She started to cry again then. "Oh God, Sam, I don't want her to die."

Listening to her tore at his heart. "We won't let that happen. The first thing he told me when I described it to him was that kids with AML do really well and often have full recovery, particularly at Bethanie's age. Just hang in there. I'll see you tomorrow. Text me your flight number. I'll pick you up."

"You don't have to do that. You can come to the apartment."

"Fuck you," he said, and she smiled. Same old Sam. Same old godsend in every crisis for her entire life. He even had the right doctor in his back pocket.

She called the pediatrician after that, brought her up to date and gave her Dr. Jeff Armstrong's email address at Sloan Kettering so she could send him Bethanie's test results digitally.

"I'll handle it right away," she promised. Coco called British Airways after that and got two business class seats for the next day. She wasn't sure if she should take three, in case Ian wanted to go with them, but she could always call them back. She went to pack then, and was just finishing when Ian came home. He was hoping that everything had gone well, but he'd almost been afraid to come home and hear bad news. Coco had waited till he got home so she could tell him in person, not by text or on the phone.

"Did the doctor call you?" he asked, instantly worried when he saw Coco's face. She gave him the rapid version.

"She's got leukemia. They want to start her on chemo. I'm going to New York tomorrow with her. Sam has a client who's a star pediatric oncologist at Sloan Kettering. He'll see her day after tomorrow. I don't know if we'll do treatment here or there. Do you want to come with us?" He didn't answer her at first, but sat down facing her.

He was as pale as she was. He couldn't believe what he had just heard. It had hit him like a hand grenade.

"I'll let you get settled first. Call me after you see him. I can come over later if you stay." She nodded. It didn't even seem strange to her that he wasn't flying with them. Nothing did. Not after the news she'd had. Bethanie woke up crying then, and Coco went to comfort her.

They were leaving on a nine A.M. flight to New York the next day. She had texted the information to Sam. They were landing at noon New York time, and had to leave the house at six A.M. to get to the airport in time to check in. Coco was frantic all day, and Ian stayed in his office.

Bethanie went to sleep early, still feverish, and Coco nearly crawled into the kitchen while Ian cooked dinner, which he did almost every night when he was there. She knew he was due for another writing spell sometime soon, but she didn't know when. He never warned her ahead of time or knew himself when he'd be ready to start. It just came to him and he left.

She could only eat a few mouthfuls for dinner. They were packed and she had put in all of Bethanie's favorite toys, stuffed animals, and blankets, in case they stayed. All she took were jeans, sweaters, and running shoes for herself. She expected to be at the hospital for however long they were there.

"I can't believe this is happening," she said to Ian when she stopped trying to eat and put her fork down.

"Don't give up," he said sternly. "She's tougher than you think, and if this guy is any good, he'll cure her."

"They have a good success rate, but it's not a hundred percent," she reminded him. "Some kids don't make it. And the chemo will make her very sick. She'll lose her hair." But as long as she didn't lose her life, Coco could live with it. He looked as distraught as she did, and cleaned up the kitchen when she went upstairs to take a bath. He had said very little all day since she told him the news. He looked disoriented and distracted.

When he walked into her bathroom half an hour later, she knew something was wrong. She could see more bad news coming. From him this time.

"Are you okay?" she asked, and he shook his head and she could see that he was crying.

It took him a few minutes to compose himself. "There are things that you don't know about me, that most people don't need to know. But now you do. I told you that my father killed my mother. He was insane, a drunk, a drug addict. He'd been in and out of jail and mental hospitals. He killed my mother in a senseless rage. I had a little sister too. She was ten years younger than I was. She was seven. He killed her too, when he killed my mother. I was out and when I came home, I found them, all three of them. I never recovered from it. I never really loved anyone or got attached to anyone from that day on. Except you and Bethanie for the last four years. My sister is why I never wanted kids. I never wanted to be that close to anyone again, or love anyone that much. In a way he killed me too. What you see now, and have for the last four years, is what's left. It's what I could patch back together after he killed Weenie and my mother. Her name was Edwina. She called me Eeny.

"I found them after he did it," he repeated, looking distraught. "I can't even tell you what that was like." The tears were pouring down his face, unchecked. She tried to reach a hand out to him but he wouldn't let her. He couldn't bear the tenderness of her touch, and the flood of memories too. "A piece of me died with them. A big piece, the biggest part of me. I've never been able to have a normal relationship since and still can't. When I get too close, I run and disappear till I have distance again. That's why I disappeared when you had the baby, but I fell in love with her anyway.

"I can't be here for you now, Coco. I can't do it. It would kill me. I've been closer to you than anyone in my life. But I'm not husband material, or father material. If anything happens to her, it will kill me. And now she's sick. You're a strong woman, stronger than I am. I'm just a shell, Coco. I'm not a man." He was crying and she put her arms around him, still soaking wet from the bath, and she held him while he cried. "I want to go with you tomorrow, but I can't. When you leave, I'm going to go far from here to be alone again. Don't count on me. I can't be there for either of you. I'm like a hologram, an image, an illusion, there is nothing left inside."

"Yes, there is," she said softly. "I understand when you disappear. I'm fine with it."

"But you're not fine now, and you won't be, and neither will she until she survives this. I can't, Coco, I just can't," he sobbed and they held each other in silence for a long time. He had bared his soul to her, and loved her enough to do so.

"I'm so sorry, Ian. I love you. I'm so sorry your father did this to you, and your mother, and your sister. We're going to make it through this. They'll just have to cure Bethanie." She was being strong for him, as well as for her daughter and herself.

"You'll make it through this. Please God you both will. But I can't do it with you. When you leave tomorrow you have to let me go." He was the Phantom of the Opera, hiding in the darkness, and he had let her see beneath the mask. "Let me go, Coco, if you love me. I don't want to let you down," but he already had. He wanted to be there for her and Bethanie, but he knew he couldn't. He was being honest with her, more than he ever had been in his life.

They lay together all that night and never slept. She was wide awake, as he lay with her, stroking her face and her body, as though to be sure he would remember every inch of her. They didn't make love, they couldn't have, with what was happening to Bethanie. They just lay there loving each other, as Ian silently said goodbye. She wondered if she would ever see him again, and didn't think so. She was fighting not to lose Bethanie, and she was losing him at the same time, and she knew there was nothing she could do to stop him. She *had* to focus on Bethanie first and give her every ounce of her strength. She didn't have enough for him too and he knew it. He had none for her.

He watched her leave the next day for the airport in a cab. He held her tight for a minute, and hugged Bethanie.

"You take care of your mama for me, right, Miss Beth?"

"Yes, Mr. Ian," she said in a weak voice and smiled at him, as he steeled himself not to cry in front of her. His eyes met Coco's for a long moment. He kissed her through the cab window, as she felt four years vanish in the mist. And then the cab pulled away and he stood there without moving. Then he went inside to pack his bags. It was time to hit the road again. For Ian, it was done. And for Coco and Bethanie, the fight had just begun.

Chapter 16

Sam met them at the airport in New York. He looked serious, but broke into a smile when he picked Bethanie up in his arms.

"Hiya, Uncle Sam. Where's Nathan?" She smiled at him. She and his oldest son were friends on FaceTime, and the same age.

"He's at school, where you should be. What are you doing in New York?" Coco had brought a stroller for her in case she felt too sick to walk or was tired, and Sam set her gently in it, and pushed her after they came out of customs.

"I'm here because I'm sick. They're going to make me better."

"That sounds like a good plan." He exchanged a glance with Coco, who looked exhausted and tense, but was putting a good face on it when he kissed her. He didn't ask her how she was. He could see it. She looked as though the world had come to an end.

The porter followed them with their bags. Sam had brought a car and driver so he didn't have to park in the garage. He wanted to make everything as easy as possible for them. The driver picked them up quickly, and the porter loaded the bags into the car. Then they headed to the city. Sam came to the apartment with them. Theresa was waiting and took Bethanie to the kitchen to get something to eat. Coco hadn't been to New York since her last visit with Ian six months before. Theresa still took care of the apartment that Coco couldn't seem to let go of, as though she expected her parents to be there if she came home. But they weren't. Things were looking faded and tired, although Theresa kept the shades closed when no one was there, which was all the time.

"How is she?" Sam asked her quietly, as they sat down in the den. Theresa had put fresh flowers around the apartment for them. They reminded her of her mother, who used to have flowers everywhere.

"She's tired. Sick. I can't wait to see the doctor tomorrow. I keep hoping they made a mistake, but I know they didn't."

"I'll go with you," Sam said quietly. "The appointment is at ten o'clock. Tamar said to tell you how sorry she is." She had given birth to their fourth child, a son they had named David, a few weeks before. She'd had a caesarean section the last two times, and it had worn her out. "She says she's done, but I don't believe her. Four is a nice number, it works for me." She knew what a devoted father he was. He helped Tamar with the kids as soon as he came home from work and on the weekends. But he couldn't nurse them or give birth to them. "How's Ian?" He was used to his being part of the furniture of her life, on an erratic basis, but they had been together for a long time. She hesitated when he asked and Sam looked at her strangely.

"Something wrong?"

"Yeah, I guess so." She was too shell-shocked and shaken up to react to it. The full impact hadn't hit her yet, but she knew it would later, when she was alone. "He left today."

"For where? Another book?"

"No, according to him, for good. He couldn't deal with Bethanie being sick."

"Are you serious?" Sam looked stunned. "Tell me he didn't mean it."

"I think he did," she said quietly. "You were right a long time ago, he's badly damaged. Some pretty awful stuff happened to him when he was young. I knew some of it, but not all until last night."

"So awful that he can't stick by you?" Sam couldn't imagine it and didn't want to, and what it must have done to her, to have brought her daughter with leukemia to New York, and have her man walk out on her. He was furious thinking about it.

"He can't do it, Sam. His father murdered his mother when he was seventeen. And his seven-year-old sister, and then killed himself. Ian found them. He says he hasn't been a whole person since. He says he can't love anyone, but he loves us and I know it. The thought that Bethanie could die is too much for him. He said he was leaving me. He was packing when we left. He's a broken man. And right now I have to worry about Bethanie. I can't take care of him too. Maybe he was right to go. I didn't want him to, but I can't fix what they did to him. When he feels too much, he runs."

"Oh my God, Coco. What else?"

"This is enough. It's just about Bethanie right now. I'll worry about me later. And Ian, if he comes back. But I don't think he will." She felt as though he had died, and a part of her with him, but he had died a long time ago. He was just a shell with a beating heart that was still bleeding twenty-eight years later. Right now she needed every ounce of her energy for her daughter. "Everything okay with you?"

"We're fine. I think Tamar is depressed this time. She's been very quiet since the delivery. It happened last time too." He knew more about childbirth and the aftermath than most men.

"I never had that, but I'm a one-time mom, so what do I know?"

"You're twenty-eight years old. You don't know what could happen in the future. You might meet someone and have more kids."

"Yes, I do know. Either Ian will come back, or some other dazzling guy will come along, someone broken or different or exotic or famous or brilliant and unusual and knock me right on my ass, and it'll turn out like this again. Guys like Ian don't go the distance. They can't. And that seems to be my specialty, as you said a long time ago. Four years was a good run." She seemed ready to let him go, which surprised Sam. But she knew from everything he'd said that she couldn't hang on to him. The falling stars had turned to dust in her hands the night before.

"I hope he comes back," Sam said in a low voice.

"So do I, but I'm pretty sure he won't. Bethanie will take it hard. She loves him, and he loves her. It almost killed him to see us go. He wanted to come with us, but he didn't have it in him. Now we need to focus on what's going to happen here." She was determined. Every fiber of her being was focused on Bethanie.

Sam left a little while later, and picked them up at nine-thirty the next morning to go to Sloan Kettering. He had taken the day off from work to be with them.

Bethanie came bounding out of Coco's old childhood room to greet him, and she looked better after a night's sleep. Coco didn't. She hadn't been able to stop herself. She had called Ian, and he didn't pick up. She had no idea where he was or if she'd ever see him again. She thought she wouldn't, but she still hoped.

The news at Sloan Kettering, after Dr. Jeff Armstrong reviewed the bloodwork and examined Bethanie, was somewhat encouraging. He concurred with the diagnosis they'd gotten in London. Bethanie had AML. They had caught it early and he thought the odds were good, but she was a very sick little girl. He recommended their standard protocol for the disease, which was six weeks of intense chemotherapy, which would make her feel awful and she'd lose her hair. He wanted to start the next day. Ideally, they hoped she would go into remission after the first intense round of chemotherapy. She had a ninety-five percent chance of remission, and even cure. The length of treatment would be about six months, depending on how she responded. And he felt that a full cure was entirely possible. He recommended that she be treated in Boston, Paris, or at Sloan Kettering, rather than go back to London, and he would treat her himself if they stayed. He was impressive in every way. Coco could tell he was brilliant.

"I want to get her treated here," Coco confirmed. He nodded agreement and looked at her intensely. He was a tall, powerfully built man with sandy blond hair and deep blue eyes. He was very serious, and rarely smiled, except when speaking to his patients. He described the protocol to her. Bethanie would be in the hospital for six weeks, for chemo and to protect her from infection, and then she could go home for some of the time, and Coco could stay at the hospital with her as much as she wanted. There was something cold about him, but at the same time he inspired confidence. You could tell that he was used to being in command. He wasn't sympathetic when he spoke to Coco, but he had been very gentle when he examined Bethanie.

He explained that they were going to put a port in to administer the medication more easily. "We start tomorrow then," he said as he stood up. They had a hard six months ahead of them, but Coco wanted to get started. "When you're finished here," Dr. Armstrong told her, "you'll need to choose between those three cities for follow-up. Paris, Boston, or here in New York. We follow the same protocol." After he left the room, she thanked Sam again. And she knew she had to call Leslie and tell her. She couldn't work until the end of the year, and London wasn't on the list for follow-up treatment. There was so much to think about. She considered sending a text to Ian that they were starting tomorrow, but it would only torture him. She had to go through this alone, with Sam's help when he had time. But she couldn't lean too heavily on him either. He had a business to run, four children, and a depressed wife, and his mother hadn't been well for the last year. There was only so much he could shoulder. She didn't want to burden him.

But he took them back to the hospital the next day to start treatment, and then left to go to his office an hour later. He said he'd call and check in throughout the day.

The first treatment didn't seem to have too violent an effect, but they increased the dose progressively, and by the end of the first week in the hospital, Bethanie was as sick as they had predicted. Her immune system was depressed from that point on, so she couldn't leave the hospital. They were living in a bubble, and she felt sick and slept a lot of the time. Coco spent hours with her on her lap or reading to her until she fell asleep. She stayed at the hospital with her. She went home every few days for fresh clothes, but other than that, Coco never left her.

She texted and called Ian several times, but got no response. It was an endless six weeks. Sam came to see them every day.

*   *   *

The star physician, Jeff Armstrong, checked on Bethanie several times a day. He came to see her repeatedly during her chemo treatments, and he stopped to chat with Coco in the hall whenever he saw her. He surprised her when he mentioned a gala evening to benefit the hospital, and suggested that she should go. She didn't want to leave Bethanie, but she felt obligated to once he suggested it, and asked Sam if he would go with her. But he had to be at home with the kids. Tamar still wasn't doing well after her C-section, so Coco bought a thousand-dollar seat and went alone. She hadn't brought anything dressy to wear, but found an old evening gown in her closet that still fit her. It wasn't exciting, but she wore her hair up, and stopped at Saks to buy a pair of evening sandals and a big rhinestone brooch that looked real, and a black satin evening bag. She wasn't in a festive mood, and she was shocked when she found herself at the head table, seated next to Jeff Armstrong, who offered her a private tour of their research facilities the next day. She couldn't turn that down. She didn't want to be rude to him after all the personal attention he was giving Bethanie.

The tour of their research facilities the next day was fascinating and intense. He explained every detail to her, and gave her a two-hour tour himself, and then stopped to visit Bethanie, and as he left he bestowed one of his rare smiles on Coco. She could feel the strength he emanated. He exuded power and a brilliant mind. As she thought it, she recognized the early signs that were always so attractive to her. Supreme intelligence, a man at the top of his field, and unlimited success. The flash. It defined every man who was attracted to her, and whom she was drawn to like a moth to flame. She reminded herself to be careful. He had an important function in her life. He was trying to save her daughter, she didn't want to become too personally involved with him. During the benefit dinner he had mentioned the kind of donations they were trying to elicit in their fund drive. He suggested a million dollars and upward, which was obviously not for himself, but for research. There was clearly an ulterior motive and an agenda behind his random moments chatting with her in the hall. A donation was certainly possible, though perhaps not quite that large. If they cured Bethanie, she would be forever grateful, but it made her uneasy that he saw her as a source of money and was preying on their plight, however subtly.

"Do you like to sail?" he asked her one day in the hall, and she said she did, but hadn't in a long time. "I have a small sailboat I keep tied up at the Chelsea Piers, if you'd like to come out with me sometime." He was very attractive, somewhere in his mid to late forties. He reminded her of a younger Ed, or a more professional-looking Ian. He was definitely a type, her type. He was at the top of his field, as Ian was. She had called Ian several more times, and he still hadn't responded. But Jeff Armstrong made it clear that he was eager to spend time with her during their lengthy stay in New York.

"I don't think I should leave Bethanie right now," she said with a warm smile, and she mentioned him to Sam when he came by that night. He brought a drawing from Nathan to Bethanie. She was still very sick, but on the whole, she was holding up well.

"I think I have a problem," Coco told Sam, after he told her how Tamar was. She was still depressed, and the baby was colicky. Nathan had hit his head at school that day and had to be picked up and brought home.

"I'm turning into Mr. Mom," he said with a sigh. He was doing all he could for his kids, and Tamar was despondent. He said she cried all the time.

"I think Jeff Armstrong is hitting on me," Coco shared with him, looking worried. "He suggested I buy a ticket to the benefit, which I did to support the cause, and he had me seated next to him, which was a little awkward. He invited me today to go sailing with him on his boat. And he wants a million-dollar donation or more. I can't afford that, though I'll certainly give them a healthy donation if they cure my daughter. I can't put my finger on it, but he's just a little too friendly for my taste. He's also what I always fall for. I'm not here for that, I'm here for Bethanie. But he's so damn smart and attractive. He's the flash you always talk about, Sam, which is my nemesis." He laughed at her.

"You're just too damn beautiful and sexy for your own good."

"Like hell I am. I look a mess. I'm not feeling sexy. This isn't the time or the place. And I'm still in love with Ian," she said sadly.

"Did Jeff tell you he has a gorgeous Chinese wife? She's a professor at Columbia Medical School. She's a knockout. She lectures all over the place, she probably couldn't make it to the benefit." He looked startled that Jeff had gotten personal with her. It seemed inappropriate to him.

"So what's he after? Just money?" she asked him innocently.

"That, and you. You're a doubleheader, Coco. You're young and beautiful *and* you can make an enormous donation. Not many women your age can."

"I don't want to be the object of his attentions, particularly if he's married. Here we go again."

"Just keep saying no. He'll get the message eventually." Sam thought it was funny and Jeff was harmless. He was a busy man and an important one. He wasn't going to stalk her. But Coco didn't trust herself. He was a very attractive man, she was lonely and scared, and

he was cast in the role of savior, which made him even more dangerous for her. She knew herself. And she did not want a married man,
under any circumstances, savior or not. All she wanted from him was
that he save her daughter.

He asked her to lunch the following week when he saw Coco in
the hall when Bethanie was sleeping. He wasn't being overly pushy,
but he was persistent, and married. She saw him in the cafeteria a
few days later, and he sat down at her table.

"Are you avoiding me, Ms. Martin?" he asked with a sultry look
and a voice as smooth as silk. She decided to be honest with him, she
didn't know what else to do.

"I understand you're married," she said quietly, looking him in the
eye. His attention was flattering, but his style and everything he represented was dangerous for her, like a drug she had detoxed from
and didn't want to dabble with again.

"That's true," he said easily, as though it didn't matter. "My wife
and I have an understanding. She's a very busy person. And so am I.
It's hard to keep a marriage working well sometimes in those condi-
tions. The life went out of our marriage years ago, and you're a very
intriguing woman," and also nearly twenty years younger than he
was. It was Ed all over again, with a different job. Same guy, same
style, same line. She almost wanted to laugh, and suddenly he was
no longer attractive, just another married guy at the top of his field
who was full of himself, and thought any woman would be lucky to
have him. He was a classic narcissist.

"I'm very touched by your offers," she said coyly, feeling like an
idiot flirting with him to get him off her back. "It's hard for me to
concentrate on anything right now except my daughter. Maybe when
she's better," she said and he nodded. She could almost see him put

her in the fridge for later, as a midnight snack. She didn't want to anger him so he'd lose interest in Bethanie, which she knew he wouldn't. He was too much the consummate professional for that, and indeed a brilliant researcher and physician, but he was also a horny, bored married guy looking for a new playmate. Like Nigel, or Ed, or so many men. At least Ian had never cheated on her, that she knew of. It wasn't his style and he was an honest man. Men like Jeff had a massive ego that needed to be fed, like white mice to a boa constrictor. She had no desire to be anyone's white mouse. He left her alone at her table then, and didn't invite her to join him again. He had struck out, which men like him didn't like either. She knew the type too well, and was proud of herself for resisting his advances.

It was late June by then, and in mid-July, six weeks after they had started treatment, Bethanie was in remission. She was able to leave the hospital for a while, and be treated as an outpatient. Coco was able to take her to Southampton and drove her there herself. Bethanie had lost her hair, which she hated, and she was wearing a little white eyelet hat, like she'd worn when she was a baby.

They made a sand castle and had a nice time. They slept in the same bed. Coco had to force herself not to think of her parents and Ian, the people she had loved and lost. Jeff Armstrong never crossed her mind. All she could think of was Bethanie, in remission and hopefully on her way to a cure. She was becoming one of their success stories, and Coco had never been as grateful in her life, nor as proud of herself for resisting a brilliant, successful, and charming married man. The flash hadn't worked its magic this time.

Chapter 17

The next four and a half months went by very quickly during the latter part of Bethanie's treatments. She was firmly in remission, and able to be treated as an outpatient, living at home. Coco went to a museum occasionally, when she could get away. They went to Southampton several times in July and August. In mid-August, Bethanie turned five, and they had a birthday party for her at the hospital, and another one at home with Theresa, Coco, and Sam. His children couldn't visit, because her immune system was still compromised, but in September, after four months of treatment, the doctors were pleased with her progress, and considered her cancer-free. Coco was hoping they might get back to London by October. Leslie had been managing the business without her, and Coco wanted to go back to work. She longed for their life to get back to normal, and for Bethanie to be a healthy little girl again. Bethanie had asked about Ian several times, but there had been no sign of him since they left London. Coco just told her that he was away writing a book, which Bethanie was used to, and knew they couldn't call him then.

She asked her mother one day on the beach in Southampton why they had no daddy. Coco told her that some people just didn't, and Bethanie was satisfied with her answer, for now. She would tell her the truth when she was older, in the gentlest way she could. Coco had heard from Leslie that Nigel was living in Dubai and entertained in Sussex, whenever he came back to England. She had no idea what he was doing and didn't care.

She had dinner with Sam whenever he had time, which wasn't often. Tamar was still depressed five months after David's birth, and he seemed like he was losing patience with her. He was doing almost everything for the kids, and he and Coco had dinner wherever he could eat meals that weren't kosher. He had just turned thirty, leading the life his parents had wanted for him, but not the one he had wanted when they went to school.

"Tamar has been talking about going to law school," he told her, looking irritated. "I don't know who she thinks is going to take care of the kids if she does, unless we hire a full-time nanny, which costs a fortune. We have a woman who comes in to help part-time and has kids of her own. My mother isn't up to it anymore. And I can't do any more than I already am. I haven't had a day off from work or kids in four years." He loved his children, and his wife, but Coco had the feeling he was drowning, and didn't know what she could do to help him. He asked if she had heard from Ian, and she said she hadn't, and he stopped asking, not wanting to upset her.

Bethanie went trick-or-treating around the hospital, and finally in November, Jeff and his team declared her cured. There was no sign of leukemia in any of her tests. Technically, she was in remission, but he thought there was a strong possibility that the disease would not return. They had a party to celebrate it with ice cream and balloons in the pediatric ward.

She was officially discharged from the hospital. All the nurses and doctors came to say goodbye to Bethanie. And on the last day when she went to thank Jeff again, Coco handed him an envelope with a five-hundred-thousand-dollar check in it. It was less than he wanted, but it was an enormous gift.

She had dinner with Sam that night. They were leaving for London the next day. She had been there for six months. It felt like an eternity to her.

"Do you think you'd ever move back here?" Sam asked her wistfully. He had loved having her nearby during Bethanie's treatments, and being able to see her anytime he wanted, even every day for a short time. He told her that she had gotten him through a hard time. Tamar's depression had finally started to lift. She said now that she didn't want to have any more children, and this time Sam believed her. The last one had taken too big a toll on her. Sam admitted to Coco he was relieved. "Four is a lot of kids."

"I don't think I'd move back," she said. "I'm going to keep the apartment here, though. I've been thinking about selling the house in London. It's too big for us, and it has bad memories for me now." She tried not to think of Nigel there, but the house was more than she wanted to deal with. "And I've been thinking of going back to school."

"You too?" He was surprised. "That's all Tamar can think of. I'm beginning to think she was too young to get married, and I sure was. Some of my friends from college aren't even married yet. And I've been married for five years, and have four kids."

"Do you regret it?" she asked, and he hesitated.

"Sometimes. It's a lot with my father's business to run." He still considered it his father's and not his own. "I'd rather have a smaller office and deal with bigger clients. I'm slowly getting into investment advising full-time, which I like a lot better than accounting. My mother is opposed to it, and so is Tamar, but it's a much more exciting and lucrative field for me, although it involves more risk."

"Then you should do it," she encouraged him. "You can't live your life for everyone else." He nodded, wondering if it was true. He had for years, and his family seemed to like it better than he did.

"What about you? Where are you thinking of going to school?"

"You'll think I'm crazy," she said, with a look of mischief in her eye that reminded him of when they were in high school, which he thought were the best years of their lives.

"I've always thought you were crazy." He smiled at her. "Good-crazy. You do things, most people don't and just waste their lives, like me."

"Don't be so tough on yourself. You do things too. You have four kids, what more do you want?" He didn't say it, but he wanted his dreams back. Coco hadn't given up her dreams, she had invented new ones. "Jeff says that Bethanie needs to be checked at a university hospital where they use the same protocols as he did, which means Boston, New York, or Paris. I've been thinking about doing my last two semesters at the American University in Paris. I'm tired of New York after the past six months, and I don't want to go to Boston. But Paris might be fun for a year. I need to see what's happening with my business, but Leslie seems to be doing fine without me. I could spend a year in Paris, and maybe go back to London then. I think I've become a nomad, like Ian. I'll see what I decide when I go back."

Sam couldn't take them to the airport, and Coco and Bethanie left quietly the next day. Bethanie had been incredibly brave and she had come through it, and with luck she would never have a relapse. Coco had sent a text to Ian to tell him that Bethanie was in remission, and hopefully cured. He hadn't responded, but at least he knew. She felt she owed him at least that. It was going to be strange going back to the house in London and not seeing him there, or Bruce lounging in the kitchen, waiting for Ian to come home or for someone to give him a meal.

The house in London was immaculate and silent when they walked in. Bethanie rushed to her room to check on her dolls and stuffed animals and they were all there. There was a note from Ian, that he had left on Bethanie's bed, and it brought tears to Coco's eyes when she read it to her.

"Miss Beth: When you read this, you'll be home and all well again. Have a wonderful time in school, play with all your friends, be good to your mom, and remember to tell her how much you love her. I am going away to ride camels and write a book. Always remember that I love you. Bruce and I will miss you. A big hug and all my love, Mr. Ian." There was no mention of his coming back or seeing her again.

And there was no note on Coco's bed when she went to check. And what could he have said to her? She knew what they had shared and how much they loved each other. It was enough. But when she went to bed that night, she noticed the galleys of his next book on her bed table. She had read it when he finished writing it. She opened it to the dedication page, just as she was meant to. He hadn't dedicated it yet when she'd read it. There was a lump in her throat the size of a fist. "To the four women I have loved and always will, Weenie, my mother, Coco, and Bethanie, with all my love, I.K." And beneath it he had written in the familiar brown ink he used, "I love you, Ian." He had put it on her bed table when he left, and it had waited for her for six months.

The last six months had been an incredible odyssey, through Bethanie's leukemia, losing Ian the day they left, and now coming home to an empty house. She wasn't sure what to do next, but tomorrow she would go to her office, find out what they were working on, and call the American University in Paris. She wanted to live her life now. She didn't want to waste a moment of it, and Paris seemed like a suitable destination for a while.

She checked on Bethanie, who was sound asleep. She had put Ian's letter on her bulletin board. As she slipped into her own bed, between crisp clean sheets, Coco wondered what chapters would come next. With Bethanie cured, she could turn her attention to the business of living again. And wherever Ian was now, she hoped he was happy. She knew that she would always love him, and that he would love her, as best he could.

Coco dropped Bethanie off at her school the next day, where they celebrated her. Everyone stood up and cheered when she walked in, and they had made posters welcoming her back. When Coco walked into her office shortly after, she hardly recognized it. Leslie had done some redecorating, and hired three new assistants, who were already busy. They had spoken regularly, FaceTimed daily, and Leslie had sent her frequent emails. The business was continuing to grow, and Coco didn't feel as though they needed her desperately. She talked to Leslie that morning about going to Paris to go back to school, and Leslie smiled broadly at her.

"Do it! You've had a hell of a year, you deserve whatever you want to do." Coco was feeling the same way about it. She wanted to celebrate life after going through hell in New York. Bethanie's recovery was a major victory, the only one that mattered.

She spoke to the admissions office at AUP, and although she was applying late, they were willing to let her start in January. She promised to send them her transcript from Columbia, and then she marched into Leslie's office with a grin.

"I have a new client for you."

"Really? Who? A VIP?" Leslie asked.

"Of course! Me! I want you to find me an apartment or a house in Paris for a year. I don't think I'll stay that long. I'm going to take as many credits as I can, to graduate. But I'd rather take the house for a year, in case we want to stay a little longer after I graduate."

"That's a tall order. I don't have great contacts there, and I don't speak French, but one of the new girls does. I'll see what I can do."

She was beaming when Coco came to work a week later, and handed her a folder with a description and photographs of a house in it. It was very sweet, small, and on the Left Bank, with three bedrooms.

"The difficult we do quickly, the impossible we do faster. What do you think?" Coco looked it over and then smiled at her and handed the folder back.

"I'll take it."

"Just like that? Don't you want to go over and see it?"

"I don't need to. I trust you." It looked a little like the house they had found for Ian when he was consulting on his movie when he first came to London. It had the same kind of quaint fairy tale feel to it. Coco wrote a check for the deposit. She had already filled out the forms for AUP. And the day before her twenty-ninth birthday in December, she got an email telling her that she had been accepted as a second semester senior at AUP and with the credits she had, she could graduate in June.

She looked into schools for Bethanie, and found a small bilingual school, which sounded perfect, and they had room for Bethanie.

Coco celebrated her birthday with Bethanie and Leslie. She had a new man in her life and seemed happy with him. At forty-five, she was no longer looking for Prince Charming. She loved her business and was content with someone more human scale. He was a talented furniture designer who had been one of their clients, and had moved to London from Copenhagen a year before. When Coco met him, she liked him a lot.

Coco bought a Christmas tree and she and Bethanie decorated it. She was grateful for every day they shared. And the day after New Year's Day, they left for Paris. Bethanie started school a few days later. Coco showed up for her first class at AUP with a bag full of notebooks and pens, and she felt like a kid again as she went from class to class, and enjoyed talking to the other students. She also felt like the old lady in the group. She was twenty-nine, and she looked just like one of them.

She dropped her books at the end of her second class, and a student in a blue and white striped sweater helped her pick them up. He looked like an overgrown boy, and said he was from Vermont. He had a mane of dark hair, and told her he was twenty-three years old when they had coffee together between classes. She told him she had dropped out of school eight years before, and didn't say why, and she had decided to graduate now. He treated her as though she was his age, which was refreshing. He wasn't a famous author, or a researcher, or a captain of industry, or a gigolo, he was just a boy and treated her like a girl. She invited him for dinner that weekend, and he brought two friends with him. They had fun playing with Bethanie, and he said he was the oldest of seven children.

They went to the movies together, and were in two of the same classes. Several students were older than she was. Being there was like diving into a pool of cool water. It woke her up. She felt alive. She was learning new things and remembering old ones, reading books that had new meaning now that she was older. It was like starting life over without tragedy, and they had long political discussions in cafés near the school. She felt young again, after the painful months they had spent at Sloan Kettering, and although she had promised herself she wouldn't, she wound up sleeping with Jimmy one afternoon at her house when Bethanie was still at school. There was a freshness and simplicity to all of it. It wasn't complicated. It was real. And she had found a babysitter Bethanie loved, a young French girl, which gave Coco freedom to go out sometimes.

"You're the most exciting woman I've ever known," Jimmy said to her. He had dark hair like hers. She was only six years older, but had lived several lifetimes. She told Sam about him, but didn't admit to sleeping with him. She wasn't in love with him, but she liked him enormously. His whole life was ahead of him, and he had everything to look forward to. He was some kind of computer genius, and wanted to get a master's in physics at MIT after he left AUP. He had three roommates so they went to her house at lunchtime and made love, and sometimes he joined her and Bethanie for dinner in the evening. Bethanie thought he was her friend, and they played for hours sometimes. He had endless patience with her, and when they went to the park, all three of them rode the swings. Paris was just what Coco and Bethanie had needed. It was healing.

Leslie called her a few times to ask her advice about various new clients. She went back to London to help out during school vacations, and Jimmy came with them, and met up with friends in London. She hadn't had such a carefree time since she'd been in college the first time. Going to school made her feel like a kid again.

She was startled when she got an email from Ian. She had stopped hoping to hear from him. He was still in Marrakesh, living in an old palace he had rented, and working on a new book. He wanted to know how Bethanie was doing, and if she was still in remission, which he said was the main reason for his email, but he wanted to know how Coco was too. He said he thought of her every day, but he didn't ask to see her.

She told him that she was going to school in Paris and enjoying it thoroughly. It was the perfect counterpoint to their six months of hell in New York. Her life in Paris was a little piece of heaven. She said she was happy to hear from him, but didn't ask to see him either. She thought it would be too hard to see him and not be with him, and it was clear that he didn't want to open that door again, but he missed her. She had torn a scab off an old wound without meaning to, when Bethanie got sick and they were afraid they would lose her. He said he wasn't strong enough to lose anyone again. He sent them both his love, and didn't say anything about coming to England or where he would go next.

And after a week in London, she and Jimmy and Bethanie went back to Paris and went back to school.

Coco went to Giverny with Jimmy in the spring. They explored

Versailles together. When Coco graduated, he looked at her mournfully. He was going to Scotland for the summer to stay with friends, back to Vermont after that, and then sailing in Maine, which he did every summer with his family, and then starting graduate school at MIT in the fall.

"Does this mean it's over, Coco?" he asked her sadly, the night before he left for Edinburgh.

"I think so, don't you?"

"These were the happiest six months of my life," he said, as though he was being banished from Brigadoon.

"Mine too, and the easiest." And then she realized something that made her smile. She was the flash for him. "Now you need to go and play with children your own age, and I do too."

"Why? We're good together." He didn't see why it had to end, except that he was going to Boston and she was going back to London.

"But we wouldn't be good together if we tried to make it last. That was never our intention. It just happened, and it made everything more fun."

"Do you want to meet me in Scotland?"

"No, I don't." She had never told him she loved him because she didn't, and she didn't want to lie to him. The truth was much sweeter, that they were special friends, and neither of them would ever forget the brief time they had shared in Paris. It would be a sweet memory for both of them with nothing to spoil it.

Saying goodbye to him was one of the more grown-up things she'd ever done. She didn't try to stretch their affair, keep it or make it grow or drag it into her everyday life. She kissed him when he left and he cried. "Now go find a nice girl in Vermont and fall in love with her, and don't go looking for the wild, exotic, exciting ones. They don't last. That's the best advice I can ever give you. If you chase that, it's foam on the sand and you'll wind up alone like me." He waved at her as he disappeared into the metro to get to his train to Scotland at the Gare du Nord.

She left for London with Bethanie the next day. They gave up the house in Paris. Bethanie had liked her school there too, and was speaking French. Coco packed her diploma, and then they went home. She had allowed herself to be a child for a season, and now it was time to go home and be a grown-up. She remembered now that childhood and youth didn't last forever, and it was just as well. She had begun to miss being an adult and working. She felt renewed and refreshed and ready to go back to London, to pick up the reins of her life again.

Chapter 18

When Coco came back to London in June, Leslie was happy to see her. There were changes in her life too. Her Danish boyfriend of the last two years had proposed to her. He had never been married before, and Leslie had been divorced for ten years. They were doing it at the beginning of July. She wanted Coco there to run the office when they went on their honeymoon for two weeks. Coco was delighted for her and happy to do it.

"Did you leave the Boy Wonder in Paris?" Leslie teased her. She had gone over to visit twice, and he had come to London so they'd met. "For a minute I thought you were serious, and then I realized you were just having fun." She had assessed it correctly.

"He's in Edinburgh now, and then he's going home to Vermont."

"Was he heartbroken when he left?"

Coco smiled at the memory. "Just a little. He'll get over it. Things like that aren't meant to last. Nothing does, except the real thing, but that's hard to find. My friend Sam says that I fall for the flash every time, and I have."

"We've all had our share of those," Leslie said. She'd had her own good times. But this time she had found a good one, and had decided to grab it before she missed her chance. "We've had an interesting proposition I wanted to discuss with you. It's from an investor in New York. He loves our concept, and wants to open an office there. He wants one of us to help him set it up. You know the city and I don't. He wants to add to our operating capital, set up an office, hire a staff. It would increase our business exponentially. What do you think?"

"Are you asking me to move to New York and run it? I wouldn't want to do that. I'd rather live here," she said. "I'm not ready to live in New York again." She couldn't wait to leave after her six months there.

"No, I think he wants us to help him set it up, show him how we work, and then we can go home. I thought three months might do it, till he's up and running. Does that appeal to you?"

"I would do it for three months. I owe you for the last year, between New York and Paris. I'd have to put Bethanie in school in New York while I'm there, which is fine at her age. When does he want to start?"

"Mid-September, I think. He's already found office space in SoHo, and he's interviewing staff now."

"You wanted to open a New York office when you started," Coco reminded her. "This is our chance."

"Will you do it?"

"Yes, I will," Coco said, wondering if she'd regret being stuck in New York again for three months. But having a fresh influx of operating capital was appealing, and she could spend time with Sam. "I could go as soon as you get back from your honeymoon. That would give me two months to help him set up and stick around for a month after he opens. I'd be back mid-October. That should work." And she had the house in Southampton where she and Bethanie could spend weekends. And Bethanie would only be in school in New York for six weeks, which would be an adventure for her.

"I'll get to work on it, and tell him you'll do it. Thank you, Coco," she said warmly. "This is a great opportunity for us. We could use our model to open in a number of cities eventually, with the right partners. This one came highly recommended by our bank and a mutual friend."

They were working on resource lists for the New York office four days later, when Coco got a text from Sam. He was coming to London to see an important investment client and he wanted to have dinner with her. He had successfully developed a whole new aspect to his business, and his firm had grown.

"Do you want to stay with me? Plenty of room," she texted back, and he responded that he was staying at a hotel, which was close to where he had several meetings lined up. She said she would love to have dinner with him. He was arriving the following week, and she was going to tell him then about her coming to New York for three months.

She was busy with Leslie on their New York project until he arrived, and she picked him up at the commercial hotel where he was staying. She thought he looked unusually serious and was probably tired. She took him to one of her favorite Italian restaurants where they could talk.

He waited until they had ordered dinner and a glass of wine for each of them before he dropped the bomb. They hadn't spoken as much recently, he was busy, and she had a feeling that his life wasn't running smoothly, or he was overwhelmed. He seemed stressed whenever they talked, his texts were short, and they never Face-Timed anymore. She assumed that broadening his business had him swamped. She wondered too if Tamar was still depressed. He looked at Coco after a sip of wine. "We're getting a divorce." There had been no hint of it till now. She was stunned.

"You're what? Are you kidding? When did that happen? How did I miss that? Are you in love with someone else?" She assumed that it was his decision, not Tamar's.

"No, I'm not. Tamar is leaving me. She said she was too young and didn't know what she was doing when we got married. She thinks I'm too liberal. I'm not Orthodox enough. She says she feels suffo-cated by our life. She can't deal with the kids and doesn't want to. She wants to work, after law school. And it all falls to me. She thinks I robbed her of her youth," when in fact she had impacted his im-measurably, and cut it short. "She wants to go to law school. She's been saying it for a while, about law school, not the divorce. That's new. My mother will have a stroke. Sabra and Liam are getting a di-vorce too. He cheated on her with his secretary. My whole family appears to be falling apart, except for the two religious fanatics, who seem divinely happy. My sister, the nun, and my brother, the rabbi. The rest of us are a mess." He looked depressed when he said it and she smiled.

"Holy shit. What happened?"

"Sabra and Liam don't get along, and he's cheated on her before. They fight all the time. They're a nightmare to be around. And Tamar has had some kind of epiphany, which doesn't include me. We tried counseling, which I didn't want to tell you. It just got worse." He didn't look heartbroken over it; he looked shocked. And Coco was even more so.

"Do you think she has someone else?" It seemed so unlike her. But he was busy, working to support a family of six.

"She's been going to a different synagogue. I suppose she could be in love with the rabbi, or someone there. She doesn't think I'm religious enough for her. And I'm not. I wanted to go to a Reform temple, not the strict Orthodox synagogues she prefers. This is going to kill my mother," he said mournfully. He viewed his mother as fragile, which she was not.

"Your mother is a strong woman, she'll be fine." She had no doubt of that. "What about you? How are you?"

"I'm shocked. I never thought she'd do this. I know she's been unhappy and depressed since the baby. But not to this extent. She told me a week ago she wants out. I wanted to tell you when I saw you."

"Can you work out some kind of decent arrangement for the kids?" Coco asked him. They were still so young.

"We're trying. I think the last baby put her over the edge. It almost did me in too. He's colicky, he cries all the time. I suggested a nanny, not a divorce. She wants both." He looked hurt and she felt sorry for him. "If you want to make it work, you can. She doesn't want to. She just wants out. It will be complicated with four kids and her in law school, and I'm busy."

"Just like that? With four kids? No warning? No negotiation?"

"Not that I know of. She says she warned me, but she didn't. Or I didn't hear it. I feel like such a failure." He had tears in his eyes.

"It's not you, Sam. She's been a mouse since you met her. And now she turns into a lion." Tamar was twenty-eight, and coming into her own. She suddenly wanted independence and freedom, and every-thing she'd missed.

"She wants me to have custody, and she'll have visitation. So she's walking out on the kids too." Coco was floored and would never have seen it coming. Not Tamar. "The irony is that I felt like I was drowning for a long time. We started having babies so quickly, which was what *she* wanted, and our families expected of us. She's so ada-mant about anything religious, and she's never been interested in the world or the community until now. I almost had an affair two years ago, with a girl who worked for me. I fired her so I didn't do anything stupid. And now Tamar wants out. I'm not happy either, but I'm not walking out on her, or complaining about her religious convictions. I don't blame her that we got married. I got pushed into it by my par-ents, but I've lived up to my side of the deal. We have nothing in common, and nothing to talk about. I love my kids, but I'm always running between them and my work, and trying to keep her happy. She complains all the time. And my mother expects me to keep my father's business alive to honor him. What he created is antiquated and should be shut down. It made sense when he set it up, but now it doesn't. It supported all of us, but it was a different time and he was a different man. He thought small. He was always afraid to do anything big. I'm much more interested in the investment side of the business, not the accounting, which was our bread and butter, but it's stale now. There's no magic or creativity to it." He was trapped be-tween the world he grew up in, and what he wanted to do himself, grow wings and fly. And Tamar and his mother were holding him back. After burdening him with four children by the age of thirty, now she wanted out. It seemed so unfair. "At least you followed your dreams. I never have," he said. "And what am I going to do as a divorced man with four kids?" He looked woebegone, and Coco touched his hand.

"You'll manage and do it well." He was the best husband she knew, the best father, son, and friend. He covered all the bases, and had for years, with no one's help. He thought the same of her. They had both managed in hard circumstances, with no support from their partners. Even Ian, who was a kind man, was not there when she needed him. Once Bethanie got sick, he had run away and she had to face it alone. He was still hiding in Marrakesh with his books and his dog, afraid to live. At least she had taken chances, even if she made mistakes and got hurt. The wounds healed. And she knew Sam's would too.

"I don't understand people," Sam said, "how when things get tough, they just walk away, instead of putting some effort into it." Walking away wasn't his style or hers. But Sam had a lot on his back now, especially if he had to shoulder Tamar's responsibilities and his own. "Maybe she'll come to her senses, but I don't think so."

"Even if she does," Coco said bravely, honest with him as she always tried to be, "then you're stuck in a marriage you never wanted, with a woman I'm not sure you ever loved. You said you loved her, but you married her out of duty and respect for your parents, and for her. You can't stay with someone for fifty years out of respect."

"My parents did," he said.

"They loved each other too. My mother always said not to play by other people's rules and to think outside the box. I took it too far, and tried to win the unwinnable with impossible people. I knew Ian was damaged, even though I didn't realize how extreme it was. And the warning signs were there with Nigel, but I closed my eyes. I knew he wanted a glamorous life and had no money. I just didn't see or didn't want to see that he was after mine, and every piece of ass that walked past him. And I knew Ed was married. There are a million men like him out there, cheating on their wives. It's the oldest story in the world."

"You were young then," Sam said with a forgiving smile.

"I still knew, but I can't afford to be stupid anymore, or blind. You were right, I get dazzled every time. There's no substance there. It's all sparkle with nothing behind it. Even now, I just spent six months playing with a sweet boy fresh out of kindergarten. I need to get serious about my life too. I should sell my house here. It's too big and it makes no sense. It used to remind me of Nigel, now it reminds me of Ian. I need something that's mine. And my parents' apartment is depressing. I have to let go of that too. Growing up is hard," she said, and he smiled.

They had been leading grown-up lives for a long time and taken on adult responsibilities while they were still children. "I'm coming to New York for three months, by the way. We have a new investor, who wants to set up an office there. I'm going to get him started. Maybe I'll put my parents' apartment on the market when I'm there. I'd like to keep the house in the Hamptons though, and take Bethanie there in the summer. I guess I need to figure out my life too." It felt like she was starting from scratch after Ian, the interlude with Jimmy in Paris, and Bethanie getting sick. She'd gotten her degree, now what? And she hadn't been serious about her business either, from the distance in the past year. Fortunately, Leslie had been there to run it and did it well. "I'm almost thirty, I feel like I need to act like an adult." He smiled again.

"You've had a lot of curveballs thrown at you," he said generously. "Your parents dying, Bethanie's leukemia, bad men. All things considered, you've handled it pretty well. And I *am* thirty, and my life is a mess."

"That's not your fault either. And it's not a mess. You got married too young, and married the wrong woman. Maybe you need a little more flash in your life, and I need a little less . . . until the next dazzler comes along and sweeps me off my feet." But they both knew she wasn't an innocent anymore. She hadn't fallen for Dr. Jeff Armstrong's game, no matter how seductive, handsome, and successful he was. His being married had stopped her cold, and he was one of the biggest narcissists she'd ever met. He had cured Bethanie, though, which was all she wanted from him. Bethanie had been checked regularly by the team of doctors that he had referred her to in Paris, and she was still healthy and free of the disease. She was cured, which was all that mattered to Coco.

"I have a couple of interesting clients here, for investments," Sam said. "I'd like to cultivate a few more. Right now, they are mostly Americans living here. If you know of any prospects here, please let me know."

"I'll think about it. And I'll see you in New York soon," she said, as they got up from dinner and left the restaurant. "What are you going to do about Tamar?" she asked.

"Wait and see what she does. She said she was going to see a lawyer when I left, to try and work out some kind of separation agreement. She took the LSATs, she wants to start law school in January, if she gets in. She'd like to specialize in tax law, which actually would have fit with what I do, but I don't think we're going to be running a business together," he said ruefully, "just sharing our kids, although they'll live with me most of the time. They're young to have divorced parents and a split living situation," he said with regret.

"Maybe it's easier that way," she said, trying to encourage him, "when they're younger."

"I was thinking about moving the family to the suburbs, but I won't if I'm going to be single. I'd rather be in the city."

"You're going to have fun, Sam." He was still younger than most men getting married for the first time. Being divorced at thirty-one, which he would be soon, wasn't a death sentence. He had taken a five-year detour into marriage, and it hadn't worked out. He still had a long life to live, and time to meet the right woman. And he loved his children and was devoted to them.

"At least I'll see you while you're in New York." She was looking forward to it too.

She dropped him off at his hotel, he hugged her and got out of the car. "Thank you for cheering me up."

"You do it for me all the time." She smiled at him. He always had. And so had she. It was so damn hard being a grown-up, at any age.

Coco and Bethanie attended Leslie's wedding. Bethanie was the flower girl and Coco the maid of honor. And as soon as Leslie returned from her honeymoon, they flew to New York.

They spent the first weekend in Southampton enjoying the hot weather. Bethanie loved it and so did Coco. She freshened up some things in the house, and moved them around, which made the house feel like hers, not her parents'. They went for long walks on the beach, built sand castles, collected shells, and put them on a table to dry. Sam came out for the day with his children. Tamar wasn't with him. She had seen a lawyer, and he had hired one. They were working on a separation agreement, but were still living in the apartment together. He said it was very tense, and she had applied to law school at NYU and Columbia, after doing well on the LSATs, which didn't surprise him. She was boring, but bright, and had been a good student in college.

Their children played in the sand, while he and Coco watched them. He had brought a babysitter to help with the baby and the others. Bethanie and Nathan were best friends, until they fought over a shovel, and Bethanie hit him with a bucket and Coco had to scold her and remind her to be nice.

"It starts early," Sam said with a grin.

They made lunch for the kids and ate the peanut butter and jelly sandwiches that were left over. It was simple and fun.

"How's your investor?" Sam was curious about him.

"He's a really nice guy. He was a real estate agent, and loved what we were doing when a friend told him about it. He's gay, and his partner is a decorator. It's a great setup for them. They're married and have two adorable adopted little girls. Only one of them is the investor, but they're both really nice guys. They already have a great roster of potential clients, mostly corporations bringing people to New York from other cities, or internationally. That's where we really shine." Leslie had done most of the work for the past year when Coco was away, but before that they had both put a lot of effort into building the business, and Coco had invested the most money. It had really paid off for both of them.

They'd given Sam's children an early dinner. He gave the baby a bottle, and knew they'd sleep most of the way home.

"I had a really nice day. I'm glad you're keeping this house. It reminds me of when we were kids."

"Me too." She smiled nostalgically. "It reminds me of my parents mostly. They loved it here. They were so great together. Why can't we find people like that?"

"They weren't complicated," Sam answered her. "Most people today seem to be. There are too many options and choices and wounded people running around. Like Ian, although he was an extreme case, and fame makes it all harder." She nodded. He was right, except that Tamar wasn't complicated. He just hadn't loved her enough to marry her, or at all. She had always been a mistake.

"My parents were always perfectly clear about how much they loved each other. That never changed. It just got better," Coco said with admiration, wishing she could find a situation like theirs. "They believed in each other."

"We make odd decisions, and pick difficult people. Anything is acceptable now. You have to get it right in the beginning. I don't think you can take an impossible situation and make it work, no matter how hard you try. None of your choices were the right ones, no matter how appealing they seemed at the time," Sam said to her. "And neither was mine. It was never right with Tamar and I knew it, and it wasn't that appealing, except to my parents. I should have followed my instincts. Instead, I tried to do the noble thing." She nodded. He was right about that too. He was a smart and a good man and he was going to be fine, Coco was sure of it. Women were going to be crawling all over him when he was free, although the four kids might scare them at first, but he was a great dad, and a good husband, or had tried to be.

He left the house in Southampton with a wave, after he hugged her, while Coco and Bethanie stood in the driveway waving back. They had had a wonderful day.

On Sunday, Coco and Bethanie drove into the city. Monday morning she left Bethanie with Theresa, met with Evan, their investor, and got to work. The storefront office they had in SoHo was great looking, and Jack, his partner, had done wonders with it, to make it inviting. They worked hard, and she liked the staff they had hired. It suited their image, and the style of the brand. They were bright young people with lots of enthusiasm and energy and were going to be a credit to Leslie and Coco's business. Evan and Jack were going to visit them in London in December, and bring the crew so the staff of the two offices could meet, and get to know each other, to make things run more smoothly.

It was a long week. They were officially going to be open in seven weeks. She wanted to go to the Hamptons again that weekend but it was pouring rain on Friday, so she didn't. It was after seven when she got home, and Sam called her as she walked in the door. He sounded grim.

"Can I come over?"

"Sure. Something wrong? You sound pissed." She looked in the fridge after they hung up, there wasn't much there, but she could make him a salad if he was starving.

He arrived twenty minutes later, and he looked livid when he took off his dripping raincoat, and followed her into the den, which was her favorite room. The living room was beautiful but always felt too fancy. Her parents had loved the den too.

"What happened?" she asked him. He looked furious.

"You were right. My mother heard it from a friend at shul. Tamar's been having an affair with the rabbi of the other synagogue I told you about. I love that when religious men, leaders of the community, go around sleeping with other men's wives. It's no better than priests having affairs. Apparently, it's been going on for eight or nine months, ever since the baby. Supposedly, she went to him for counseling about our marriage, and they fell in love. He's fifty-five and a widower, with no kids, and she's only twenty-eight."

"That should be fun," Coco said.

"My mother is crazed over it. She didn't believe it at first, but she checked it out with a few other people, who knew all about it and confirmed it. She came to my office to tell me. It's good for her to know that rabbis aren't all saints either. But Tamar is a piece of work."

"What are you going to do? Did you tell her you know?"

"Not yet. I want to talk to my lawyer first. He was gone for the day by the time my mother left my office. She alternately cried and raged for two hours." He smiled at that. "My day was shot to hell. I'm not surprised, and yet I am. I never thought she'd do something like that, she's such a moral person, and so meek. I couldn't imagine her cheating on me. It's been going on for nearly a year. It certainly says how miserable she must be with me." He felt guilty about that too, as though everything was his fault.

"I think she's miserable with herself. It's hard to be miserable with you." He always made her feel better about life, not worse.

"She doesn't think so. I never thought I'd say it, but I do want her to move out now, and leave the kids with me. She can have visitation, but I want custody. She says she doesn't want custody and I do, although can you imagine my being alone with four kids?" That was a tall order and he worked hard and long hours. "We have a part-time nanny now anyway. We have ever since she's been depressed. And apparently, not as depressed as I thought. Her rabbi boyfriend is strict Orthodox. She loves that. My mother's friend said he's a nice guy and deeply religious." Sam knew more about him now than he wanted to, thanks to his mother. He had looked him up on the Internet after his mother left his office. Rabbi Israel Seligson was a good-looking man. And old enough to be Sam's father, and Tamar's. Maybe that was what she was looking for. He no longer knew. He wondered if he had suggested law school to her, but she had mentioned it before. It would be a big status symbol for her to be a rabbi's wife, more so than being the wife of an accountant, or even an investment advisor.

"Are you hungry?" Coco asked him, to distract him.

"Yes, I want a ham sandwich and a shrimp cocktail," he said, glaring at her, and she laughed.

"That bad, huh?"

"Worse. She betrayed me, Coco. She lied to me. We haven't had sex since David was conceived, which was almost two years ago. But still, she slept in bed with me every night, and she was having an affair with him. How does that work with all her religious principles? And his?"

"Maybe she thought it was okay because she wasn't having sex with you. There's no telling how people justify things to themselves. Look at Nigel. At least she wasn't doing it with him in your bed while you were at work."

"Who knows? Maybe she was, when the nanny took the kids to the park. Anything's possible." Coco knew that was true. She felt sorry for him. He felt abused, and he wasn't wrong. It had turned out that Tamar was human, even if not exciting. "I don't know how I'm going to look her in the eye all weekend and not say anything. I want to talk to my lawyer first. At least my mother won't give me a hard time about a divorce now. She thinks she should be stoned in the street." Whatever happened next, it was a hard way for a marriage to end, feeling cheated, lied to, and used. She'd been there herself.

Coco made a salad for both of them, and put some chicken on a plate, and Sam left at eleven, after venting for several hours.

"Do you want to have dinner tomorrow night?" he asked as he left, and she looked regretful.

"I can't. Evan and Jack invited me to dinner with some of their friends. Anytime next week is fine."

"I don't know what's going to be happening next week. It may be explosive. I don't want to make plans yet. Have fun tomorrow," he said, kissed her cheek, and left. She read for a while afterward, thinking of him off and on, and then went to bed. There was no question in her mind, or his. Sam had some rough times ahead.

Chapter 19

Coco was impressed when she got to Evan and Jack's address. They had an elegant brownstone in the East Seventies. Evan was in his early thirties, and Jack in his late forties. They had a spectacular home and exquisite taste, with impressive art and beautiful furniture. The floor set aside for their daughters would have been heaven for any little girl. They were three and four, and there were murals of ballerinas in their rooms and a big playroom with a view of the garden. The girls came downstairs with their nanny in little pink smocked dresses, with matching bows in their hair, to curtsy and shake hands with the guests. They were beautifully behaved, sweet children. Evan had already suggested that Bethanie come to play some afternoon.

The guest list was as impressive as their home. They moved in elite social circles. Jack was on the boards of the Metropolitan Museum of Art, the Metropolitan Opera, and the New York City Ballet, while Evan was involved with MoMA. Coco learned in the course of dinner that they had been together for ten years, and she already knew they were stable, successful, interesting people. There were several couples at the impeccably set dinner table whose names she recognized: a famous female writer, who was Ian's main competitor; a famous literary agent and his wife, a successful artist; and a well-known art collector, Charles Bartlett, whom they sat next to Coco, and was easily the best-looking man in the room. He was fascinating to talk to and had homes in London, Sardinia, Tuscany, Saint Bart's, and a triplex apartment in New York, decorated by Jack, and a plane to circulate between them with ease. He was originally an oilman from Texas, was one of the most famous venture capitalists, and was somewhere in his mid-forties. He'd been married and divorced twice, first to a famous actress, and then to a major Russian ballerina. Coco felt totally out of her league sitting next to him, and was glad she had bought a new dress for the occasion. It was a black lace Oscar de la Renta. She had been afraid it was a little too revealing but her dinner partner seemed to enjoy it, and the other women were so well dressed that Coco was glad she had gone a little overboard with a new dress to impress her hosts.

Despite his myriad houses in fabulous locations, and famous art collection, part of which he had just lent to the Tate in London, Charles was surprisingly unassuming, fun to talk to, and had a great sense of humor and the ability to laugh at himself. She had to force herself to tear her attention away and make an effort to speak to the man on her other side, who was a well-known artist. But Charles Bartlett was clearly the most interesting guest. And when they moved back to the living room for coffee, he came straight to Coco and sat down next to her.

"I hope it's not rude to say, or upsetting, but I knew your father. We did a few deals together. He was a wonderful man, and I met your mother too. I felt terrible about what happened. You must have been just a kid then." He was so compassionate when he said it, that she was deeply touched, and he won her heart immediately.

"I was in college. It was awful. I moved to London afterward, but I was pretty lost for a while."

"I'm so sorry." He changed the subject then, and had her laughing again a little while later. He stayed close to her for the rest of the night, and by the time the evening ended, she felt as though she had a new friend. Almost as soon as she got home, Evan texted her. "Charlie Bartlett wants your phone number. Okay to give it to him?"

She appreciated his asking, and texted back immediately. "Perfect, no problem. Thank you for a fabulous evening. So much fun. See you Monday."

Charlie Bartlett called her the next morning and invited her to brunch at the Carlyle. They walked through Central Park afterward and he left her reluctantly when he put her in a cab to go home.

He called her again on Monday, and invited her to a gala dinner at the Metropolitan Museum that she had frequently read about but never been to. He had lunch with her in SoHo when he dropped by to see the new offices, and took her to dinner at La Grenouille on the weekend. It was a full-court press with a massive bouquet of red roses, and every evening she spent with him was more fun than the last one. He had to go to London and Dubai the following week, but as soon as he got back, he took her out to dinner again, and invited her to see his incredible Fifth Avenue triplex that made her parents' apartment look like a hovel in comparison. She was impressed that when she went to his apartment, somewhat hesitantly for a drink, he didn't try to get her into bed. He treated her like a very attractive woman he was smitten with and courting, but not like a piece of meat that was his for the grabbing. He was a total gentleman and she loved the little bit of Texan drawl he still had. It was a challenge to keep her head and not fall head over heels in love with him. He was everything any woman could have wanted and more. His obvious fortune far exceeded hers so he wanted nothing from her. He was kind and funny, intelligent, and had a great time with her. She hadn't had a bad moment with him yet, and he kept coming up with more fun things to do. He knew about every play, every exhibit, and every new restaurant in New York. She was working hard in the daytime, and playing hard at night with Charlie. She wanted to ask him where he'd been all her life while she wasted her time with sleazeballs like Nigel and Ed, and cripples like Ian. There was nothing wrong with Charlie Bartlett, and he felt the same way about her. She was starting to ask herself if this could be happening, and if it was real. It was almost too good to be true, and if it wasn't real, his performance was seamless. He appeared to be the perfect man in every way.

He waited two weeks to kiss her, and when he did, it was both gentle and searing at the same time, and quickly became highly addictive. They did a lot of kissing and groping and wishing after that, but Coco didn't want to rush into anything. She wanted to savor each moment and let it unfold. He was in no rush. He wanted things to happen the way she wanted them to, however that was. She had never been around a man as easy to get along with, and so eager to make her happy, whatever that meant to her.

Sam sensed something different about her, and questioned her about it when they had dinner.

"What's up? I saw you on Page Six twice last week." Everyone in the city read it, about the movers and shakers, and the high-end local gossip. "How do you know Charles Bartlett?" Sam was impressed.

"He's a friend of Evan, my investor."

"He's got a great reputation in the world of finance. He's supposedly a pleasure to do business with, and an honest guy."

"He's an incredibly nice man. He knew my father. I think I've really met a great guy this time. I'm taking it slow. We've been out a lot."

"That doesn't sound slow to me."

"What's happening with Tamar?" They hadn't spoken in a few days, and the last time they had, things were stressful for him, which was no surprise, given the situation. He had confronted her about the affair with the rabbi, and she admitted it. She was in love with him. Enough so to give up custody of her kids.

"Amazingly, it sounds like she's really going to let me have custody, with reasonable visitation for her. The rabbi must not want four children under five underfoot. But she wants a lot of spousal support, and possibly a settlement. I can't believe it, but it's down to that now. I think she may move out soon. I'll have to prepare the kids." His whole life had unraveled in a matter of weeks, and she felt like hers was just starting again. She felt reborn with Charlie. He made her feel like a very special fairy princess and as she thought it, she heard a familiar ring in her head. Someone else had made her feel that way . . . Nigel . . . and Ed in the beginning . . . and Ian . . . She wanted to be sure this wasn't a replay of all the mistakes she'd made before. But it didn't seem like it. He seemed perfect in every way.

She and Sam talked for a while, he was tired and irritable, and stressed by his negotiations with Tamar over money while still living with her. She wanted a hefty sum for having given up five years of her life. His mother had declared war on her, on Sam's behalf, which complicated matters further. The baby had an earache and had kept him up all night, and Nathan had stomach flu. Tamar was doing nothing to help him with the kids. They were his problem now. In her mind, she had already left.

"Sounds like real life to me," Coco said gently, but the good news in her life was that Bethanie had just been checked at Sloan Kettering again, and had come through with flying colors, with no sign of leukemia at all. The treatment had worked. Everything else in Coco's life was insignificant compared to that.

She and Charlie had been dating for a month when he invited her away for a weekend at his house in Saint Bart's. It was a loaded question, and she understood the implication, but they had seen a lot of each other, and she was dying to sleep with him. She accepted, and they were planning to go down on Friday morning on his plane. They were going to spend a night on his boat, which was docked in Antigua and he hadn't mentioned to her. It was a two-hundred-and-fourteen-foot sailboat he'd had built by a famous shipyard in Italy, and was the envy of experienced sailors. He was taking her to a party in Palm Beach on Sunday night, and they were flying back on Monday morning in time for both of them to go to work. It all sounded perfect. On her lunch hour she bought a white silk dress at Chanel in SoHo to wear on his boat. It was just going to be the two of them all weekend, until they went to Palm Beach for the party, which was going to be a big event. She had a new dress for that too. She'd been doing a lot of shopping lately, for their busy social life. It was easy for him. He either wore suits or black tie. The lifestyle was familiar to her, although it wasn't what she would have chosen to pursue on her own. She was happy with a simple life, doing things with Bethanie or Sam and his children. But it was exciting being out with Charlie. He made her feel beautiful, sophisticated, and young.

She spoke to Sam on Thursday night, before she left. She didn't tell him where she was going, he had enough problems these days with Tamar and a divorce, she didn't want to bother him with her new social life and budding romance. She had a faint suspicion he wouldn't approve. He was negative about everything these days. And there was an unreal quality to her relationship with Charlie. Her parents hadn't lived that way, even though they could have. They didn't like to show off, and Coco never had either. But it was fun being with Charlie, it was all so glamorous and exciting.

"Do you want to have dinner tomorrow night? The nanny will stay late if I need her to," Sam asked her.

"I can't, I'm sorry, Sam."

"Another black-tie event on the Bartlett circuit?" he asked, sounding a little snide about it, or maybe just jealous that she was having fun and he wasn't. Nothing about his life was fun at the moment, neither his battles with Tamar about the spousal support she wanted, nor his kids, who seemed to be constantly sick now that the two oldest were in preschool and brought every bug home to the two younger ones. Sam had had a cold for two weeks, and a bout of stomach flu himself. He was run-down and tired, and discouraged. "I seem to be in purgatory at the moment," he commented, and she laughed.

She didn't answer his comment about what she was doing on Friday night, and felt guilty and like she was letting him down when she hung up. Theresa was going to babysit for Bethanie for the weekend. It didn't seem fair that she was leading the life of a fairy princess and Sam was the drudge in his, with Tamar badgering him for money, in love with another man, his mother kibitzing from the sidelines and putting her oar in, and his four children constantly sick. It was definitely a nightmare, and a little too real. And Tamar made no pretense of helping him at all.

Charlie picked her up in his Bentley on Friday morning, and drove her to Teterboro in New Jersey where his plane was waiting. It was a Gulfstream, which comfortably accommodated a dozen people, and could travel long distances without refueling, so he used it to go to Europe frequently. There were two flight attendants to serve them, and they had a hot breakfast waiting. The captain and copilot were pleasant and professional. They took off twenty minutes after they got there, while Charlie and Coco had breakfast, with *The New York Times* and *The Wall Street Journal* neatly folded next to them.

They flew directly to Saint Martin, where his boat picked them up to take them to Saint Bart's, avoiding the ride on the terrifying puddle jumper that usually landed there. The boat was beyond fabulous, with every imaginable comfort and filled with priceless art. A Rolls was waiting for them with his houseman driving in Saint Bart's, and they went straight to his house, which had a magnificent view of the ocean, and an enormous pool.

He had given her her own room, so she would have privacy, and enough space for her things, and they could move at the pace that seemed most natural to them. There was no pressure on her at all, although they both knew what would happen that weekend and why they were there. They had waited a month for this. The house was filled with flowers, and her room was as well. He opened a bottle of champagne for her when they arrived, and they sat by the pool for a little while, before they went to put bathing suits on, before having lunch at the pool.

He sat admiring her, as she looked at him, and an odd question popped into her mind. He made everything so easy for her, and himself. He was a man who liked his comforts and the fruits of his huge success.

"Does this ever seem unreal to you, Charlie?" she asked him and he smiled.

"No, why would it? It's my real life and the way I want it. Some of us are lucky enough to live the way we choose. I have no encumbrances, no children to worry about, and this is the way I want to live." She wondered if he ever felt guilty about indulging himself to that degree, or missed going to McDonald's, or riding the subway or doing the things that other people did. Her father had built a successful empire and amassed an enormous fortune, but she couldn't imagine them sitting by the pool, surrounded by servants, waited on hand and foot, with their own plane, and a yacht in the harbor. At a certain point, it became excessive, and she wondered where that line was for him, or if it even existed.

She was enjoying it thoroughly, but it didn't feel real. It was the flash to the highest degree, the Mount Everest of consumption. She wondered if maybe Texans just did things bigger, but she also couldn't imagine him taking care of four young children like Sam, or even like her with Bethanie. She liked to be comfortable too, but in Charlie's lifestyle, you missed the simple, precious moments that she also enjoyed. The times when you could be alone, or made dinner, just the two of you, which her parents had done. Charlie was always surrounded by employees and liked to be waited on.

They swam before lunch, and ate the lobster prepared by the French chef he kept there. After lunch, they dozed in the sun for a while. She awoke to his touch, as he sat on her chaise and gently stroked her back. She had unhooked her top, and he had told her she could swim topless since everyone did in Saint Bart's since it was French, but she didn't feel quite ready for that with him yet. She turned her head to look at him with a sleepy smile and he leaned down and kissed her.

"Do you want to go down to the boat for a while?" he asked her, and she nodded. She put her top back on, and he drove her to the port in a Ferrari. When they got there, his yacht was nestled among several others, and they were welcomed aboard by the crew. They took off for a little while and enjoyed the sun and the breeze on deck.

"I can never decide where I want to be when I'm here, at the house or on the boat. I love this boat." He was an expert sailor, and they sailed for a while, and then slowly came back to the port in a light wind. Every moment she shared with him was perfect. She couldn't imagine real life intruding on them. She would have loved to have Bethanie with her, but these were adult moments that weren't meant for children. His life was entirely geared to adults in a life of supreme luxury. She was being cared for like a child, without a care in the world. In Charlie's world, one felt totally safe and protected and shielded from anything unpleasant.

As she sat at the rail, she had a pang again, thinking of Sam, and how real his life was right now, how real hers had been at various times and how painful. Even Charlie couldn't prevent bad things from happening, like what had happened to her parents, or Bethanie getting sick. The safety of Charlie's world was an illusion. He was as vulnerable as everyone else. He just didn't know it, and protected himself well, and her.

When they got back to the house, she bathed and changed for dinner. She was going to wear the white silk Chanel that night, which seemed appropriate. As she brushed her dark hair, she met her own eyes in the mirror, and knew what she was doing. She was hiding, and chasing the fairy tale again. It was the flash in all its glory. And all of a sudden she knew where she wanted to be and with whom. All she didn't know was why she hadn't figured it out sooner, or how he'd feel about it.

She put her brush down and turned away from the mirror. She wanted to call Bethanie, but she didn't want to upset her if she was having fun. And she wanted to call Sam, and he was very definitely not having fun. He wasn't on a yacht or a tropical island. He was probably cleaning up after his kids, with no nanny on the weekend. With luck, no one had an earache or diarrhea.

She took her white silk dress off, folded it, and put it back into the suitcase. She put on the white jeans she'd brought with a white T-shirt and white ballet flats, packed the rest of her things, and walked out to find Charlie in the living room. He was waiting for her with another bottle of Cristal in a silver bucket and two chilled champagne flutes.

He looked surprised but not displeased by what she was wearing. He had been thinking about what lay ahead for them later that night, and so had she, and she knew she couldn't do it. She had to be honest with him, and herself.

She looked apologetic as she approached him, but she had awoken from her stupor, and she was wide-awake now. The luxurious fumes of his life had inebriated her for weeks. But now she was stone cold sober.

"Charlie, I know this will sound crazy, but I have to go home." She sounded calm and serious and no longer playful.

"Did something happen to your daughter?" He was instantly sympathetic. "Did they call you from home?" He knew how sick she had been before.

"She's fine. But I'm not. I shouldn't be here. I know better. This is what I do. I get caught up in someone else's fairy tale, and try to live their dream with them. This is your dream, not mine. My dream includes a little girl who gets sick, very sick last year, and cries, and gets chocolate ice cream all over my jeans, and a job I love, which isn't glamorous, but I have fun doing it, and people you probably wouldn't even want to know. This is your reality, not mine. I need to go home." She was the first woman who had ever said that to him. He was angry for a minute, and then he respected her for it. She was her own person, and a brave girl. He only knew a fraction of what she'd been through, but she was a strong woman, and he knew he could love her if she'd let him. But it didn't seem like that was going to happen. "If you get me to the airport, I'll catch a flight back to New York. You don't need to send me, or fly me back." She didn't want to inconvenience him on top of it, or cost him anything. This had been her mistake.

"Will you spend the night?" he asked hopefully, thinking that maybe he could persuade her if she stayed.

"No, I won't. I don't trust either of us, particularly myself." She smiled at him. "You're an incredibly appealing man. I think I already love you a little bit, and I'd rather stop now. It just gets messy later, and everyone gets hurt." She was too wise for his game. He wasn't a player but he used all the wiles and comforts he had to win. She wasn't going to let him. She knew she had stopped just in time before something stupid happened and then it would take months or years to undo it, and repair the damage.

"I'm sorry it's only a little bit." He smiled at her. "You're a remarkable woman." And now that she didn't want him, he wanted her even more. "I'm not letting you take that suicide flight out of Saint Bart's. I'd never forgive myself. The boat can take you to Saint Martin. It will only take an hour. You can catch the first flight out, or spend the night on the boat if you have to." He wanted to go with her and try to change her mind, but he didn't. He knew better, and not to chase a woman who didn't want him. He could see that Coco had made up her mind and nothing would stop her. Not even him.

"Thank you, Charlie. And I really mean that. Thank you for making it easy, even this part. I'm sorry I can't stay."

"I thought it was too good to be true, and I was one lucky guy."

"You are a lucky guy, and a great one, and I've been lucky to be with you. I just need to be doing something different." She reached up and kissed him on the cheek then. He had been a total gentleman throughout, even now. He could have told her to walk home if she didn't want him. Instead he was providing his two-hundred-foot yacht to help her make her getaway. She was back in the hall with her suitcases five minutes later. He kissed her, for real this time, and meant it, and she thanked him again and followed the driver outside to the Rolls. He drove her down to the port, and she boarded the boat. They set sail fifteen minutes later, after they cast off the lines and started the engines, and she was in Saint Martin at ten o'clock. One of the crew members accompanied her to the airport in a cab. She had missed the last flight, but there was one at seven the next morning. She went back to the boat to spend the night, as Charlie had offered. They put her in the owner's cabin, and she had a good chance to see everything she missed. The Picassos on the walls, the Warhols, the rest of his art, the luxurious cabin, and the man himself was so enticing, and she had turned him down. Maybe she was crazy, but she hoped she was right. She didn't want to spend more years of her life, chasing the flash only to discover later it wasn't real. Charlie was the best of his kind, but it wasn't the life she wanted.

A crew member took her back to the airport at five-thirty A.M., she checked in at six, and thanked the crewman who left her there. The flight was full and nothing like the comforts of the flight down from New York on his plane. But she felt good in her own skin, pleased with herself, and a little nervous about what she was about to do.

They landed at nine-thirty, she got her bags, and was in the city at eleven, and left her suitcases with her doorman. She didn't want to go upstairs and see Bethanie yet. She was still wearing her white jeans and T-shirt, and a red sweater. It was chilly in New York, but a sunny day.

She took a cab to Sam's apartment, and the doorman let her go upstairs. She rang the bell and was startled when Tamar answered and opened the door. The two women stood there looking at each other for a minute, and Coco could see that she'd been crying, and she looked like she was packing. There were boxes and suitcases all around her.

"Hi, Tamar. I'm sorry to barge in on you. Is Sam here?" They could go for a walk since Tamar was home, but she shook her head.

"No, he took the kids to the park." And then she started to cry. "This isn't as easy as he thinks, you know. It's very hard."

"I'm sure it is." There were children and human beings involved, and two men. "I'm sorry." She didn't want to engage her further and hear the whole ugly story. She was on Sam's side, not Tamar's. She thanked her and left, and ran across the street to the park to find him. Their apartment was in the same building as his mother's, which she was sure wasn't easy for Tamar either, to have your mother-in-law breathing down your neck. She'd never had one, but it didn't look pleasant to her, and she knew his mother and how tough she could be. Especially now that she knew Tamar had betrayed her son.

She saw Sam from a distance at the playground alone with the four kids. He looked surprised to see her as she approached him in her white jeans and red sweater with a purposeful look. He had the baby in a harness strapped to his back, and was helping Nathan tie his shoelaces. Ruth was clinging to his leg, and he had an eye on Hannah in the sandbox, happily shoveling sand into a pail. He needed ten hands and four sets of eyes to keep them in check. And there wasn't a bottle of Cristal or a yacht anywhere in sight.

"What are you doing here?" he asked, trying to keep an eye on her and the children at the same time. "Theresa said you were in Saint Bart's when I called you last night."

"I was. I just got back."

"Short trip," he commented.

"Very." He could guess who she had gone with, her life was a million miles from his now. He didn't resent her for it, he just had no frame of reference given where his own life was.

"How did you know where I was?" he asked her.

"Tamar told me. I went to the apartment. It looks like she's packing."

"She's moving out next week. We told the kids yesterday. They seem okay. I'm not sure how much they understand." Coco nodded. "Why did you come back?" He was curious about it. She had a strange look on her face, half guilty, half scared. "Did something go wrong?"

"I forgot something. I almost made a terrible mistake, but I stopped it in time."

"Did he do something bad?" He frowned.

"No, he was actually incredibly nice about it."

"So what did you forget?"

"Something I knew in fourth grade, and somehow I managed to forget by fifth grade, and for the last twenty years. I don't know how the hell I forgot it, but I did."

"And what was that?" He didn't know where she was going and he was bouncing a little from one foot to the other, to keep David quiet in the frame on his back.

"That I love you, Sam, always have and always will. That you're the only man in the world I love, and who knows me and loves me anyway. I don't know how the hell I got so distracted with all the glitter and the glamour and the bullshit. Saint Bart's was just more of the same, private jet down, fabulous house, two-hundred-foot yacht, gorgeous swimming pool, lots of champagne."

"Shit," he said, grinning at her, "I'd have stayed. No one takes me on trips like that."

"All I could think of while I was there was you," she said, "and our kids, and everything we've both been through, and what you're going through now with Tamar. I love you, Sam. You're the flash for me. The only flash I want. I'm yours if you want me. You're the only man I've ever really loved." There were tears in her eyes and he stood staring at her with a look of wonder. She thought of her parents. She wanted what they had, and this was it, with Sam. It was real. Charlie's life wasn't, or Ed's or Nigel's. Ian was real, but he was broken. Sam was whole, and so was she, even after all they'd been through.

"You walked out on all that for me?" She nodded. "You're crazy, and I love you too. I've thought about it over the years but I thought you wouldn't want me. I'm not fancy enough or glamorous enough."

"This is what I want. You, and the kids," she said simply. He pulled her into his arms then and kissed her for the first time, while his children stared at them. Sam was smiling when they stopped kissing.

"You're nuts to give all that up for me. But if this is what you want, we're all yours. I have an idea too. I want to close the accounting side of my business, and only handle private investments. I can do it from anywhere. What do you think if I come to London, with the kids, and try working from there, at home?" She smiled. Suddenly it all made sense. These were the children she had been waiting for. The enormous house Nigel had made her buy with rooms for all the children they never had were going to be filled with Sam and his kids, and Bethanie. And maybe more of their own.

"It sounds great to me." She thought about it then. "I'd better keep my parents' apartment for when we come here. I think I'll redo it and spruce it up a little." It had all finally fallen into place, and taken twenty years to do it, with a million detours and good and bad men, and Tamar leaving him for another man. There was a reason for all of it. And it started in fourth grade. It was suddenly all so simple. "Your mom was right."

"About what?" He looked puzzled.

"If we kept hanging around together, we'd wind up getting married one day."

"It took you long enough," he complained.

"That's not so bad . . . twenty years." She turned and smiled at him, while they continued to keep an eye on the kids.

"I'm hungry, Daddy," Nathan came to report to him, and Sam looked at Coco with a question.

"McDonald's?"

"Perfect," she said, and went to scoop Hannah out of the sandbox.

They walked out of the park together a few minutes later, with his arm around her.

"I love you," he whispered in her ear.

"I love you too," she whispered back, and they both smiled. Just like when she was in fourth grade. Finally. They were back to where they started and were always meant to be. It just took a long time to see it, and the lessons they had learned hadn't been wasted if they led to this in the end.

It had been a long road for both of them, which had finally led them safely home.

About the Author

DANIELLE STEEL has been hailed as one of the world's best-selling authors, with almost a billion copies of her novels sold. Her many international bestsellers include *Royal, Daddy's Girls, The Wedding Dress, The Numbers Game, Moral Compass, Spy, Child's Play, The Dark Side, Lost and Found,* and other highly acclaimed novels. She is also the author of *His Bright Light,* the story of her son Nick Traina's life and death; *A Gift of Hope,* a memoir of her work with the homeless; *Expect a Miracle,* a book of her favorite quotations for inspiration and comfort; *Pure Joy,* about the dogs she and her family have loved; and the children's books *Pretty Minnie in Paris* and *Pretty Minnie in Hollywood.*

daniellesteel.com
Facebook.com/DanielleSteelOfficial
Twitter: @daniellesteel
Instagram: @officialdaniellesteel